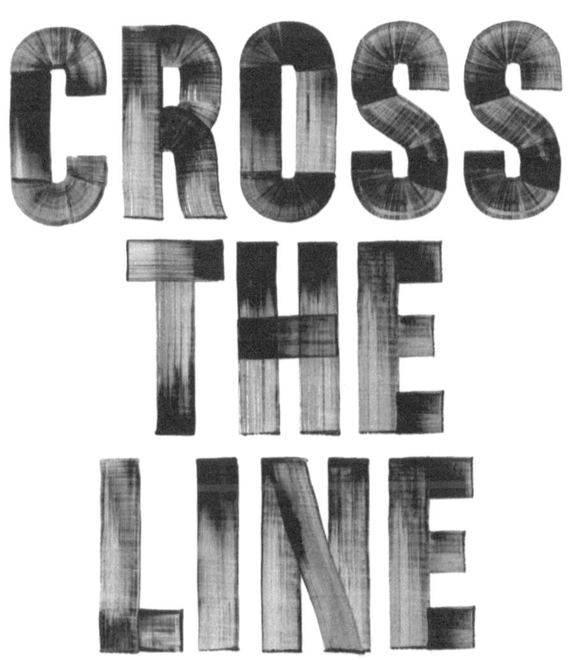

S. MASSERY
S.J. SYLVIS

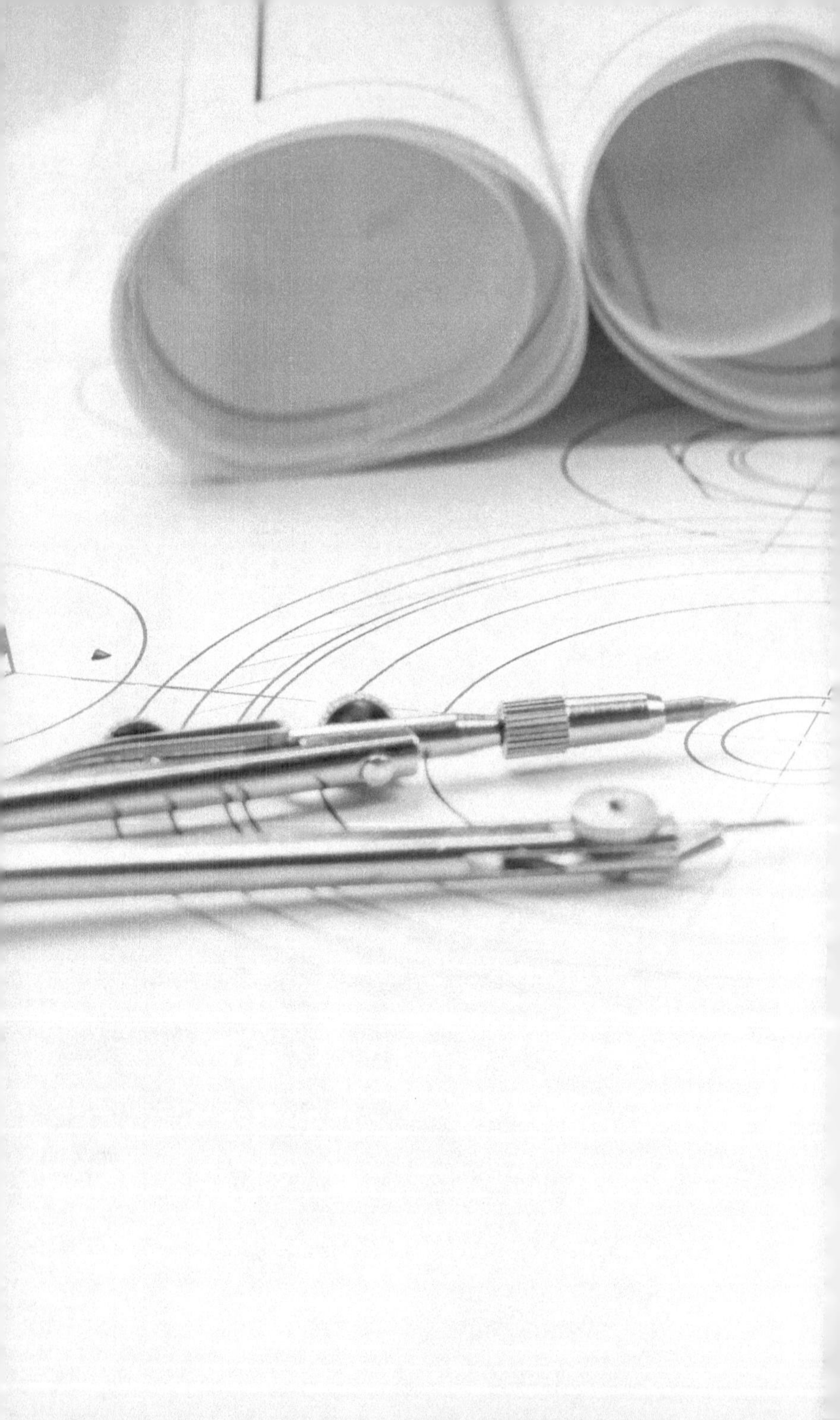

A NOTE FROM THE AUTHORS

Dear reader,

We hope you enjoy Cross and Scarlett's story! This one is a tad darker than the previous books in the series. It includes step-siblings, bullying, blackmail, a medium amount of physical violence (the hero fights), talk of sexual assault (but not described on-page in detail), plus spice and all things nice.

It's not necessary to read the previous books in the series prior to this one.

Happy reading!

xoxo,
   Sara & S.J.

SHADOW VALLEY U READING LIST

Sticks & Stones

Join Wren fight off her growing attraction to her brother's best friend in this forced proximity, enemies-to-lovers hockey romance

http://mybook.to/svu1

Heart of Thorns

Thorne is desperate to put his parents' meddling to an end —so much so that he talks the prickly black cat, Briar, into faking being his girlfriend, in this fake dating, grumpy/sunshine football romance http://mybook.to/svu2

The Christmas Playbook

Things take a turn for the worse when Rhys and Mira—childhood neighbors turned strangers—discover they've been double-booked at the sold-out ski resort. Add in a dysfunctional family, a la Home Alone, some Christmas cheer, and a golden retriever football player…

http://mybook.to/thechristmasplaybook

Cross the Line

Cross and Scarlett are enemies at first sight, and the friction worsens when they're forced to live together at Shadow Valley University…

http://mybook.to/svu3

SCARLETT

I STARE at myself in the full-length mirror. My blonde hair is pinned behind my ears, and I drop my attention to the plunging neckline of my bridesmaid dress—or would it be considered a best woman's dress? I'll be standing next to my father as he marries Sofia, the woman I met no less than twenty-four hours ago when they picked me up from the airport.

She seems nice, and she's gorgeous, but not in the way I expected. The women my father has dated over the years were nothing less than gold diggers who spent more time in a salon chair than at a desk in school. Sofia is naturally pretty with her golden skin and rich brown hair that could put any Pantene commercial to rest. She's smarter than I originally gave her credit for, too. She's bilingual—speaking both English and Spanish—so at least I know there's something in between her ears other than air.

"Look at you, sweetheart."

I raise my attention from my cleavage to my dad in the reflection of the mirror. He stands with his shoulder resting along the doorjamb in his pristine suit and salt-and-pepper hair gelled to perfection.

I turn and glance down at my pink dress again. "Does this look okay?" I nibble on my lip. "It was all I had that was appropriate."

I've been studying abroad for most of the summer and didn't exactly have time to shop for a dress before walking off the escalator and meeting my new future stepmother for the first time. I picked it up at a local boutique in Barcelona while spending the weekend jumping from club to club with Lucia and Emmy. It was either this or a skimpy red dress, and I highly doubted my father would approve of that.

"You look perfect," he answers, making an obvious attempt to keep his gaze away from anything below my shoulders.

I smash my lips together to hide my amusement. He wants to say something about the deep V cut in the worst way. I just know it.

"Well." I sigh. "Is it time?"

My dad's hands disappear into the pockets of his trousers. "Before we go, I want to talk to you about something."

"Dad." I cross my arms and do my best to keep my face even. "You don't need to have the sex talk with me."

He chokes on air, pounding his chest with a closed fist. I burst out in laughter at his reaction. His cheeks turn red, his dark eyebrows crowding above his dark, navy eyes with irritation.

"Scarlett Wallace," he warns. "Don't kill me before I walk down the aisle."

I shrug, a smile still on my lips. "I'm just trying to lighten the mood."

He eventually places his hands back into his pockets and shakes his head. "Well, I guess you're fine with me and Sofia marrying, then? Since you're making jokes." He chuckles, his body losing tension.

I don't know if I've ever seen him so…concerned before. Maybe when he first started dating again after Mom passed away, but that was years ago.

"Dad." I walk toward him, my heels clicking against the marble floor. I pat his chest and smooth out his lapels, attempting to calm him. "I'm not a kid anymore. It's not like Sofia is stepping in and raising me. If you're happy, then I'm happy."

His deep breath fills the space between us, his shoulders evening out.

"Plus, she's way better than bimbo one, two, three, and four," I add.

His mouth flattens, but he doesn't argue. Instead, he puts his arm out for me to take, and we head down the long, quiet hall toward the French doors. The wedding isn't big. There are only about forty people in attendance, most of whom are family and some employees of Wallace Security. My father, the CEO of the business, draws a fine line between business and pleasure. However, those who have been around since the start of WS are as close to family as they can get without sharing a bloodline. Naturally, they'd be here.

After I've walked down the aisle with my dad and smiling at familiar faces, it's obvious that Sofia doesn't come from the same sort of lifestyle. There's maybe a handful of people I don't recognize, and none of them have the same golden skin tone that Sofia gets from her ethnicity—in short, they're all white.

Close friends? Maybe she was adopted?

To be honest, I don't know much about her.

I know they've been dating for a while, but with being away at Yale and then in Spain for a summer program, I've sort of been cut off from everything.

It was freedom mixed with books, salty air, and margaritas. I loved every second of it.

My dad centers himself at the altar, and I glide past him into position a few feet back. He glances over his shoulder at me and smiles, then panic sets in on his face.

"Wait. I forgot to mention something to you." His voice is pitched low.

My stomach falls. This was too good to be true. "She's pregnant, isn't she?"

"What? No." He shakes his head and follows it with a quiet laugh. His voice lowers even more. "Sofia and I won't be having any children together, Scarlett."

Whew. My dad was amazing when I was younger, and he still is, though a little hit or miss in some spots, but I couldn't imagine him having a baby with his new wife at the age of fifty-one.

"Sofia and I both decided that we're past that stage in life. I have you, and she has Cross."

Wait, what?

"Who's Cross?" I whisper.

"That's what I forgot to mention. You've been away, and with the wedding planning, and picking you up at the airport last minute…" The music shifts, and everyone stands. "Cross is Sofia's son."

"So I'll have a stepbrother? How old is he?"

How could my father forget to mention that?

He doesn't answer. Instead, he stares down the aisle, his jaw slacking. I stare at his profile and almost forget about the whole mention of my new stepbrother. Happiness blankets his expression, his eyes crinkling at the sides when he smiles. I can't remember a time that my dad has ever seemed so content before. Maybe he used to look at Mom like this—something I've likely forgotten over the years. Either way, he seems so at peace that I can't even be angry about the whole 'you have a surprise stepbrother' thing.

It's not that big of a deal. I'm hundreds of miles away most of the year, with the exception of major holidays.

With everyone's attention directed down the aisle, I pull myself back to the present and do the same. But instead of focusing on Sofia dressed in white, my attention goes to someone else—the person walking her down the aisle.

My entire body seizes. I blink several times, trying to right my vision.

I pray that the guy walking Sofia down the aisle isn't my new stepbrother, but with the same flawless deep-tan color of skin, I don't know who else it would be. He has the same shade of dark-brown hair, too, though his is perfectly messy, paired with a jawline that is edged with too much sex appeal. The closer he gets, the more I observe. He has to be close to my age and—*why is he staring at me like he wants to rip my head off?*

He hands off Sofia, pulling his scowl away from me at the last second and smiling at my father. I don't know the guy, but even that seems forced.

"Thank you, Cross," my father murmurs.

Ding, ding, ding. That's definitely my new stepbrother.

After Sofia and my father assume their rightful positions, I lean slightly to the left to get a better read on Cross. The muscles in his temples flick, like he's grinding his jaw.

Is he angry? Does he not like my father or something? Maybe he is protective over his mother?

Cross quickly jerks his gaze to me, catching me red-handed staring at him. I freeze, my entire body filling with shock. He narrows his eyes, appraising me. Apparently, I don't pass the vibe check, because he loses interest fast. His attention slides away, leaving me fuming.

My teeth clamp together.

Excuse me?

I shoot him a dirty look, although I have no idea if he catches it.

Two can play that game, jerk!

Sofia may be kind and warm, but her son? That's a totally different story.

CHAPTER 1

CROSS

SIX MONTHS LATER

"THANK YOU FOR MEETING WITH ME." My advisor ushers me into her office. "Are you all squared away on your classes for this semester?"

I take a seat across from her and kick my legs out. "I am. Your email sounded urgent…"

"Right." She lifts the glasses hanging around her neck and puts them on, then directs her attention to her computer screen.

It's at an angle, so she still has line of sight on me, but I can't see it. I do, however, see the reflection in her glasses. She clicks around painfully slow.

She is probably the oldest employee in the financial aid office, so the lack of technological skill is…understandable.

Her email *was* urgent. She listed off times for today and tomorrow that she had available, saying that we needed to resolve a matter before classes start on Wednesday.

So here I am, bright and early on Monday morning. It's barely eight, but I've already been up for hours. I snuck in a session with my trainer at the gym to prepare for an upcoming fight, and that somewhat lessened my anxiety surrounding *this*. I'm in the best shape of my life, and lacrosse season will be starting next month.

Honestly? I hate finance stuff. I wasn't exactly raised with the best role models when it came to finances. I know how to make food out of the random shit in the pantry and fridge, and how to stretch a dollar, but when it comes to…I don't know, building wealth? That's a phrase the new stepdad throws around a lot, and I haven't been able to admit I have no fucking idea what he's talking about.

So being in the financial aid office…

"Ah, yes, here we are." She clears her throat and glances my way. "I'll just dive right in, shall I?"

I gesture for her to continue, my stomach knotting.

"Your GPA has dipped below the requirement for some of your scholarships. Most importantly, the athletic one." She faces me. "We're a Division I school, which means our GPA requirement is a two point three. As of the end of the fall semester, you have a two point two."

I swallow. I knew I wasn't doing so hot in those freaking business classes, but after the final, I tuned everything out. I didn't want to know how much I sucked.

Clearly, I should've done some extra credit.

In order to make Shadow Valley University *work* with my nonexistent funds, I received a handful of scholarships. My tuition is completely covered by the athletic scholarship, while smaller, academic ones go toward housing.

"Okay," I say slowly. "How do I fix it?"

Her expression melts into one of pity. "If you can raise your GPA above a two point three by the end of the semester, you will be eligible to renew the scholarship for your senior year. You should've been made aware of this by your academic advisor last semester."

I press my lips together. Last semester…nope. I

vaguely recall some emails, but I figured it was about picking classes. I was all set in that department.

"So…do I still have a scholarship?"

"You do," she says. "I was able to do some finagling. As long as you meet with a tutor for your classes this semester, the athletic one remains in place."

"In other words, I need to pay for housing." My voice comes out wooden.

She nods. "We can give you a week if you'd prefer to stay in the same dorm, but there are some other options." She plucks a brochure from a stack off to the side and slides it across the desk to me.

"Anything else?"

"That was it, hon. My email is always open if you have any questions. Otherwise, we'll see you next week."

Fuck.

I get up and stride out of the financial aid office. I force my body to remain loose, the same way I do before a fight, but it's really just trying to hold off the internal panic. Housing… Shit, it's not even *remotely* affordable. I could try to find a roommate for some off-campus apartment, but my fights wouldn't cover rent.

I get paid good money when I win, but there's no guarantee. Plus, it's not exactly inconspicuous. When lacrosse season rolls around, I need to focus on that. Even if fighting is my first love, lacrosse is what keeps me in school.

Shaking out my limbs, I leave the administration building and climb into my car. I've been spending the last week with a teammate, essentially couch surfing, because my mom and her new husband are entertaining the *other* one.

Scarlett.

Since the wedding, I've managed to avoid being in the same room with her for longer than a few minutes. And *she's* managed to tone down the disgusted looks. She had no problem showing me her true colors when my mom and I walked down the aisle.

The sick part is, I was happy for my mom. She seemed to have found a genuinely good guy, and he's *still* as into her as he was before he put a rock on her finger. Too bad he has baggage in the form of a prissy, holier-than-thou daughter.

Well, maybe she's not so holy. The dress she was wearing left nothing up top to the imagination. She probably had to use tape to give herself that sort of cleavage. It was just tacky, you know?

Anyway, I'm more of an ass guy, and she was a bit lacking in that department.

That's not the point. I'm grateful Miss Yale hasn't been around, because my mother doesn't need that negativity. Her new husband, Robert, took her on a Greek island-hopping honeymoon, and she came back practically glowing.

But when Robert told us his daughter was coming home for the holidays, I started planning my exit. I stuck around through New Year's then packed my bags and hit the road.

My phone chimes with a new email. I click on it, then start the car. I drop my cell on my thigh to rub my hands together.

Winter is not my season. It's always fucking cold. It's kind of funny how much the hockey guys seem to relish it. You can always spot them because they never wear jackets. *Maybe* a puffer jacket if it's below zero, but that's rare.

I saw them all in a snowball fight on campus a few weeks ago, and not a single one was in anything thicker than a sweatshirt.

Crazy.

The email finally loads, and I scan its contents. It's from my advisor in the financial aid office, where I just came from.

Hi, Cross!

Just following up from our conversation. I've attached the invoice for our residential housing, to be paid on January 20th—one week from today, as discussed. Please don't hesitate to reach out with any questions.

Here is a link for tutors. We recommend finding one for each class.

Sincerely,

Maureen Bladwell

I open the attachment and gawk at the amount. There's no way. I drive back to my teammate's house slowly, racking my brain for a solution that doesn't involve my mother. But, like her ears were burning, she calls just before I pull into the driveway.

"Morning, *Mamá*," I answer.

"*Mijo*. I got an email from your financial aid office yesterday…"

My smile fades. "Oh. I just left her office—"

"Why didn't you tell us you were struggling?" She sounds hurt that I didn't open up to her.

"I—"

"The important thing is that they're being lenient," she continues. "But it seems like the housing is a situation. Is that right?"

I cover my face. "I didn't want you to have to deal with this. I'm going to figure something out."

"*Escuincle*, you know better than to keep things from me."

She just called me a brat, which is pretty familiar. Growing up, I heard *escuincle* come out of her mouth more than my name. I drop my hand and roll my eyes, but her tone warns against argument.

"Robert has already fixed it," she declares.

I sit up straighter. "What? How?"

"He's been looking to invest in a property in Shadow Valley, and he bought a house recently. It's been undergoing some repairs, but it's vacant—soon to be fully furnished. And since you now need somewhere to stay…"

"*Mamá*, I can't accept that."

She scoffs. "Robert just texted you the address. There's a delivery truck coming today, so you'd be helping out a lot if you were there to receive it. And…"

I hear Robert in the background but can't make out what he's saying.

"There's a key under the mat," she finishes. "Okay?"

Damn.

"Okay. Yes. Thank you."

"You're welcome, *mijo*. Robert says he'll call you about the details of the house later this afternoon."

My head hurts from the whiplash of the morning.

Inside, my teammate, Nate, is in the kitchen, making

some sort of green smoothie. He grins when I enter and offers me a glass.

I shake my head and take a seat at the breakfast bar. "You're never gonna guess what happened."

He pauses a beat, withholding my smoothie just out of reach. "You tell me right now."

I laugh then dive into the story. By the time I'm done, we've both drained our glasses, and I'm getting antsy to check out this house Robert bought.

"It kind of sounds too good to be true," Nate comments. "But, hey, maybe my couch will recover from your imprint from the last few weeks."

"Fuck off, dude."

I've been living out of a bag, so there's not much I need to collect. Nate reemerges in workout clothes while I'm loading my car.

"Don't be a stranger," he says. "Good luck with Stepdaddy's house."

I flip him off, and his laughter reaches me. I slam the door shut and start the engine. I go to my messages with Robert and click on the address, which auto-populates in my maps app. It's only five minutes from here. And, zooming in, it seems like it's about a similar distance to the school.

Maybe this won't be so bad.

I repeat that thought when I pull up to the curb in front of it. The house is two stories, white with dark-blue shutters and a matching dark-blue front door. There's even an attached garage. The front lawn will probably look nice in the spring when the grass comes back to life.

The spare key is easy to find. I let myself in and wander around, whistling under my breath. It seems half-furnished…in progress. I imagine whatever's being delivered today will have the rest of Robert's vision.

Or whatever assistant he assigned to the job, I should say.

It's kind of nice, though. Quaint but definitely not my style. Although, as a twenty-one-year-old dude, my style is black sheets and no headboard. Ha. Maybe this experience will get me over that. I hear headboards are in.

I go down the main hallway that opens up into the kitchen and dining area.

"Damn."

It's being renovated. What seems like new cabinets have been installed, sans countertops. They've laid plywood across to make do. The stainless-steel appliances are installed, but there's plastic on the floor. There's not even a sink.

At least my mom wasn't exaggerating.

There are two bedrooms upstairs, both furnished.

With headboards. That's how you know it's luxury living.

The mattresses are still covered in plastic, and tags hang off the dressers.

It's like it was all stocked in a hurry.

After examining both rooms, I take my pick and drop my bag on the bed. It crinkles loudly, but that will be a problem for later.

Downstairs, the front door opens. The hinges kind of squeal—probably the next thing on Robert's to-do list. But it's weird that a delivery guy would just let himself in…

I tense. My instincts take over, alarms going off in my head. I step lightly, creeping across the room.

Heavy footsteps on the stairs make me go still.

"Shit," someone swears.

Not the voice of a delivery guy.

"Damn this heavy suitcase." It's a girl, followed by the distinct *thump-thump-thump* of something hitting every step.

What the fuck?

I go into the hallway just as a familiar blonde-haired bitch reaches the top step.

My good mood tanks. She's lugging a huge purple suitcase behind her, struggling to get it up beside her, and she doesn't immediately spot me. I'm not sure what the fuck she's doing or why she's here, but I can guarantee this circles back to Robert.

Can't I just have *one* win?

But no.

It is satisfying watching her wrestle with that suitcase. There's a chance she's about to drop it and send it sailing back to the bottom. Maybe put a dent in the nice drywall her daddy will have to pay to fix.

So, scaring her is just the icing on top. This will be good.

I open the camera on my phone and hit *record*.

In my deepest voice, I boom, "What the hell are you doing here, Wallace?"

The scream she gives me is guaranteed to go viral.

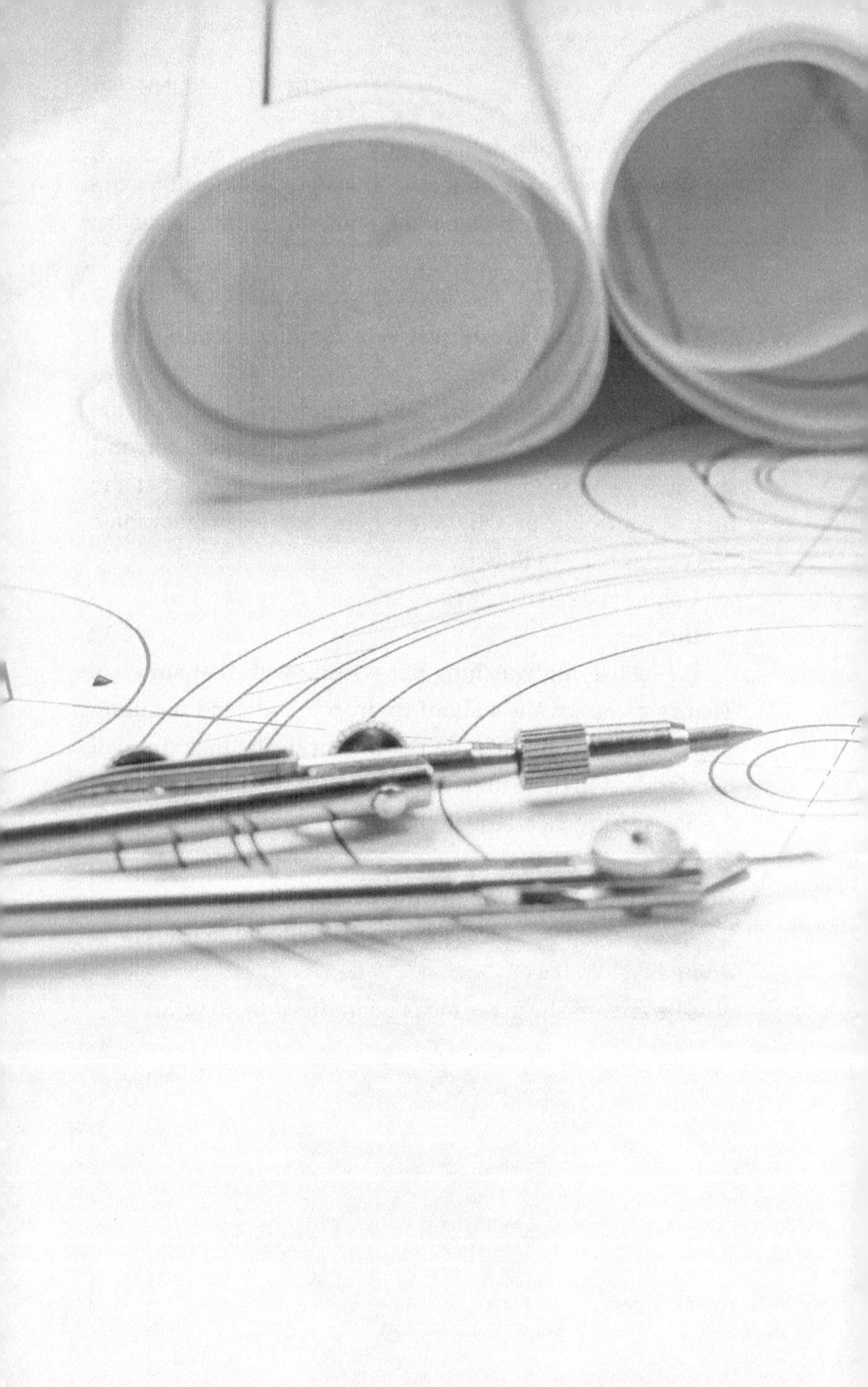

CHAPTER 2
SCARLETT

I SINK DOWN to the floor and cover my ears with my hands. My scream echoes throughout the near-empty house, filtering through my palms, right along with Cross's cackle. I shake in my crouched stance, and a tremor of blinding fear cuts through me.

"Gold." Cross's voice is muted. "That was fucking gold."

I release my ears, my arms prickling with fear.

"Jesus, get up." Cross snorts. "It's not like I'm holding a knife. I didn't even cover my face."

I scowl at him and stand on two wobbly legs. "You're an asshole."

Cross—too hot for his own good, unfortunately—shrugs. "I've been called worse."

"I'm sure you have," I mumble.

Lugging my suitcase behind me, I push past him. I stick my elbow out far enough to dig into his stomach, which admittedly is as hard as a rock.

"Oof."

I smile to myself and continue down the hallway.

I want to ask what he's doing here, but I really don't want to let on that I'm blindsided by his appearance. I've had one too many surprises lately, but if he's here for any reason other than running an errand for my father, I'm going to scream.

Again.

"That's my room," he quips from behind.

My teeth clank together. I stop rolling my suitcase across the wooden floor and spin around to face my stepbrother.

I make a face.

It still feels so odd to say that.

Stepbrother.

Every interaction I've had with him has been awful. If he isn't pretending to be nice to me in front of my father and Sofia, he's sending me scathing glares and doing shit like jumping out from behind walls to scare me half to death.

When I left for fall semester after the wedding, I thought, *good riddance.* Out of sight, out of mind.

But then I ended up back at home for the holidays, and that was where I stayed. Cross was hardly around—not that I would've noticed much with everything that was going on—but I overheard my father comforting Sofia when she expressed how upset she was that he seemed to be pulling away.

I'm certain he was absent during the holidays because I was home, but who am I to care?

"Your room?" I repeat.

"Yeah." He straightens to his full height. "*My* room. Didn't realize you were hard of hearing, Wallace."

I should've known this was too good to be true.

My father knew something was up when I announced that I wasn't going back to Yale after the holidays.

"You're the smartest in your class, you have a full ride to Yale, and you don't want to go back?"

"No."

"Something happened."

"Nothing happened —"

"You don't have to tell me what happened, but don't give up on school because of it. What if you transfer? To Shadow Valley?"

I know exactly why Cross is here. My dad probably bribed him to watch out for me, or maybe he thought I'd feel more comfortable if I had him around...safer. *As if.* I'd rather live alone, because I'm not sure being in the same house as Cross would be considered *safe.*

The question is, does Cross know that's why he's here?

I fold my arms and put all my weight on one foot. "So you mean to tell me that we're roommates?"

His eyes narrow, like he's just as put off by the thought as I am. "We're sharing a house, not a room."

I roll my eyes. "Housemates, then?"

Cross is busying himself with his phone, a half-smile overtaking his lips at whatever is on the screen. "Whatever you want to call it. Just don't say it in public."

The only thing worse than sharing walls with my rude, offensive, careless, *jerk* of a stepbrother is going back to Yale.

"Did you know?"

Cross lifts his gaze to mine quickly. Those brown eyes, rimmed in thick black eyelashes, narrow again, but he doesn't answer. He just stares a hole in my face.

We stand in uncomfortable silence.

I clear my throat. "What did your new stepdaddy give you to get you to agree?"

Anger flashes across his face. "*Stepdaddy*? You've got to be kidding me."

I feed off his emotions like I'm starving. I lean back on the doorjamb, my suitcase touching my leg. He's blocking the other two doorways, which gives me nowhere to go but into the room he says is his or down the stairs. Neither seems like a good option.

"Surely you didn't opt to share a house with your spoiled brat of a stepsister..." I throw out the same insult he flung at me the last time we spoke. Something in me demands I keep poking the bear. "You either didn't know, or my father bribed you." I tap my finger against my chin and pretend to think. "What does Cross want?"

He advances on me, his jaw clenched. He stops a hair's breadth away and braces his hand on the doorframe over my head. He's so tall that he effortlessly leans down into my space. It takes all of my willpower not to cower.

"One, I can't be bribed," he intones.

I hold my breath and angle my chin with a feigned boldness. My heart pounds so hard my chest aches.

"And two..." Cross grabs on to my suitcase. "I don't want anything from your father."

His brown eyes darken. I open my mouth to push him a little further, because although I know he doesn't like me, and he is intimidating, the old Scarlett never would've let him get away with talking to me like this.

My therapist said it's okay not to be the same Scarlett I was before, because I've been through something that is life-changing, but I can't help but reach for that girl who stood up for herself and was fearless.

"Except a free place to live?" I bat my eyes innocently.

Cross bares his teeth, and I bite the inside of my cheek. My mouth fills with blood, and my pulse thrums violently.

His phone vibrates, and he pulls it out of his pocket. A familiar number flashes across the screen, and he instantly becomes irritated. He lets a growl out right before he answers.

"Hello?"

I lean closer, trying to hear what my father is saying. I'm almost so swept away in eavesdropping that I don't notice Cross dragging my suitcase away from me.

"What are you doing?" I hiss.

He ignores me and continues talking to my dad. "Yeah, she just arrived. I'm helping her with her suitcase right now, actually."

He is?

Just when I let my guard down and think he's going to put my suitcase in the other bedroom, he winks and chucks it down the stairs.

My jaw falls open with a silent gasp.

It thuds down every step until it finally stops on the landing then bursts open. I stare at it, then turn and face Cross. I catch a glimpse of his smug expression as he slips past me into his room.

"You…fucking…asshole—"

He flips me off without turning around.

With anger guiding my steps, I lunge toward him.

His door slams in my face. I jerk back just in time to save my nose, and that only pisses me off more. The lock cuts through the pounding in my ears.

I let out a shriek and slap the door.

My hand stings but not quite as hot as the embarrassment coloring my cheeks.

It's okay, I tell myself woodenly. I descend the stairs and crouch next to my case. I slowly close and re-zip it, warring with my emotions.

Being stuck in a house with Cross is still better than going back to Yale.

Barely.

But it is.

CHAPTER 3

CROSS

"SOMETHING GOT YOU TWISTED UP?"

As a reply, I hit the bag Tyler is holding with extra power, and he lets out a hard breath. He waves me off, takes a step back, and plants his hands on his hips. The expression on his face is pure stubborn, middle-child energy. He's not moving until I start talking.

I straighten from my stance and sigh. "It's nothing."

His expression morphs into worry. "Your dad hassling you again?"

Tyler has been my best friend since second grade, when I was the new kid in class with a black eye—the one that came from my father. He made me practice lying, even at seven, before I was allowed to leave the house. It left me with some, uh…anger issues.

Perfect for taking out on bullies.

Tyler and I sat next to each other, and it didn't take long to notice that some of the boys in the other class liked to steal his lunch. When I went searching for a fight, Tyler was there, telling the teachers the other ones started it.

Immediate best friends.

I joined the lacrosse team with him in sixth grade.

He was dragged into the world of underground fighting because of me.

I slept on his couch for a week in tenth grade when my mom was in the hospital and my dad sat in jail. He beat her so badly there was no lie big enough to cover the truth.

My only regret is that I wasn't there to save her from it in the first place.

But then I got accepted to Shadow Valley U on a lacrosse scholarship, and Tyler was *happy* for me. He got a partial scholarship, and the coach liked him just fine, which he said was better than nothing.

So, here we are.

Except, he's living with his boyfriend this year, and I'm stuck with *Scarlett Wallace*. The bane of my existence. Her pinched expression—from the wedding, yes, but also from two days ago—is etched into my mind.

And somehow, after I slammed the door in her face, I've managed to avoid all signs of her.

Her dad did a shit job talking me off the ledge, too. He just mentioned her needing a change of scenery, someone to look out for her, *blah, blah, blah*. All I heard was that the fancy Ivy League school she attended was getting boring.

She wants to slum it with the heathens of SVU for the next year and a half.

"Cross," Tyler pushes. "Your dad?"

I shake my head sharply. "Nah. He has a no-contact order. He'd get in trouble if he reached out."

Doesn't mean it can't still happen. Say, some stranger showing up with a typed-up letter from him, the note full of threats about me *talking*, but it's always left unsigned. Because he's not an idiot.

I've never been so glad to change my last name to my

mother's. *Lopez* is connected to so much rich Mexican history. Leaving it behind in favor of my father's—boring *Martin*—felt almost sacrilegious.

If I were religious.

I'm not, though. Not even remotely.

"There he is!" a deep, familiar voice booms out. "I told you, 'If I had to bet, Cross Lopez will be working the bag today.' And I was right!"

I swivel to face the large man making his way across the gym floor. Stanley Griggs is the owner of the gym. He was once a trainer for some famous MMA fighters, but now he mostly arranges under-the-table fights. He's the one who got me into it a few years ago. He gave me the address of some shitty warehouse across town, and it wasn't until I showed up that I realized what he had in store for me.

I won that first fight by the skin of my teeth, and Stanley slapped some cash in my hand. Said there was more of it if I wanted in.

That was the beginning of my addiction.

"Mr. Griggs," I greet him, shaking his hand. "Nice to see you, sir."

"Kiss-ass," Tyler says under his breath.

Stanley either doesn't catch my best friend's attitude or he is good at ignoring him. Either way, he smiles brightly and herds me out of Tyler's earshot. "I have some people I'd like you to meet. They're very well connected in, well…our sort of show."

I swallow and nod. He keeps promising me that these fights will lead to a professional fight. A legit one. But it's never been the right time, or he can't get their agents to agree to fight someone…well, he didn't *say* I was an amateur, but he definitely implied it.

"How's your mom?" Stanley asks.

"She's good. She got married over the summer."

He whistles. "A gorgeous lady like her? I'm not surprised someone snatched her up."

I force a laugh. "Yeah. He treats her well, so…"

"That's important, Cross."

We climb the steps to Stanley's office on the second floor. The wall of windows gives him an aerial view over his gym, just the way he likes it. But right now, the blinds are drawn, hiding who waits within.

Before I can enter, Stanley grasps my arm and tugs me to a halt. "What's the one thing you need more than anything in this life, Cross?"

I stare at him. "What?"

He gives me a look. "Come on. What is your one desire?"

"A professional fight—"

"Yes!" He shakes my arm. "Hold on to that, okay? These are good guys. The offer might sound…well, I should just let them explain. I've already been negotiating up on your behalf."

That's not unusual…

"Okay," I agree.

"Okay," he echoes.

He releases me and opens the door, and leads me inside. Two men sit on the couch along the right wall. They're both in forms of business casual. They wear slacks and dress shoes, but one has a black polo shirt, the kind golfers would wear, and the other is in a pale-blue button-down.

That doesn't give me much to go on. There are no logos on their clothing, and the dress-shirt guy has a briefcase at his feet. The other one has propped his ankle up on his other knee, but he drops it, and both rise at our entrance.

"This is Cross Lopez," Stanley introduces. "Cross, these are colleagues of mine, Jason and Alex Webber."

Brothers, then.

"Nice to meet you, Cross," Polo Shirt Guy says. "I'm Alex."

"Jason," the other one adds.

They both shake my hand, then Stanley motions to the upright chair that sits facing his desk.

"Pull that over," he says. "Make yourself comfortable."

I do, and Stanley settles his frame into the lone armchair. I sit up straight and try to get my attention off the sweat drenching my shirt. I didn't notice it until right this second, under their scrutiny.

And suddenly, my hope ratchets higher. He asked me what I wanted. Are they going to give that to me? My chest tightens. I press my lips together so I don't blurt out my questions.

"We've heard a great deal about you, Cross," Jason says. "From Stanley, and others. Good things. Impressive things."

I glance at the gym owner, who's still smiling, and nod carefully. "Thank you, sir."

"Because of this, we think you'd be a perfect fit for an upcoming fight." Alex holds up his hands. "Now, it's still in the same format as before. It's not sanctioned. However, if you can do this for us, we can guarantee you a match against Wilmer Fox."

My jaw drops.

Wilmer Fox is a rising star in the fighting world. I think even my mom knows who this kid is. He's only twenty-three, two years older than me, and he's practically a household name.

"Name the day, and I'll be there," I promise. "I'll beat anyone you put me up against."

Alex and Jason exchange a look.

My stomach knots. Did I say something wrong?

"The problem is…" Alex meets my gaze. His light-blue eyes hold no warmth for me, no kindness, but there is an honesty there. "We don't want you to win."

My shoulders hike. "Excuse me?"

"Now, son," Stanley murmurs. "This sort of *ask* would come with other benefits as well."

"What?" My voice comes out hoarse.

"Cross." Jason picks up the briefcase at his side and balances it on his knees. "We know you want to fight Fox—we can make that happen. You lose one fight, and you can cement your name in the MMA world going up against Fox."

"It's asking a lot," Stanley says. "You see the boy's hesitation, Jason, don't you?"

Jason flicks the clasps on the briefcase and opens it. He takes a second then swivels it around to show me.

Stacks of cash. Bundles—or whatever they're called. A fucking ton of them. It's more money than I've seen in my life.

"H-how much?"

Jason smiles. "Twenty thousand dollars."

My eyes widen.

"That you can take today, Cross," Alex adds.

I gulp. Twenty thousand bucks could solve my living arrangement with Wallace. It could be a fund to get the fuck out of Shadow Valley. Or better, it could be the cash to get my mother out of this relationship if it ever turns sour. I don't know if it will—she's historically not chosen the best men to date—but I've got to protect her.

Which means accepting this deal, even if I'll never be able to look at myself the same ever again.

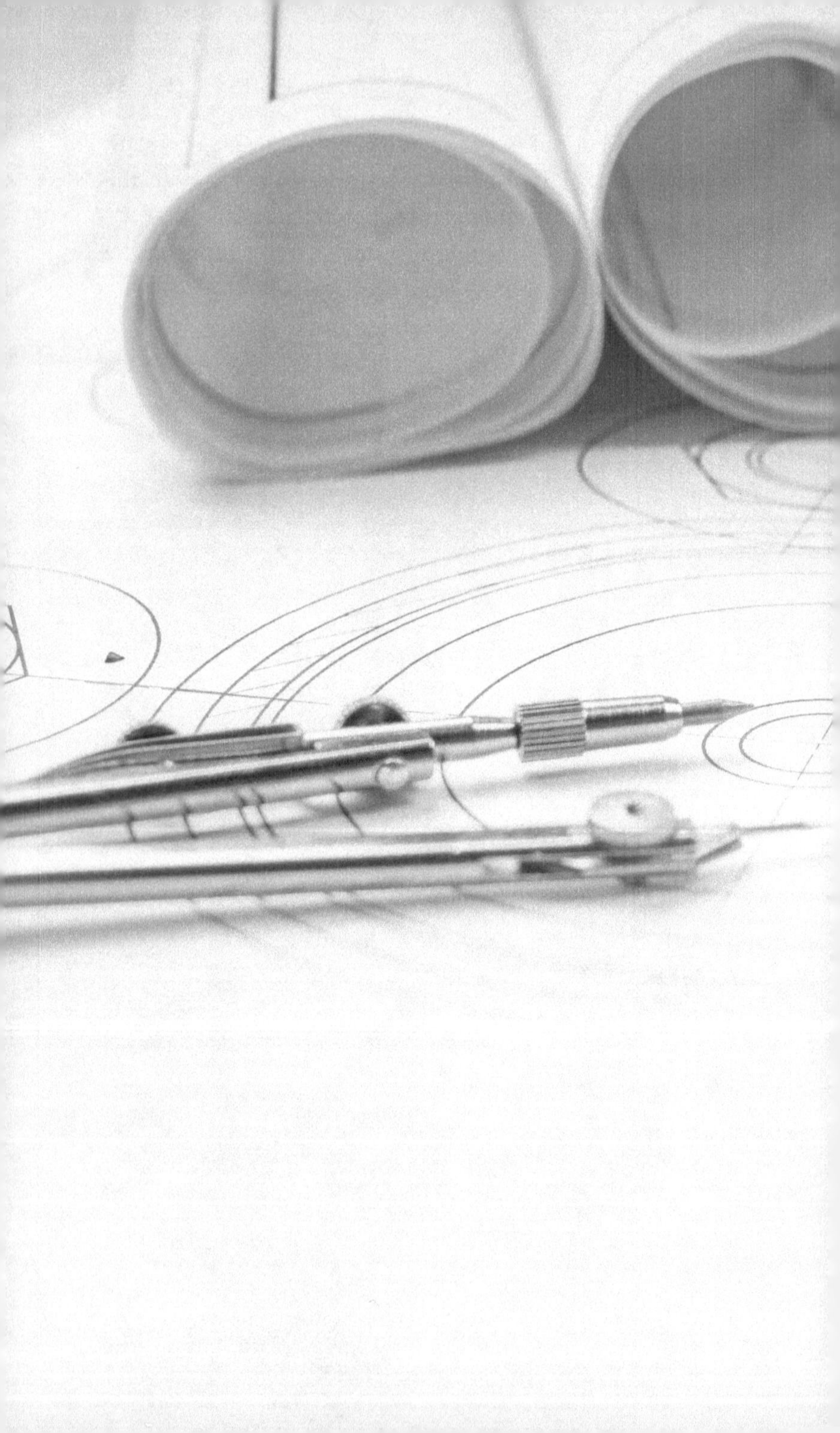

CHAPTER 4
SCARLETT

"COME IN, COME IN!" An older woman with crescent glasses perched on the tip of her nose places her hand on the small of my back to usher me into her office. "Take a seat, Scarlett."

Once she is back in her chair, she quickly begins typing on her computer, and the next thing I hear is something being printed from behind her. She spins in her seat, pulls out the piece of paper, and smiles.

"Your schedule." She slides it across her desk. "Very ambitious class choices, but given your background at Yale, I think you'll do just fine."

I smile and glance at the course load. It's heavy but doable.

"Though, may I make a suggestion?"

I focus on my academic advisor. Her expression is cautious at best.

"Sure?" My agreement comes out like a question.

"Tutoring." She clasps her hands together on top of her desk, appearing pleased with herself.

"Tutoring?" I repeat.

Didn't she just say that I'd do *just fine* with my course selections?

I clear my throat and try my best not to offend her. "I think I'll be okay, but if I need help, I will look into tutoring."

Not.

A wheezy laugh leaves her. "No." She shakes her head. "I think *you* should tutor. With your test scores and impeccable GPA from an Ivy League like Yale? Some of our students could really benefit from having a tutoring session with you."

I see myself in the reflection of the glass cabinets behind her desk. My smile seems painful, which is exactly what it'd feel like to tutor my peers at Shadow Valley.

"It would be a good way to meet some of the students, maybe make a friend or two? Your father said—"

I perk up at the mention of my dad. "My father?"

My body flushes. A rush of scorching heat washes over my skin like a warm summer's rain.

What does she mean by *my father*? Is he blasting my business to anyone who will listen?

The next few minutes of the meeting are a blur. I nod and agree to things that I want no part of, yet somehow, I leave with my name listed with the others under **student tutors for peers.**

As soon as I'm around the corner and out of sight, I dial his number with a vengeance.

It rings once before he picks up. I don't even take a breath before laying into him.

"Are you serious, Dad? Do you want everyone at Shadow Valley to know that I came home from Yale with my tail tucked between my legs? Not to mention telling my academic advisor that I'm friendless!"

That's right. She said the word *friendless.*

I have friends! They're just back at Yale.

My father sighs, waiting for a beat to speak. I lean against the stone wall and stare out into the courtyard.

Shadow Valley is so much different than Yale, and I'm not just speaking about the architecture. The air is fresher, the students less uppity. I can't say I feel at ease here, especially not at home with my new housemate, but I'm not checking over my shoulder every few seconds or hiding from a cluster of guys, wondering if *he'll* be in the mix, so at least there's that.

"Sweetheart." My father sighs again, his breath loud inside my ear.

I can picture him now, squeezing the back of his neck where most of his tension settles.

"What did you tell her?" I ask.

He pauses.

"More importantly, what did you tell Cross?" I roll my eyes even though he can't see me. "Why didn't you tell me that we'd be housemates?"

"I didn't think it mattered…"

Cross and I have an unspoken pact to put our differences aside when we're with our parents, so of course my father doesn't see the issue with it. In fact, he probably thinks I feel better with Cross there.

But I don't.

"I didn't tell Cross or your academic advisor anything other than you transferred to Shadow Valley to be closer to home."

Which I suppose makes sense, considering he doesn't actually know what happened at Yale.

I raise an eyebrow. "And…"

"And I asked Cross to watch out for you, maybe take you to a campus event if he happened to go to one."

I scrunch my nose. "A campus event?"

"You know." He chuckles. "Somewhere you can make a friend or two."

I choke on a silent laugh. Cross does not want me to be friends with his friends and vice versa. I'd rather never see Cross ever again, thank you very much.

"You don't have to worry about me. I know how to make friends," I argue. "I don't need my stepbrother's help with that." I lower my voice and mutter, "If anything, he needs *my* help."

A faint laugh comes from around the corner, and I peek forward to see who's listening. A girl with pretty auburn hair, holding a similar paper like the one in my hand, slaps her hand over her mouth. She lowers it to mouth the word *sorry* at me, then rolls her lips together.

"I'm not worried," my dad argues. "And what was that about helping Cross? I couldn't quite hear you."

I shut my eyes and shake my head. "It's nothing. Listen, I gotta go, Dad. I just got my schedule and—"

"Right! Okay, well, just give me a call later. I, uh… installed some alarms at the house, by the way. Cross has all the information. I told him to pass it along to you."

Lovely.

I'm mid-hang-up when the eavesdropper places her hand over her heart.

"I am so sorry," she blurts out. "I did not mean to overhear your conversation. I just walked out here from meeting with my academic advisor"—she points behind her to the same doors I exited from—"and couldn't help but laugh at the dig about your stepbrother."

I give her a half-smile. "It's okay. I'm glad I could amuse someone."

"I'm Sawyer," she introduces herself, holding out her hand.

I shake it gently. "I'm Scarlett."

She glances at my schedule. "So you're a transfer, too?"

"Yeah," I say. "Where are you coming from?"

"A small college in a Podunk town." She laughs sarcastically. "You?"

"Uh…" I'm hesitant to tell her the truth, because when people find out I went to Yale, they automatically assume I'm a genius. I'm not. I'm just an great student who likes to excel in all aspects of life. "Yale."

"Yale," she repeats. "You're far away from home, then?"

I shake my head. "Technically, this is home, so I've just moved back."

To live with my stepbrother, apparently.

"Oh, darn." She sighs. "I was hoping there was at least one other person here who was approachable, who could be clueless with me. I don't even know where the coffee stand is."

A laugh bubbles out of me. "Don't get me wrong, I still don't know where anything is. It's been a few years since I've lived in Shadow Valley, and I've never even been on this campus before." I glance around for a coffee stand and come up empty-handed. I turn back toward Sawyer. "If you want, we can go find coffee together. My first class doesn't start until tomorrow, so I'm free."

Hope illuminates in her blue eyes. "Really?"

"Yeah, of course," I say with more enthusiasm than I've had in a week.

Sawyer and I walk down the stone steps.

"Plus," I continue, "my dad thinks I need my stepbrother's help to make friends at Shadow Valley. I'd love nothing more than to prove him wrong."

Sawyer grins. "I can definitely help you with that."

We make our way through the center of campus, trading stories about our old schools. It makes me ache for the school I used to love. The familiarity of it. My *friends*. But no. One stupid decision ruined everything.

I swear, we circle the whole interior of the campus and come up blank.

"Maybe the dining hall has coffee," she says. "I could eat something anyway."

I nod fast, my cheeks heating. "Told you I didn't know my way around."

"We could ask someone." She tucks a lock of her red hair behind her ear. "Be extroverted and shit."

"Pass."

She laughs. "I'm glad I found you, Scarlett."

Ditto.

The student center, at least, is easy to locate. A quick peek at my watch reveals we're right in time for a late breakfast. The worker looks at both of us like we're idiots when we don't know what to hand her to get in, then she sighs heavily when Sawyer and I go digging for our student IDs.

At least I got that yesterday. *Sheesh.*

On the way in, we pass a corkboard covered in flyers.

"Uh, Scar."

I jerk. It's been a minute since anyone has called me that—it was a thing at Yale, but I haven't talked to those friends in…a while.

Sawyer taps my arm. "Is that you?"

I focus on where she's pointing, and the blood drains out of my face.

There's a flyer—no, there are at least seven—plastered to the board. A selfie from my Instagram is front and center, with red block lettering above and below it.

WANTED: in desperate search of new friends.

Must be able to handle random fits of nonsense, unpleasant body odor, and barking.

At the bottom, there are tear-away pieces that have my school email address on it.

What the actual fuck?

BARKING?

Unpleasant body odor?

This has Cross written all over it.

My face burns. Mortification screeches through me, and my nails scrape at the corkboard in my hurry to rip them all down. The papers tear and crumple, but it doesn't seem like I'm moving fast enough.

Everyone is staring.

Sawyer is probably going to ditch me immediately— who wouldn't?

When they're finally all down, my chest heaves. I turn around and mentally brace for the horrified expression my new friend—*new ex-friend, more like*—must have.

But she's not. She loops her arm in mine and tugs me deeper into the dining hall. She makes a beeline straight for the trash bin, where she takes the papers from my hand and stuffs them down.

"There," she says. "Now, I can't wait to hear the story behind that."

"You're not going to dump me?"

She laughs. "You kidding? Things just got interesting, girl. You're stuck with me."

CHAPTER 5
CROSS

MY PHONE CHIRPS. The incoming alert is from the security system that Wallace—my mom's new husband, *not* the demon living across the hall from me—forced on us. I was around when they showed up and installed it, but Scarlett was nowhere to be found.

It's not my fault she missed the instructions on how to shut off the alarm system.

That's what the text is: an automated message that the silent alarm has been triggered. Wonder how many family codes she tried to type in?

And how long is it going to take her to give up and call me?

The text has asked if it was a mistake or if emergency services should be dispatched. Another minute, and I think I'll get a call.

Bzzzz.

Yep.

"Hello?" I answer.

"Mr. Lopez? This is Nick with Wallace Security. The

silent alarm is currently going off at your residence. Do you require assistance?"

I sigh. "No, Nick, it's just my bumbling idiot of a stepsister. You can kill it."

"Kill—"

"The alarm, Nick. Thanks, buddy." I hang up on him and finish stapling the last flyer up in the library announcement section. The dining hall ones disappeared, but this is just phase one of my mission to make Scarlett's life hell.

Honestly? I don't give a fuck if she receives a single email—although, I do rip some of the tags off, just to give people the idea that someone's interested. I just live for her embarrassment and suffering.

Once my handiwork is done, I head downstairs and check in for my first tutoring session. It's a grudging act, but I'd rather not dig myself into a deeper hole.

In a way, it's good that the security system works. With twenty grand hidden in my closet, it's nice to know who's coming and going. Plus, there are little sensors on all the first-floor windows, too.

Scarlett won't be able to so much as crack a window without me knowing.

I smirk. The control of it all is going straight to my head. And I haven't even seen her reaction.

"Your tutor isn't here yet," the girl at the desk says. "Take a seat, okay?"

I grimace. "How long do I have to wait to get credit for showing up? Like, if they don't?"

"Fifteen minutes."

I start the stopwatch on my phone and flash it at her. "Great. Thanks."

She sighs and motions me into the room. I saunter past

her and scan my options. There are five round tables, all covered in gaudy, overly colorful plastic tablecloths. Each one has six chairs. This room must double as something else…

Two of the five have students seated at them, their heads bent together over textbooks.

Gross.

I drag out a chair at the farthest table and drop into it, keeping my back to the wall so I have a clear view of everyone coming in and out. I drop my phone on the table and lean back, crossing my ankles. The stopwatch ticks onward, first one minute then six. Only nine more and I'm free.

What I should be doing is focusing on my upcoming fight. It's tonight, but the location is still undetermined. I'll get a text an hour prior, along with everyone else on the list. From there, it spreads by word of mouth. Invite only.

Of course, tons of extras usually show up. Half the students at SVU end up in the crowd. That'll be fun, letting them all see me lose…

As it has every time I've thought about it since that meeting, my stomach cramps. I can't believe I'm willingly doing this. In my spare time, I've been apartment shopping. But part of me likes the idea of making Wallace uncomfortable, and how am I to do that from somewhere else? Giving up the house is like giving in.

The memory of coming downstairs and finding her sitting next to my mother on the couch, watching a movie, rears its ugly head. The hatred that rushed through me in that moment was hard to control. I had to leave the house before I exploded.

In that regard, she's already taking pieces of my family that she doesn't deserve.

I drum my fingers on my thighs. My phone shows twelve minutes when someone rushes into the room.

My lip curls.

"Sorry, sorry," Scarlett apologizes to the girl at the desk. "Who am I tutoring?"

She turns around, and I grimace.

"You're kidding me…"

My thoughts exactly. Not that I'd ever admit it out loud.

I watch Scarlett visibly shut off her disdain for me. She puts her shoulders back, stands straighter, and marches through the room. She stops across the table from me, her expression carefully blank.

Her honey-blonde hair is caught up in a messy pile on top of her head. She's wearing glasses, which I haven't seen on her before. It, plus the dark eye makeup, makes her green eyes pop. Unfortunately. Paired with the over-sized zip-up sweatshirt that reveals a peek of a v-neck tee, sweats, and sneakers she's got on, I'd say she's really trying to *not* impress whomever she thought she'd be tutoring.

I file that information away, only because I suspect she had no idea her tutoring session was with me. Hell, I'm still a bit in disbelief that the universe conspired so hard to force us together again.

"Cross, what a lovely surprise."

My eyebrow leaps up of its own accord. "Careful, Wallace, or else I'd think you arranged this."

Anger flashes across her face. "Trust me, I'd never."

"Of course." I hit *end* on my stopwatch and show it to her. "But unfortunately, you're more than fifteen minutes late. So, I'll be going."

I grab my bag and stand. She moves to block me, and I

look down at her. She's average height for a girl, but I can still easily see the top of her head—and down her shirt. Her tits are pressed together in her bra, and I catch a glimpse of black lace before she drills her finger into my chest.

"You want to touch me, Wallace?" I lean in. "Start lower."

She jerks back.

"Or at least flash your tits and make it worth it."

"Ew, you pig." She crosses her arms, but all it does is lift the only promising asset she has. "You're my *stepbrother*."

"Emphasis on *step*, if you want to go there." I grin. "If you're shy, we can always role reverse. I can tutor you on how to give the perfect blow job."

Her jaw drops. "This conversation is only getting worse."

I shrug. "I'm trying to leave, Wallace. You're the one standing in my way."

"Because—" She grimaces. "I was within my fifteen-minute window. You're the one who made me late anyway."

"How's that?" I make a show of looking around. "I was here the whole time, waiting on you."

"The stupid security system," she hisses. "It wouldn't stop beeping and declaring me an intruder."

"You kind of are." I tilt my head. "Any thoughts about going back to your Ivy League?"

Her expression goes cold. "No."

"Shame. Now, if you'll excuse me…" I brush past her. I show the desk girl my stopwatch, frozen just past fifteen, and make a face at her. Then I keep moving, lest the demon behind me decides to give chase or something.

Damn.

I was hoping for a chill tutor that would kind of do a whole bunch of my work for me.

I stop in my tracks.

That's it.

Scarlett is the perfect person to do just that.

No, no, I don't think she'd actually do my work out of the goodness of her heart. But she probably would do it if I blackmailed her into it…which means my mission to move out, which was already paused, is now on hold indefinitely.

As is my avoiding her.

I glance over my shoulder, but she hasn't reappeared. No doubt she's trying to get this to be my fault, like some last-ditch effort to keep a spotless record. Too bad it's been tarnished before she's even begun.

I pause and glance at the bulletin board. The flyers are still in place, which means she probably rushed by and missed them. There are a few of the tear-away pieces gone. I type in her email and send her the security system alarm code. With any luck, it'll get lost amongst the spam.

Step one: find one of Scarlett's deep, dark secrets. A girl like her has to have a few skeletons in her closet.

Step two: use it against her. Mercilessly. And get some decent grades while I'm at it.

My phone pings as I'm walking out. Anticipation and nerves burst to life inside me when I see who's messaging.

STANLEY

Got early word on the fight location. Be there at 10PM sharp.

Another text immediately follows with a map pin.

I click it and zoom in, nodding to myself. The fight is at

an abandoned factory I've been to before. It's on the other side of town, sandwiched between businesses that haven't been so unlucky as to go bankrupt in this economy. By ten, though, it should be all cleared out.

ME

Got it.

I switch over to my text thread with Tyler.

ME

Need some last-minute prep before my fight tonight. You around?

TYLER

Yeah, just leaving my ma's.

Race you to the gym.

You're on.

Running drills and hitting something will help me feel better—especially since I'm going to be taking a beating later tonight.

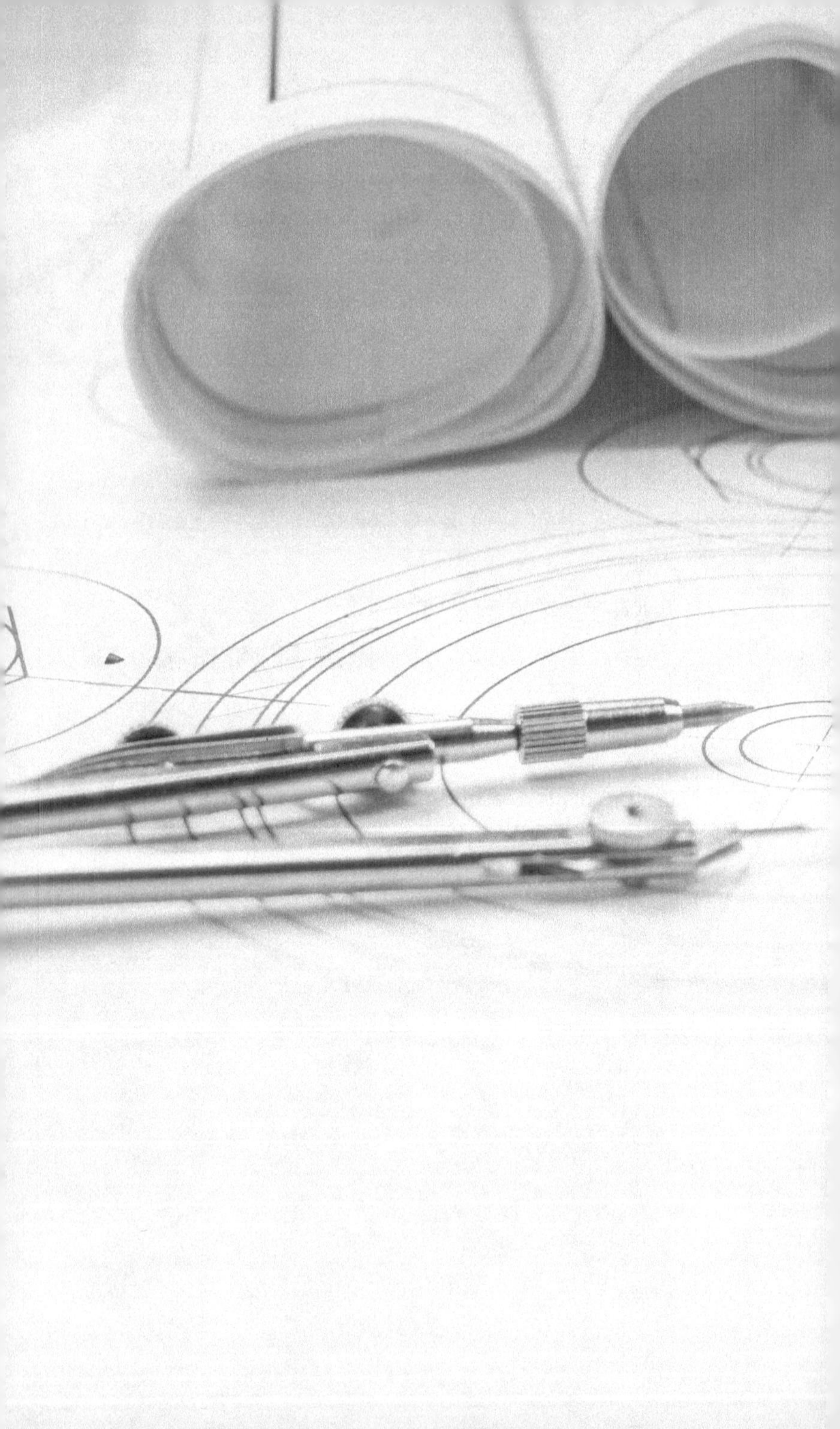

CHAPTER 6
SCARLETT

MY INBOX IS full of junk, and by junk, I mean emails from that *hilarious* flyer Cross has pinned all over campus. Another ping and I mutter how much I hate him. I crumple yet another flyer on my way to the parking lot and throw it into the trash before spotting my car.

It's dark, but thankfully, there are several streetlights lining the walkway. My lucky architecture compass stays in my purse as a steady reminder that I have some sort of protection, but it does nothing to calm my already rising blood pressure from the substantial number of students who now have my email.

Doesn't Cross understand that I'm a private person?

I quickly shut my door and lock it, relishing the safety of my car.

Of course Cross doesn't understand that I don't want people privy to my life. He doesn't know me, and the little bit that he did learn was from a judgmental standpoint at our parents' wedding where I was much different than I am now.

I was the life of the party, clanking glasses full of liquor with my dad and Cross's mother, dancing most of the night away. Where I once smiled a lot and didn't meet a stranger, now I'd rather be holed up in my bedroom with that new security system set so no one can touch me.

Shit, that's right...

I consider calling my dad to tell him that Cross has the code and has yet to give it to me, but that's something a bratty stepsister would do, and that's not how I want to play this game with him. He'll just throw it in my face that I went running to Daddy Dearest and call me a spoiled brat again.

After clicking on Cross's name, I quickly type a message.

Short and to the point.

ME

What's the security code?

My phone doesn't buzz until I pull up to the curb of our house. There aren't any lights on—not even the porch light. Either Cross isn't home, or he's being his typical asshole self and wants me to fumble in the dark.

CROSS

emailed it to you

I roll my eyes.

ME

You can't even text in complete sentences? Probably shouldn't have ditched your tutor.

With a pleased smile, I open my inbox. I check my spam folder when I see nothing but a few emails from professors with updated syllabuses. My lips flatten immediately. There are even *more* emails in my spam from people on campus finding those flyers. I flare my nostrils, exhale deeply, and delete them all.

Eventually, I find the email from Cross.

666#.

How fitting. The devil picked the Devil's number—something he probably did on purpose.

I hold my mace with a steady grip and race up the front steps, careful not to trip. I let myself into the house quickly, and the beeping of the security system immediately starts up.

It takes me a moment to locate the box on the wall. I jab the light switch and examine the panel. With shaky fingers, I enter the code.

It flashes red and reads *error* then goes back to beeping. Louder.

What the hell?

I reenter the code.

Nothing happens.

The beeping continues, followed by the word *intruder* in a robotic voice.

I angrily text Cross.

ME

> You're an asshole. What is the CORRECT code?

Cross and I are about to go toe to toe if he keeps this up. I was willing to play nice. After I accepted my future at SVU, my plan was to keep my head down and finish my degree. But now I'm stuck dealing with this.

When he doesn't text back, I try it again.

The police are going to show up if Cross doesn't text me back, and then I'll go to prison for murdering him.

Bzzzz.

I frantically drop to my knees and grab my phone.

Cross's name flashes, and I quickly answer it, only to pull it away from my ear right away. Loud noises echo in the background, and it sounds like he's at some raging house party.

"What the hell are you doing?" he shouts. "How hard is it to enter a fucking code, Scarlett?"

Angry heat covers me with his patronizing tone. "Hmm, I don't know. How hard is it to give me the correct fucking code, Cross?"

"What are you talking about?" he snaps.

I repeat the code he gave me. "666 pound. That's what I entered!"

The chatter in the background of the call lessens, and then I hear a door latch, shutting it out completely. "It's 669 pound, stupid."

"You typed it incorrectly!" I exclaim. "Maybe you shouldn't skip out on those tutoring sessions."

"Maybe you shouldn't show up late," he retorts.

I rush over to the panel and enter the correct numbers. The beeping stops, and the house falls blissfully silent.

I exhale loudly. "Okay, I got it."

"Great. Can you fucking stay put? I'm busy and don't have time to deal with your stupidity."

"My stupidity?" I shout. "And what are you so busy doing that—"

I jerk backward mid-sentence when the phone beeps.

He hung up on me.

A fiery line of annoyance zips down my spine as I stand in the middle of our dark house.

I bristle at the thought of it being *our* house.

Sighing, I throw my bag off to the side. The front door

locked automatically behind me, but I check one more time before heading to the kitchen to grab a bottle of water.

After drinking nearly all of it, I throw it into the trash and huff.

I knew Cross was an asshole from the moment I met him. But the more time I spend around him, which isn't much, the more I realize just how big of an asshole he really is.

Can you fucking stay put? I'm busy and don't have time to deal with your stupidity.

The fucking nerve.

I stomp my way down the hall and head toward the stairs. The annoyance I have for my stepbrother at the moment is at an all-time high. I stop in front of his bedroom door and smile deviously.

He wants to play games with me by giving out my email and insulting me every three seconds? Then I guess I'll need to level up and show him that he can't bully me into submission.

I push on his door and walk right inside his bedroom. I expected him to have a lock on the door to keep me out, just like I expected his room to be a mess.

It's not.

It's neat and tidy. Even the bed is made.

I don't even think my bed is made.

I flip on the lamp on his desk and give it a once-over. His schedule and a pile of notebooks lay on it, with a few pencils scattered on top. I take a photo of his schedule because it's always nice to know where your enemy is.

Then I start opening drawers.

Condoms.

Lube.

Loose change.

More pencils.

I change directions and go to his closet. Everything is freaking neat here, too, but something on the top shelf catches my attention.

My fingers skim the side of an old, wooden cigar box. I pull it down. It's sort of like the one my father has, but this one is so worn out that I can hardly make out the word *Forseca* engraved on the top.

I run my fingers along the grooves and give the box a little shake. Nothing rattles on the inside, and there isn't a strong scent of cigars like I'd expect, so without hesitation, I flip the box open.

Whoa.

Benjamin Franklin's face stares back at me, and my lips part.

I grip the wad of cash, and it's much more than I thought.

This is a ton of money.

Where did Cross get this much cash?

Did he rob my dad?

I roll my eyes. That's unlikely. My father is too anal to let this disappear without noticing, and although Cross isn't the nicest to me, it's obvious he cares for his mother. He likely puts up with me and my dad because he knows his mom is happy. He isn't going to ruin their marriage by stealing from his new stepdad.

Right?

I freeze mid-thought.

A noise comes from the other side of the door, and I stare at it with panic surging to my fingertips. I drop the wad of cash, as if it's going to catch on fire, and watch it float to the floor like feathers.

Fuck me.

I drop to my knees to cover up the evidence, but it's too late.

The door swings open, and my face pales. Cross, along with one of his friends, appears in the doorway.

I'm at a loss for words.

Not because Cross just caught me snooping through his room, but because he can hardly stand. His friend's arm is wrapped around Cross's waist. His face is a mess of purple bruises and blood.

"Who are you?" his friend asks.

I pop up from my knees, and that's when Cross finally notices me.

His expression switches from pained to lethal in a split second.

Shit.

CHAPTER 7
CROSS

"I'VE NEVER SEEN THAT," Tyler says. "Like, *fuck*. Did someone drug you?"

I grunt and grip the edge of the car, hauling myself up and out. It doesn't help that Tyler's car is so low to the ground that it's like sitting on the pavement. He grabs my forearm and supports some of my weight, but *everything* hurts. I may as well have gone through a meat grinder.

Definitely not my finest moment.

Why couldn't I have gotten someone who could punch hard enough to knock me out? That would've been better than the shitshow I just endured.

There's an unread text from one of the Webber brothers on my phone and another few from Stanley, but I haven't been able to look at them yet. The shame and anger swirling in my gut are too much to take, and I might snap at them.

I never want to do that again.

"Doesn't matter," I say to Tyler. "An ice bath will fix it."

He laughs under his breath. "Yeah, right. Who's gonna haul the ice bags up the stairs?"

"Me. Just call me, uh…" Ah, hell. Maybe I do need tutoring if I can't remember the name of the guy who pushes a boulder up a mountain over and over again. It was punishment for tricking the gods. And here I am, tricking literally everyone.

"Maybe you have a concussion."

I snap my fingers. "Sisyphus."

"Sissy-who?"

I groan. "Jesus, man, read a freaking book."

"You're the one who needs tutoring. Did your step-sister teach you that one?"

"Fuck off. I like mythology."

Tyler laughs in my face, but he doesn't say anything else. He just helps me get inside and up the tight staircase. We move agonizingly slowly. My ribs scream with every step, and his grip on my waist isn't helping matters.

"That ice bath is sounding better and better," I mutter.

I'm extra glad I stocked up on bags of ice earlier today. Unless Scarlett decided to fuck with me and get rid of all of them…in which case, Tyler might need to make a trip to the gas station.

"Straight for the tub, or…?"

I shake my head and move toward my room. Tyler reaches forward and shoves my door open, and light floods into the hall, which is weird because it wasn't on when I left.

"Who are you?" Tyler blurts out.

I focus, and my blood drains away from my face.

Scarlett is crouched by my desk with the box of cash open on it and loose bills scattered across the floor. There are even some in her grasp.

Caught red-handed.

The *fuck*?

My mouth opens and closes, but I don't know what question to go with first. *What the hell are you doing?* Or, *Who the fuck do you think you are?* Snooping. Stealing. Invading my privacy.

The rage that flutters through me is spurred on by my shitty night, by my pain, and I shake off Tyler to lunge across the room. I haul her up by her hair and shove her against the desk. The old cigar box—an antique I got from my grandfather before he passed years ago—slides. I reach around her and slam the lid.

I use her hair to tilt her head back, forcing her gaze to meet mine. Her green eyes are so wide I can make out the edges of her contact lenses.

"Cross," Tyler calls. "*Dude.*"

I ignore him and lean over Scarlett. She grasps my wrist, but she's trembling. Her nails dig into my skin, and it's the least pain I've felt all night. But her fear is intoxicating, and I want more.

But, at the same time, I want absolutely nothing to do with her.

"Get out," I say softly. I loosen my grip, and her silky hair slides through my fingers.

She inches away, seeming to test if I'm serious, then bolts. Tyler scoots aside to let her pass, and her door slams a moment later.

I brace myself on the desk and let out a long, slow exhale.

"What the fuck?" Tyler closes my door softly and approaches. "I've never seen you act like that. And what the hell is all this cash?" He crouches and gathers the fallen bills, dropping the pile to the desk beside my hand.

"Savings," I bite out. "Certainly none of her business."

"Try a bank next time, man," Tyler says. "Jesus."

"Yeah." I force a laugh and straighten. My body aches, but there's an underlying shame at having a witness to my outburst. "You can go. I'm gonna use carrying the ice upstairs as punishment."

"Just like your Sisyphus," he agrees. "I'm not gonna argue with you. Think about a bank…or at the very least, a safe."

I wave him off. "Night, man."

He leaves, and I sit heavily on the edge of my bed. I take a few deep breaths.

Tonight was an epic shitshow. Mentally, I warred with my desire to *crush* my opponent, and I had to stem my anger every time I let him hit me. Not to mention, I had to make it look like I wasn't *letting* it happen.

I don't know where this anger comes from, but fighting has become the perfect outlet. Better than lacrosse—although I can't deny I enjoy the camaraderie that comes with a team sport—and, hell, it's better than sex.

At least, the sort of sex I've been having in recent months.

Unbidden, the image of a naked Scarlett flashes in front of me.

No, no, and no.

The distraction I need is awaiting me. I hobble downstairs and load a bag of ice on each shoulder then carefully make my way back up. I set them in the bathroom and retrace my path. When I've got all four bags stacked together, I start the water in the tub, turn it to cold, and dump in the ice.

This is gonna suck.

But perhaps less so than realizing Scarlett has uncovered one of my secrets—even if she doesn't know the context. There was no paper trail of the Webber brothers' ask. Just the money I carted home in my duffel bag then warily transferred to the cigar box.

Tyler was right. I need to get a safe. Or put it in a safety deposit box in the bank. *Something.* Having it where anyone can find it is dangerous, security system or not.

I shut off the water and strip. Getting into the ice bath is always the worst part, and now is no different. The tub isn't super deep, which means I'll need to slide down to get my chest in the water.

"Oh, fuck me." It takes work to loosen my clenched jaw, but every inch has my muscles tensing. My knees come out of the water, but they don't hurt as much as my upper body. When it sloshes over my shoulders, I blow out a breath.

Then submerge myself.

The freezing water rushes over my face. The burn of not breathing is almost comparable to the stabbing pain in my ribs caused *by* breathing. I'm hoping they're just deeply bruised, not cracked.

I open my eyes. The world above—the drop ceiling tiles—is blurry.

And so is the face that suddenly swims over me.

I grasp the edges of the tub and haul myself up. Scarlett jumps back, her fists clenched, and her gaze falls to my torso then back up to my face. I slick the water out of my eyes, pushing my hair back, and stare at her.

She's in pajamas. Not cute ones either. Her baggy shirt does nothing for her figure, and her sweatpants, while seemingly thin material, fall straight from her hips to the floor. Her hair is pulled back, her glasses perched on her nose.

Fascinating.

"What are you doing?" she asks.

"Icing myself." I raise an eyebrow. "What are *you* doing?"

"I have to brush my teeth." Her tone is hot. "I didn't realize you were in here, drowning yourself."

She's fun to piss off. And clearly my existence does just that.

Mission accomplished.

Well, one of my missions. The *other* mission is to find dirt on her to put her even more under my thumb.

"What happened to you?" she asks.

I roll my eyes, but it's probably lost within the swelling. "Nothing. This is how I always look."

She scoffs. "Yeah, right. Fine, don't tell me."

The fact that she's still standing at the edge of the tub, a red tint to her cheeks, says a lot. She could've immediately left the bathroom or, I don't know, brushed her teeth and left me to my underwater meditation.

"You done ogling me, Wallace?"

She cringes and spins away. She tucks an invisible strand of hair behind her ear and plucks her toothbrush from its cup. Her movements are jerky, and it doesn't seem like she's fully focused on the task.

I smile to myself. The water doesn't even feel cold anymore, although cubes bump my skin. So maybe I'm just crazy.

When she's nearly done brushing her teeth, I say, "By the way, I thought that was an extra toothbrush. I used it to clean soap scum in the tub this morning."

The toothbrush falls from her mouth, and she gags and spits then grabs the cup and frantically flushes out her mouth. When she shoves herself back upright, she glares at me.

"Tell me you're kidding."

I lift my shoulder, masking the stab of pain, and mime zipping my lips.

Without another word, I sink back under the water. Hopefully she gets the message and leaves me the fuck alone—until I can find something to hold over her anyway.

CHAPTER 8
SCARLETT

"WHY THE HELL does he have that much money lying around?" Sawyer asks, whipping her attention toward me.

I make a face. "Well, it wasn't exactly lying around."

Her hand falls to my arm, and we stop walking. "What do you mean?"

A cool breeze slips between us, reminding me that, although the temperature is higher than average, it's still only January. Winter isn't over, and with the cold glares I get from Cross, it feels even cooler.

I sigh and give in to the part of the story I left out. "I may or may not have been snooping around in his room."

Sawyer's mouth opens with shock, but it quickly changes into a sly grin. "I need all the details."

We continue past the sports fields, on our way to the best coffee cart on campus. We've been on a mission to find the best barista, and so far, the guy who appears higher than a kite each time we visit makes the best hazelnut latte.

"I was so pissed off about the flyers and alarm thing that I decided to try to get back at him."

"By going through his room?" she asks. "What were you trying to find?"

"Anything useful." I snort. "But all I found was a wad of cash and then an angry-looking Cross with a lot of bruises."

Sawyer exhales, her pink cheeks slowly deflating. "You're braver than I am. I've seen him on campus, and he's..."

Hot?

I bite the inside of my cheek and rid the image of him inside the tub full of icy water. I didn't see *too* much, but I saw enough to know there isn't a part on his body that isn't muscular.

"Scary?" I suggest instead.

She laughs. "I was going to say intense. How did he get so banged up? Was he fighting?"

I shrug. "I think my dad told me that he plays lacrosse, but I'm not sure he could get those types of injuries from that."

"Speaking of lacrosse..."

I follow her line of sight and walk toward the chain-link fence overlooking the lacrosse field. Cross catches my attention right away from the tattoos on his arm. I couldn't get a good view of them last night while he was submerged beneath ice, but there are very few players who have tattoos—at least visible to the public eye.

"What's intense is how the hell he is even upright today," I mutter, "let alone practicing."

Just as the word leaves my mouth, Cross collides mid-air with one of his teammates and falls to the ground. His helmet tumbles off his head, rolling to a complete stop near the goal.

Cross doesn't move, and everyone freezes.

Except me.

I quickly hop the fence, leaving Sawyer behind. She calls out my name. I rush onto the field, my heart beating furiously. I think about all the injuries he had last night, how he winced when he opened his eyes to find me standing over him in the tub, likely from a concussion of some sort.

I push through the sea of guys holding their lacrosse sticks and find him gingerly sitting up.

"Cross! Are you okay?" I ask. I stop no more than a few feet away from him.

His teammates turn and stare at me, most of them with creased brows and confusion.

Cross blinks a few times, giving his head a slight shake. A lock of sweaty hair falls onto his forehead, and for some insane reason, I want to bend down and push it out of the way to confirm he's okay, but I have no idea why.

"He's fine," someone says from behind.

I turn and make eye contact with his friend from last night. The same one who watched Cross practically throw me out of his room like I was a piece of trash. He's giving me a look that I can't decipher.

I blink through my concern and finally say, "What do you mean? Last night, he could barely walk—"

Cross groans, pulling my attention back to him. The moment our eyes clash, he bares his teeth. "Will you shut the fuck up?"

I snap my mouth shut, just like he demanded, but it isn't to appease him. It's purely out of shock. I take a step backward when he climbs to his feet. His teammates eventually disperse, except for his friend from last night.

"I don't know what's going on, but..."

Cross towers over me like a nightmare, his jaw clenched.

"Go away," he grits out.

My shock only lasts a few seconds. I raise my chin, level my shoulders, and peer up at him. "You know, I was going to apologize for snooping in your room last night… because of this." I take my finger and jab him in the ribs. I know very well there's a massive bruise there.

He makes a noise and hunches.

"Clearly you have some serious shit going on in your life, but *never fucking mind.*" I turn and stomp off the field with a fire of anger trailing me.

Sawyer, with her mouth hanging wide open, sees me coming and quickly loops our arms together. "I don't know what the hell just happened, but holy shit."

My heart is beating wildly, my thoughts all over the place.

"Do you have plans tonight?" I blurt. "Because the last thing I want to do is go home, knowing he'll be there."

"I do," she says. "But you're invited."

***

It's just like old times.

Sawyer and I walk through the door of some house, the smell of warm beer filling the air and reminding me of simpler times at Yale.

"Jeez," Sawyer mutters. "We're overdressed."

I stuff a laugh down, because she's right.

Most of the girls are wearing practically nothing, but I'm not surprised in the least. I, too, was one of these girls not too long ago, but now, I stand in the middle of a party filled with hockey players, wearing jeans and a sweater.

The only part of my body that's showing is my shoulder, and that's simply because my sweater is oversized.

"At least we leave something to the imagination..." I try to make Sawyer feel better about the girls in crop tops and miniskirts, as if it isn't forty degrees out without the sun shining.

"Come on." She loops her arm in mine and tugs me toward the kitchen.

A keg, red Solo cups, and random bottles of vodka are scattered along the counter. A guy with a black eye is tending to a group of girls, filling their cups to the brim with beer.

Once they're done flirting, they turn to head back the way we came. They're distracted and unaware of the fact that we're standing behind them, and sure enough, the loudest—and tipsiest—of the bunch trips.

Her red Solo cup, full of cheap beer, flies from her hand. I grab on to her arms to steady her, the beer landing on my shirt, and manage to keep us both upright.

"Oh my Goddddd," she slurs. "I am so sorrrrrry."

"Holy shit." Sawyer bends to pick up the cup. "Are you okay, Scarlett?"

"I'm fine." I look at the girl's two friends, and my face screws up with annoyance. "You really should get her home. She's too wasted to be at a party like this."

The blonde one snickers.

The other rolls her eyes.

"Who are you? The fun police?" The blonde laughs at her joke while the other takes her drunk friend by the waist to guide her out of the kitchen.

I glance at my wet sweater, sticky with beer.

Sawyer comes over with a handful of paper towels and

tries to dab my face. Her expression says it all—I'm a lost cause.

"You're soaked," the guy manning the keg points out.

"Do you have somewhere she can clean up…or at least rinse her sweater?" Sawyer asks.

He nudges his chin toward the kitchen sink. "She can rinse in there."

I give him a deadpan look.

Sawyer scoffs. "Then she'd have to take her shirt off in front of everyone."

He grins. "Exactly."

I touch Sawyer's arm. "I'm just going to find the bathroom and clean up. Do you want to come? Or will you be okay out here?"

"Um…" She glances around, likely searching for the guy who invited her. "I'll be fine. Unless you want me to come?"

"Go look for Archer. I'll find you when I'm…"—I pull on my sweater—"less sticky."

We part ways, and I search for a line.

There's always a line for the bathroom at these types of parties.

Rising onto my tiptoes, I try to see over the heads of college students.

"Jesus, what happened to you?" someone asks.

I, unfortunately, recognize him right away. I drop down to my heels and fold my arms. "We really have to stop meeting like this."

Cross's friend somehow keeps finding me in the most embarrassing situations.

He chuckles. "I agree. What happened to you? Why do you smell like you took a swim in the keg?"

I roll my eyes. "Some girl fell and spilled her beer all over me. I'm looking for the bathroom."

And now the exit, because if Cross's friend is here, then that likely means Cross is, too.

No thanks.

"It's over there."

I follow his line of sight.

"Great." I sigh.

The line wraps around the stairwell. My sweater will be dry by then, and I'll still smell like a bar.

"Come on." He heads for the closed bathroom door and bypasses the line like he's some celebrity.

"Are you trying to help me? Or are you taking me to Cross so he can make fun of me?" I follow him.

He glances over his shoulder and grins. "I'm helping you. But don't tell Cross."

I refuse to talk to Cross, so he has nothing to worry about.

We make it to the bathroom, and I think there's a light at the end of the tunnel.

But instead, the door opens…and it's something worse.

Stepbrother dearest.

"Really?" I gape at his friend.

He puts his hands up, feigning innocence. "I swear I didn't know he was in there."

Cross is clearly surprised. His brows are furrowed, and his gae bounces between me and his friend.

I quickly push past him, making sure to nudge him with my elbow, and go to slam the door. Anything to get away from them.

Except, it doesn't shut, and suddenly, I'm not alone.

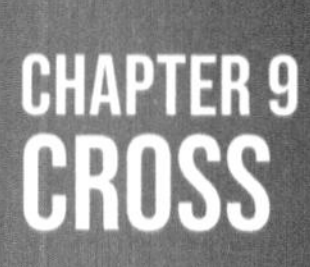

CHAPTER 9
CROSS

"I'LL DEAL with you in a minute," I grit out to Tyler then scoot behind Scarlett into the bathroom. I close and lock the door behind my back then lean on it for good measure. God only knows why my best friend was escorting my stepsister to the bathroom, but I'm about to find out.

She spins, her long hair fanning out with the movement. It carries a strong whiff of beer.

"Jesus, you smell like a brewery." I raise my eyebrow. "How long have you been here?"

"Like five minutes," she says under her breath. "And I'll be leaving as soon as you give me a minute of privacy."

I scoff. "Yeah, right. I give an inch, and you take a mile."

Her jaw drops. "Are you kidding? You've made my life impossible."

"I haven't even gotten warmed up, princess."

Ooh, she doesn't like that pet name. Her face pinches, and she abruptly turns away from me. Still, she can't hide her anger. Her reflection in the wide mirror over the counter gives her away.

Someone bangs on the door. "Come on! There's a line!"

I motion for her to get going with whatever she needs to do. It was important enough for Tyler to walk her over here…and no one would mess with him cutting the line.

"Get out," she hisses.

I scoff. "Do you not know the meaning of the word *no*?"

She pales but tries to cover up her unease with a roll of those annoyingly pretty eyes.

I cross my arms. After a long pause, she shrugs out of her sweater and turns on the tap. My eyebrows nearly rise into my hair at the sight. Her smooth, pale skin… She's wearing a bralette that extends halfway down her stomach. It covers more of her than a bikini top would. But she still angles away from me slightly as she cups water in her hand and rinses off her arms.

"What are you doing?"

"Some girl spilled beer on me," she says hotly.

"And here I thought you just had a drinking problem." I cock my head. "Why wear a sweater to a party anyway?"

"I didn't know I was coming here, genius. And I'll be leaving immediately after this."

"Right."

She's intriguing. I hate to admit it, but I can't tear my attention away from her. And she took her shirt off with barely a push of peer pressure. What else could I get her to do?

"You don't believe me?" Her eyes narrow briefly, meeting mine in the mirror. Before we can lock in, she crouches and opens the cabinet doors, digging through some stranger's shit until she emerges with a dingy washcloth.

My eyebrows rise higher, but I don't comment when

she uses it to pat dry her skin. It's probably cleaner than the damp hand towel everyone else has been using tonight.

"Okay." She tosses the washcloth on the counter. "Let me out."

"Out." I consider it. "Tempting, but no."

"No?"

I smirk. "You haven't paid the toll, princess."

She grabs her sweater, but I snatch it from her grasp.

"No, no, we're not doing *that*," I chide. "We haven't even begun to discuss your latest transgressions. They're stacking up."

"With you, every glance is a slight."

"That's true. Better only look at my feet, then."

When her gaze doesn't drop, I smile wider. Why is riling her up so much *fun?*

But then, all at once, I remember the topic at hand: the fucking embarrassment from this afternoon.

Did that hit suck? Absolutely.

Did *Scarlett Wallace* running out on the field like I'd been shot make it any better? Hell no. In fact, it opened a can of worms—questions from my teammates about the hot new girl fawning over me. I can only praise some higher entity that no one but Tyler knows she's my stepsister.

I have a reputation to uphold. Also, my coach doesn't exactly know about my fighting, and I worked damn hard to hide my injuries. So it took me a bit longer to get up today… I'm fine. Stanley got me some hardcore painkillers a while ago, and I'll be leaning on those for the next few days.

None of that matters, however, if Scarlett reveals my secrets—even ones she unwittingly holds.

And coddling me like a baby.

No, thanks.

Hard pass.

Plus, the *audacity*. In what world does Scarlett care about me?

I consider that—and then her angle. She was snooping in my room and discovered my cash, although she hasn't figured out why I have it. She won't get that from me. But perhaps that's her angle? She wants the money…or she wants me to go easy on her.

Two things that are laughable at best and infuriating at worst.

My original mission—to make her life hell—stands, no matter how worried she seemed on the field.

I lift my shirt, exposing my bruised torso. "This, Scarlett, is none of your fucking business."

She gasps.

Yes, the colors are a bit more, uh…*vibrant* than they were yesterday, no thanks to that hit today. But Coach was none the wiser, and I blamed my few mistakes on lack of sleep. Luckily, he didn't ask too many questions. Tyler did a great job of distracting him.

Tomorrow might be a different story.

I drop her shirt. It slips through my fingers, landing at my feet.

"Oops." I go to grab it and let out a pained groan.

"Oh God. No, I've got it." She immediately goes to her knees in front of me.

She reaches for it without thinking, leaning forward, and I get a great look at her tits. But just for a moment. Then, I unlock the door and twist the knob, stepping aside to allow it to swing inward. It just misses her—and she just misses *it*.

"God, Scarlett, you'd do anything to suck my dick."

I project my voice, and the loudness of it startles her.

"Why are you so desperate? I don't want you anywhere *near* me."

She flinches.

I spin on my heel and leave her there. To my satisfaction, I caught more than a few people's attention. Some even have their phones out. I hide my smirk behind a stoic expression and push through the crowd.

Tyler catches my eye, but I shake my head and keep moving.

Best not to witness Scarlett's crocodile tears and her attempts to get out of *this* one.

I get home in record time. My carefully curated buzz has worn off, along with the remnants of the painkiller I popped this afternoon. Scarlett is most likely still at the party, battling embarrassment. She seems like the type to try to put on a brave face. She'll ignore the stares because of pride.

Which puts time on my side.

Once inside, I type in the code on the security panel on the wall in the entryway. It'll reactivate in a minute, and the screen flashes red twice before going back to its normal blue to confirm.

I grab a glass of water and carry it upstairs then pause in the hallway.

My gaze goes to Scarlett's closed door.

I shouldn't...

But I could.

And *fuck* that I shouldn't. She did it to me first.

Jesus, I sound like a child with that attitude. But if I go back to my mission of blackmailing her into doing my schoolwork, I'd probably have better luck finding something in her room.

Well, it's decided.

I slip into her room and flick on the light. I'm sure I'll get a little warning with her fumbling on the keypad downstairs, at any rate—if she decides to come home.

But also, her finding me snooping would only even the score, right?

Her room is not what I expected. It's not neat—not like how I keep mine—but it's not messy either. There are clothes draped over a chair in the corner, and the comforter is lumpy and half-heartedly covering the bed.

I take it all in and focus on the closet. Everything in it is organized—boxes along the top and some tucked away, clothes on hangers. Normal shit. I give the boxes some attention, but there isn't much of note. Old notebooks and textbooks, presumably from her fancy Ivy League, photos of her posing with strangers.

I flip through a stack of pictures. The girl in these is drastically different to the one who's been living in this house. *This* one is more like the version of Scarlett I witnessed at the wedding. Even though her glare cut during the ceremony, she was quick to smile and laugh with her family. She danced.

Call me crazy, but I cannot picture the Scarlett I know now *dancing*. And she probably hasn't had any reason to smile lately.

Anyway.

I drop them back in and pick up a calculus textbook, just out of curiosity. I couldn't give a shit about differential equations, but does she write in her textbooks?

Perhaps not.

I leaf through it, and suddenly, a folded paper slips free.

It falls and glides away. I grab it and unfold it then freeze. I have to reread it three times to understand the paper prescription, then I give up and search the long medication name on my phone.

Emergency contraceptive.

Oh, shit.

I let out a low whistle.

Scarlett has some secrets, all right.

She went out and had unprotected sex...and thought she might be pregnant?

I take a picture and put it back in the calculus textbook, smiling to myself. I make sure everything is just as it was, the closet closed, the lights off, and head back to my room.

Not sure when I'll use this information against her, because it feels almost too good to be true. And too big to use on a whim. No, this will take careful planning. And when it does come out?

Checkmate.

She better start packing early. I have a feeling she'll be sprinting back to Yale by the time I'm through with her.

CHAPTER 10
SCARLETT

THE LAST THING I want to do is tutor my arrogant and cocky, tyrant of a stepbrother, but there is *no* fucking way I'm going to be labeled as a quitter my first year at Shadow Valley. Plus, I'm not willing to give him any more power than he already has by standing him up at the library out of fear.

I'm much too proud for that.

Unless, of course, it has anything to do with Yale. I'll gladly run and hide from that shitstorm.

Cross doesn't frighten me.

He irritates me, but I'm not afraid of him.

Hence why I showed up to our tutoring session forty-five minutes early. That way, this time, he can't use the excuse that his tutor is late and dip early. If he wants to stay on the lacrosse team, then he's going to sit his ass down and be humbled.

The door to the library opens, and my stomach twists with nerves.

Okay, fine.

He's a little intimidating. His jaw should be listed

beneath the word *dangerous* in the dictionary. Pair that with his toned arms, one of them covered in intricate tattoos, and I'm shifting in my seat uncomfortably.

Our gazes meet from across the quiet library, and it takes half a second for him to roll his eyes.

I force myself to smile at him, but I'm positive he knows me well enough now to realize it's as fake as the girl's boobs who just stepped in his direct path to me. His stride falters, and he tugs his backpack higher onto his shoulder. With one eyebrow raised, he peers at her from his tall height, lips flat with boredom.

His attention shifts to me, and I don't even attempt to look away.

He's caught me staring, and he uses it like ammunition.

One hand wraps around the back of her head, his fingers tangled in her long blonde hair, while his other stays on the strap of his backpack. His mouth descends like he's some kind of barbarian, and he kisses her with passion and so much sex appeal that my legs clench.

Ugh, gross.

I tear my eyes away.

Was it gross, though? Because suddenly I'm stripping out of my sweater because the back of my neck prickles with heat.

I preoccupy myself with organizing my notes and my very detailed, organized plan for tutoring so I don't look at him again. His presence is hard to ignore, though. I sense him before he's even taken a seat at the table.

"Hello, stepsister dearest." His smooth voice is like nails on a chalkboard. "Were you planning on saving my little show for your spank bank?"

That's all it takes. Less than a minute with my step-brother, and I'm already beyond irritated.

I flick my eyes to him. "You and your girlfriend are the farthest thing from what's in my spank bank, *stepbrother dearest.*"

He snorts. "Girlfriend? Yeah, right."

"Pig," I mutter.

I tense when his knee brushes against mine beneath the table.

"What was that?" he whispers.

He's so close I can smell his spicy, rich cologne.

Again, refusing to let him intimidate me, I square my shoulders and raise my head. Our mouths are way too close, especially given that we're stepsiblings.

"I called you a pig," I repeat, locking gazes with him.

His eye twitches, but suddenly, he backs away to lean in his seat with even more arrogance. "Takes one to know one."

I jerk backward. "Excuse me?" My jaw slacks with shock. "Takes one to know one? Are you saying that because of the stupid stunt you pulled at the party? You and I both know you set me up."

Am I still pissed off about that? Absolutely.

But I'll be damned if I let my own personal bully know how riled up he got me.

"Did I, though?"

Cross lifts his hip and digs into the pocket of his jeans to get out his phone. His movements are slow, his fingers swiping lazily across the screen until his smug smile appears. Alarm bells go off in my head.

He holds his phone steady and slides it across the table until it's right in front of me. He nudges his chin to it, so I follow his silent instruction and stare at the screen.

I don't have to zoom in to know what it is.

Shame drains the blood from my face. A cold sweat breaks out along my forehead, and my stomach all but drops to the floor. "Where—" I clear my throat and hastily shove the phone away. "Where did you get that?"

There's no use in deleting the photo. He's smart enough to have backup copies.

Cross leaves his phone untouched to stare at me. "Is that why you left Yale? Because you needed a new pool of dicks to choose from?"

It's as if he's slapped me. His words cut deep, the burn of humiliation stinging my skin. He has no idea what he's talking about, but I make no move to correct him.

Cross's arms rest against the table as he leans closer to me, a dirty smirk etched onto his face. "What would Daddy think if he knew his daughter was a slut?"

"A prescription for Plan B makes me a slut?" I manage to keep my voice steady, but I'm trembling on the inside.

Cross shrugs. "It's not good, stepsis. Given you came on to me at the party, and then this? I think your father will be able to connect the dots."

I narrow my eyes. "I didn't come on to you at the party, and you fucking know it."

"Shh—"

Cross and I both turn toward the girl sitting at the front desk. She puts her finger up to her lips and sends us a scathing look. We turn back toward one another, and the longer we lock gazes, the more sinister his smile becomes. My stomach turns, and it takes everything in me not to shift in my seat.

"You're shaking," he says.

Shit.

One eyebrow crooks. "That's very telling…"

"I'm shaking because I'm so angry!"

He chuckles and shakes his head. "No, you're not. You're shaking because you're afraid I'm going to show this to your father."

Of course I am!

But not for the reason he thinks.

I am the farthest thing from a slut. I've willingly had sex with two people, and the other...well, that's why I'm at Shadow Valley, arguing with my stepbrother about what he found. My dad has no idea why I chose not to go back to Yale, and if he finds out I was date-raped at a frat party, things will go from bad to worse.

"What do you want?" I quietly snap. "Are you still trying to get back at me, even after you embarrassed me at the party in front of everyone?"

Cross taps his long fingers on the table, then swipes his phone into his palm and puts it into his pocket. "You're done tutoring me."

I scoff. "No skin off my back if you don't show up."

He shakes his head. "Nah, that's not what I mean, baby sis."

My eye twitches with the pet name.

His lip rises. "You're done tutoring me because you're going to do the work for me."

I shoot up out of my seat, and my chair crashes to the floor. Cross leans back and folds his arms over his chest. He has a knowing smile. It's obvious he likes to provoke me, but I'm too angry to play it cool.

"You're out of your fucking mind if you think I'm doing your homework. I am not your servant."

"You will be if you want me to keep your dirty little secret," he says.

My mouth closes abruptly, and I stare at him from above.

I wish I could call him on his bluff, but I know he isn't joking.

Cross grabs the leg of my chair and puts it in its upright position, then points to it. "Sit."

I do as he says. His sneer catches my eye. He digs into his bag for a piece of paper that he shoves toward me.

"This is due Thursday," he says lazily. "It better be an A."

Instead of leveling him with an insult like I want to do, I slap my hand on the paper and slide it over to my side of the table. He stands with his backpack on his shoulder and towers above me.

"That's my good girl." He winks and then taps me on the head.

I almost bite him, but by the time I recover, he's already walking out of the library.

CHAPTER 11
CROSS

"STOP!"

My trainer pushes me and my fighting partner apart. I pivot, and he follows me to the far corner of the ring. I lean on the ropes and focus on my breathing, but it's hard when I'm so irrationally angry. My shoulders hunch. Recovery isn't going as fast as I want, and I'm pissed that I put myself in the position to get hurt.

Still, a few bruised ribs is better than a concussion that will follow me around for the rest of my life. At least, that's what I keep telling myself.

"Lopez." My trainer shakes my arm. "You hear the boss hollering for you?"

I straighten and pull out my mouthguard. "Missed it."

I duck under the ropes and hop down off the platform. The fighters working the bags and with partners around the edges of the huge room ignore me. Their illusion that I was unstoppable has been shattered. My reputation has been stained.

Is *that* worth twenty thousand dollars?

My gut says no, but I haven't put the money to use.

Beyond Scarlett discovering it, I bought a safe and shoved the cigar box into it so no one else could stumble upon it... or worse, steal it.

"Come on, boy," Stanley calls, poking his head out of his second-floor office.

I pick up the pace and jog up the stairs, my body only giving a mild twinge of pain. The bruises have faded to mottled green and yellow, but my shirt hides it.

The office door is open, and I enter to find the Webber brothers standing by the windows that overlook the fighters. I can't remember who is who, their features a little too similar to easily differentiate.

"Cross," one greets me. "Excellent work at the fight the other day. You really put on one hell of a performance."

I incline my chin. "So this means you'll get me in the cage with Fox?"

The other one winces. It's the barest pinch of his lips and brows, but my fighting career—if we can call it that— is based on reading my opponent.

"One more," the first says. "One more fight, and then... yes. You'll get the chance against Wilmer Fox, as we promised."

I tense. Can I really throw another fight?

"And if I say no?"

"Oh, oh—" Stanley throws his arm around my shoulders. "You're not saying that, though, right? Cross?"

I clear my throat and keep the strong urge to flip them off and storm away under control. Somehow. Slowly, I shake my head.

The Webber brothers relax simultaneously. One comes forward and holds out a card. "Text this number tomorrow at eight o'clock. You'll be given details on the fight."

I pocket the card without looking at it. Stanley releases my shoulders and claps his hand on my back.

"Good boy," he says in my ear. "Now, back to training. No excuses."

"Yes, sir," I mutter.

My skin crawls, but I hightail it out of there.

What's the worst that could happen if I *don't* throw this next fight? Give the twenty grand back? That's easy—I haven't spent any of it. With that knowledge, I swallow and keep my head high. I'm not as trapped as they'd have me believe.

I'm halfway down the stairs when I spot Tyler coming in. He holds the door for someone behind him, and my breath stalls in my chest.

What the *fuck* is Scarlett Wallace doing here?

Wind blasts through the door, nearly pushing her in, and sends her hair fluttering into her face. She brushes it back with both hands, one finger straying to slide her glasses higher up her nose.

She spots me and immediately scowls.

Feeling is mutual, sweetheart.

She winds through the gym and meets me at the bottom of the staircase, her gaze fastened on me. Her eyes are wide, her coat tugged tightly around her. Whatever she was expecting, it wasn't this.

And for that reason, I'm going to fucking murder Tyler.

My so-called best friend is right behind her, and he shrugs like he has no idea why she's here.

"What is this place?"

I redirect my attention back to Scarlett, scowl fixed in place. "What does it look like? It's a gym."

She glances around. "There are people fighting—"

"Training," Tyler interjects.

"Go away," I snap at him.

I grab Scarlett's arm and pull her away from him. Out of the corner of my eye, I spot Staney and the Webber brothers watching from the office windows above. Just what I need—more people to connect me to her and vice versa.

"What are you doing here?" I demand. I tighten my grip on her arm. "You following me, Wallace?"

She scoffs. "Excuse me, Mister High and Mighty, I'm trying to hold up my end of your blackmail."

I narrow my eyes.

She jerks free and opens her purse, pulling a small USB from within its depths. Why do women always have so many things in their purse? They're literal black holes. I've seen my mother hide so much stuff in hers, and she slings it over her shoulder like it doesn't weigh eight thousand pounds.

Okay, I'm getting off topic.

She shoves the USB into my bare chest and pauses, her fingertips on my skin.

I'm suddenly hot.

I catch the plastic gadget and her hand, too. Her lips part, and her eyes dilate. She sucks in a breath then quickly yanks away. The USB stays in my hand, against my skin.

"Your end of the blackmail," I repeat.

"The homework," she bites out. The *duh* is silent.

And unappreciated.

"So sassy," I murmur. "Might want to tone it down, Wallace. Your life as you know it hangs in the balance."

Anger flashes across her face. Interestingly, she bites back her retort…almost like you *can* teach an old dog new tricks.

I grasp her arm again and spin her toward the exit. I don't trust her to go straight there—and in a timely manner—so I guide her out. I shoot Tyler a cutting glare on our way by, and I open the door for my stepsister.

It's dark out.

"Stop manhandling me." She tries to shake me loose.

"Don't come back here." I look down my nose at her. The USB is hot in my palm, and I itch to shove it back at her, even though I assume it's my class assignment I told her to do.

The fact that she *did* it is a little shocking. I assumed more of a fight, resistance…but no. The blackmail must've been too good. Too mortifying. I could see when I revealed my knowledge that she was surprised but also scared.

Because of her dad? The man could be more straitlaced than I gave him credit for—and that will absolutely work in my favor.

Her gaze moves beyond me, back inside. "This place has something to do with how you got so injured, right? It wasn't lacrosse. It was…"

I scoff. "You're not as smart as you think you are, but I'm in a forgiving mood. So, no, this *place* didn't have anything to do with my state."

She eyes my healing bruises, which I didn't care were on display until right this second. The image of her looming over the tub, her face distorted by my underwater view, flashes in my mind.

Fuck.

"I would've given it to you at home if you were ever there," she grumbles under her breath.

I raise my eyebrow, but she turns around and speeds down the sidewalk away from me before I can ask.

Instead, I go back inside and point at a waiting Tyler.

"You. Me. In the ring."

He holds up his hands. "Dude, she said she had something important to give you—"

"Save it." God, I'm so fucking mad at him. Punching him in the face will soothe some of that, and this will make it so I don't break his nose.

Or do something irrational like chase after *her*.

CHAPTER 12
SCARLETT

"THOSE ARE HOT," Sawyer muses from beside me.

I roll my eyes. "Tattoos are *not* hot." *Said no one ever.*

I'm a sucker for a guy with tattoos, but ever since seeing Cross shirtless in the gym, I've changed my mind.

Sawyer scoffs and snaps her head over to gawk at me. "Said who?"

I look away from the movie playing on her laptop screen and shrug.

"Don't tell me." She stuffs some popcorn into her mouth. "You're into those nerdy guys. The ones with glasses who spend their mornings checking on the stock market."

No.

"What's wrong with that?" I ask.

She sighs and goes back to watching the movie. "Nothing…" She pauses. "Just sounds *boringggg.*"

I click my phone off because somehow I've ended up on Cross's social media profile. There's nothing important on there, like an explanation of why I found him training in some dark, smelly gym.

I'd only found him there because after trying to hunt him down to give him the homework *he* blackmailed me into doing, I ran into one of his lacrosse teammates, who gave me the address to the gym. He didn't tell me what kind of gym it was, and silly me to think he'd be running on a treadmill or lifting weights.

Instead, he was bare-chested and sweaty with his knuckles taped. My stomach flipped as I scanned every single toned muscle, and with the tattoos? How could I not stare?

I admit that Cross has sex appeal, but the moment he opens his mouth to insult me, I suddenly hate everything about him.

One thing is for sure, Cross is the farthest thing from boring. When our eyes meet, my body heats. Whether that's from anger or something else, I don't know.

"Boring is just what I need," I say.

Sawyer pauses the movie and turns all the way toward me on her bed. "As your only friend here, I think it's my duty to introduce you to a life of excitement."

I make a noise of sarcasm. "I had plenty of excitement at Yale."

Her eyebrows furrow. "I think that's an oxymoron."

"Don't diss the intelligent guys," I say, half joking. "They can be exciting, too."

A memory tries to slip in, reminding me of the last thing I did at Yale that was exciting, but I quickly block it and hop to my feet to stand on her fuzzy rug.

"Fine." I cross my arms. "What do you have in mind?"

Sawyer scrambles off her bed, and popcorn flies into the air and lands at our feet. She rushes over to her desk and comes back with a torn flyer in her hand. "This."

I hesitantly take the paper from her and scan its contents.

The Inner Ring - INVITE ONLY
Location disclosed after RSVP / Must have password for
entry

I make a face. "Sex parties aren't my thing…"

Sawyer stares at me as if I've grown three heads. "It's not a sex party!" She snatches the paper from me. "It's a fight."

My interest piques. "A fight?"

She nods with a thrill in her eye. "Cage-fighting. It's a thing here at Shadow Valley, and I got an invite."

I eye her suspiciously. "By who?"

"Some guy in my calc class, and you're never going to believe who's fighting."

Oh, I think I can.

"My stepbrother?" I say, deadpan.

"You knew?"

I shake my head. "Not exactly, but I saw some bruises, and then I ended up having to meet him at the gym to give him something, so I put two and two together."

Her mouth curves. "Do you wanna go? Maybe you'll get lucky and see him get his lights punched out."

The thought of showing up to his secret fight makes me far too excited.

"He'll kill me if I show up…" I say.

Sawyer's shoulders drop with disappointment. She heads for her bed, but I put my arm out to stop her.

When our eyes meet, I smile maliciously. "Which is all the more reason to go."

The stuffy basement of an abandoned building on the outskirts of town is full of college students from all over, and it sends nerves skittering across my skin. I'm hesitant to walk any farther into the crowd, especially because they took our phones at the door, but with Sawyer pulling on my wrist, I have no choice but to follow.

It's like stepping into a brand-new world.

The music thumps so loud it vibrates my chest. The only light is centered over the makeshift ring in the middle of the floor. Bodyguards much older than your typical college student stand guard, making sure the spectators don't come too close to the fight already occurring.

I reach up on my tiptoes to get a better look.

The energy buzzes when one of the guys—definitely not my stepbrother—lands a right hook to another guy's face. His head snaps to the right, and spit flies through the air.

"How's this for exciting?" Sawyer shouts into my ear.

A nervous laugh works itself out of my chest as the scene unfolds. The two guys land punches back and forth, both of them with sweat dripping down their faces onto their bare chests.

It's like UFC gone rogue, and I hate to admit it, but it is exciting.

The crowd is in a trance, and when I glance over at Sawyer, she's zeroed in on the fight, too. Flickering lights wash against her face, her eyes glittering with excitement.

The only reason I'm here is to piss Cross off and get

some dirt on him like he has on me, but without my phone, it'll be hard to prove his double life to our parents. There is no way they're aware, and who's to say he'll even spot me in the crowd?

It's *packed*.

Just how many college students are aware of this exclusive, invite-only fight? It seems like the entire school is here, plus more.

I can't help but wonder why Cross is here to fight.

Is it just a hobby?

Is it for money?

Is lacrosse not enough of a workout for him?

What would his mom think if she knew?

My lip curves into a devious smile. Even without my phone for proof, we *both* have something on each other now.

A ringing clamors throughout, signaling the end to the fight. Everyone claps and yells at the top of their lungs. Some guys exchange money up ahead, and there are a few girls that lift their shirts to show off their boobs.

My eyebrows rise with surprise, and I laugh quietly. *Wow.*

"I knew it!" Sawyer's hands fall to my shoulders. She smiles widely.

"Knew what?" I shout over the noise.

"I knew you had a wild streak. You're totally in your element!"

I shake my head and laugh again. "I'm just picturing Cross's face when he sees me mid-fight. This is what we call blackmail, babe."

Something he's familiar with.

"Is he up next?" I ask, rising to my tiptoes again.

I hope I didn't miss it—for no other reason than to make him angry, of course.

Sawyer arches a brow and leans in closer to my ear. "I think blackmail is the last thing that's going to be on his mind when he sees you."

"What do you mean?" I ask.

"You're hot, Scarlett. He's going to be hating the fact that his stepsister turns him on, is more like it."

I jerk backward and bump into a guy behind me. I mumble an apology and turn back around toward Sawyer. "That is not true," I hiss into her ear.

She shouts through a smile, "Whatever!"

Two drinks appear in front of our faces, and we take them, though I don't dare take a sip. As soon as Sawyer puts it up to her lips, I reach over and wrap my fingers around her wrist. She glances at me, and I shake my head. She squints with confusion but listens anyway.

Good girl. Never take an opened drink from someone you don't know.

The basement suddenly goes dark.

I gasp, my fingers tightening around my cup.

A voice booms over the speakers. "Are you ready for the most anticipated fight of the evening?"

The crowd is deafening.

Anticipation rushes through my veins, but I'm on edge. My chest heaves, desperate for oxygen or some type of lifeline.

So many people surround me, most of whom I've never even seen, but I've been in crowds before. I can do this.

This isn't Yale, and I'm completely sober.

It's fine—

Suddenly, an arm wraps around my waist, and a hand

goes to my mouth to muffle my scream. I'm pulled away from Sawyer, though she probably has no idea because it's pitch-black.

The sound of a door opens, and I'm quickly shoved inside from behind. My cup falls to the floor, and the sticky liquid spills all over my shoes. I spin around when a light comes on, the buzzing pulling my attention to the single lightbulb above my head.

"What the fuck are you doing here?"

Relief has my knees buckling.

If you would've told me an hour ago that I'd be relieved to see my stepbrother, I wouldn't have believed you, but here we are. Sweaty, flushed skin, with knuckles taped and an expression that could kill.

I fold my arms over my sweater and shift on my feet. Cross runs his gaze down my body, his lip snarling when he drags it back to my face. "You look like a slut."

My jaw falls. "I'm wearing more clothing than ninety percent of the girls here!"

A black sweater and ripped jeans with fish-net stockings underneath because Sawyer practically begged me to wear them. I *do not* look like a slut!

Cross advances on me. I step backward until I collide with the wall, and his hand finds its way to my throat. His thumb grips me below my jaw while his pinky rests on my collarbone. He doesn't squeeze hard, but he could if he wanted to.

"Go home," he hisses.

I should be afraid, all alone with him in this musty, empty room, but gazing up into his warm, brown eyes has me feeling strangely calm.

"Or what? You'll show my daddy the dirt you have on me?"

His eyes narrow. "I could."

My mouth curves into a smile, drawing Cross's eyes right to it.

"I wouldn't do that if I were you," I taunt. "Because now I know your dirty little secret, too."

He scoffs, his hot, seedy breath brushing against my face. "You have no proof."

I open my mouth to argue, but our attention is pulled to a door opposite of the one Cross pushed me through.

It's Tyler.

"Bro, you gotta get in the ring. They're about to flick the lights back on."

Cross squeezes my neck briefly then drops his hand and steps away. I gasp slightly and stumble forward on shaky legs. I regain my balance quickly while Cross stomps toward his friend. He grips Tyler's arm tightly, whispers something in a low voice, and then disappears.

Tyler and I make eye contact across the empty space, his lips flat with annoyance.

I send him a dirty look and flip my hair over my shoulder. I open the door I was forcefully shoved through and am met with the backs of everyone in the crowd. All their attention is on the illuminated cage.

I thankfully find my way back to Sawyer before they really start to get amped up.

"Where were you?" she shouts, eyes filled with concern.

As soon as I open my mouth to answer her, I'm saved by a wave of cheers.

Cross's name is announced, and it's as clear as glass that my stepbrother is well known around here.

My attention is immediately drawn to Cross's flickering muscles and the tattoos that cover them. He hops up and down a few times on agile feet and pops his neck, seemingly laser focused on the guy opposite him.

I immediately pull my gaze away, annoyed that I find him so attractive, and land on his opponent.

Maybe he's hotter.

I gasp.

The blood drains from my face, and my vision tunnels, the outer area darkening. The ringing in my ears is the only thing that keeps me grounded as I stare into the cage at the one person who makes my skin crawl with fear.

Nicholas Thomson, the sole reason I left Yale, is standing across from my stepbrother, and suddenly, I can't breathe.

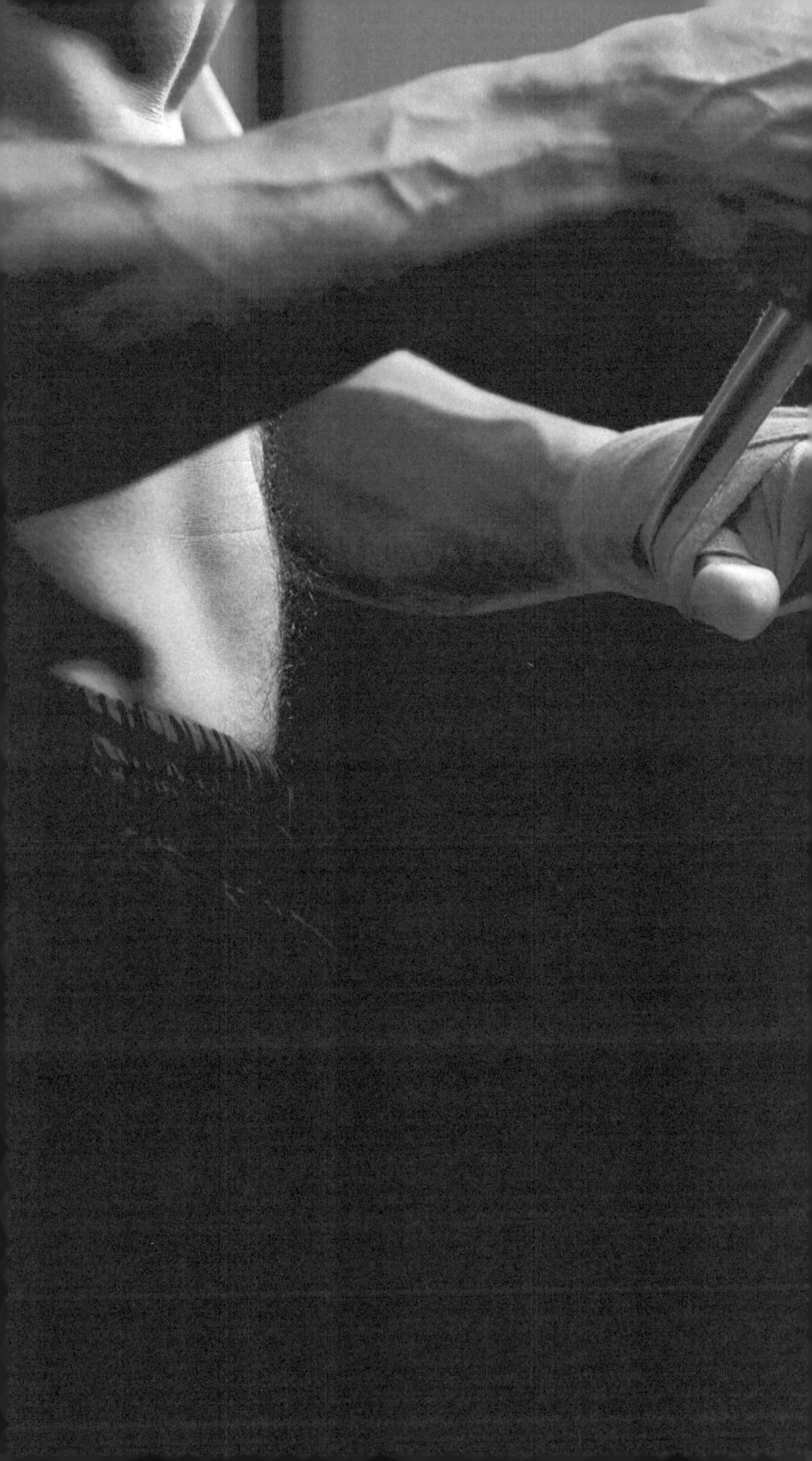

CHAPTER 13
CROSS

WHAT. The. Fuck?

My attention skitters across the crowd surrounding the cage, automatically seeking out Scarlett. I couldn't believe my eyes when I caught a glimpse of her before the lights plunged out. I was expecting the blackout after the first fight—the idiots in charge think it creates more excitement and focuses the audience after a lull.

I *wasn't* expecting the rush of adrenaline to hit when Scarlett's body pressed to mine. She immediately started trembling. Her breath on my hand came fast and shallow. Another minute and she might've passed out.

And then, in the back room, her usual vitriol returned. Like it's *my* fault.

As if. She's in my space. I never imagined she would get an invitation here.

Damn Tyler. Damn Scarlett for going to the gym and presumably putting it together.

And she wants to blackmail me!

The rotten part is, it might work.

I give up on finding her and lock eyes with my opponent. I'm supposed to lose this fight, but my skin crawls at the idea of giving Scarlett more ammunition against me. My bruises have finally faded, but the memory of that pain is sharp.

"Touch knuckles," the emcee tells us.

The guy I'm fighting isn't someone I've ever seen before. He's shirtless, like me, with his knuckles wrapped. He has no tattoos, a preppy yacht-owning haircut, and a smarmy smile. Rich, presumably.

Someone might consider him handsome, but he and I are so very different.

Why the fuck is he in this dingy warehouse, scrapping with strangers, then?

I clench my jaw and step into the center of the cage, my arm outstretched. He comes to meet me. We're the same height, but he might have fifty pounds on me. I train to be lean and quick. This guy's muscles probably came from a personal trainer having him bench press until he can't breathe.

"You know Scar?" he asks.

I tilt my head. "What?"

"Scarlett." He smirks. "We went to Yale together. But hey, I hope the sloppy seconds are worth it."

My expression drops. She slept with this prick? Dated him?

"Ohhh," the guy continues. "She hasn't put out yet."

I jerk. "Excuse me?"

He leans in. "The trick to getting her legs open is to get her blindingly drunk. Works like a charm."

I see fucking red. The slam of the cage door closing rings in my ear—the signal to start the fight. I lunge without hesitation and pop him in the nose. His cartilage crunches under my fist, and he falls backward. Belatedly, his hands come up to defend himself. I give chase, striking low.

Get her blindingly drunk.

The insinuation sits like acid on my shoulders.

He manages to bring his knee up, and I let out a hollow grunt at the impact. He shoves me away, and I allow us to separate.

Blood drips from his nose, but he doesn't seem perturbed. If anything, he seems more sinister than he did a minute ago. He grins at me, his white mouthguard bloody.

Side note: that's why I picked a black mouthguard, precisely to avoid *that* deranged look. Sure, it can be a bit of a mind game, but I don't need to fall back on tricks to win.

His muscles bunch a split second before he comes at me, and I evade, my steps light. Part of me wants him to keep talking, keep giving me evidence to stack against him, to fuel my rage. Unfortunately, he seems fresh out of words at the moment.

I drop into the zone, tuning out the roar of the crowd that's been energized by the first sight of blood. Sometimes I think the people outside the cage are more vicious than the fighters.

We reconnect, exchanging hits. I grunt when he connects with my ribs and again when he kicks at my thigh. My leg goes numb, and my knee gives out. Motherfucking Charlie horse. I stumble to the side, and I hit the cage hard with my shoulder. All the while, he's right in front of me.

I duck, protecting my head, and I manage to circle around. It's a circle—there's no getting trapped in a corner —but that doesn't mean he can't get me up against the cage and hammer body and face shots while my feet stick to the floor. That's the surest way to lose.

I just need to finish this. There's no getting out of here otherwise.

The tiniest voice of reason rings in the back of my head. I promised to lose this fight. But how was I to know he knew Scarlett?

How was I to predict she would show up here, of all places?

"Come on," the big guy pants, his fist sailing over my head. "Winner gets to take her home, yeah?"

We live together, jackass.

I dive for him. I bring him to the mat. His head bounces off, and his hot exhale hits my face. His fist catches my cheek, and I go into survival mode.

The rest is a blur.

I won. My opponent lies on his side on the mat, and he spits blood out as he comes back to consciousness.

The cage door's hinges squeal, and suddenly, Tyler is in front of me. He presses a cold compress to my brow. I wince at the prick of pain, but he just scoffs at me. He shakes his head and glances over at the guy on the mat.

I was not supposed to win. That thought filters in amidst the din, and it dawns on me that the crowd is going nuts.

Tyler leads me out of the cage, down the steps, and straight through the audience to the back room. I bump my knuckles along a row of outstretched fists. My head swims.

"Find Scarlett," I tell Tyler.

Someone holds the door open for us, ushering me through, and I crane back to check that my best friend is still following.

"You definitely have a concussion," he says with a frown. "*Scarlett?*"

"Scarlett Wallace. Maybe you're the one with a concussion."

He rolls his eyes. "Fine."

"Thanks." It physically pains me to say that in regards to him tracking down Wallace, but whatever.

I move farther into the room and sit gingerly on one of the benches. I stretch out my legs in front of me and slowly lean back. What's-his-face got some good hits in but not nearly as many as the last fight.

I see another ice bath in my future.

The door opens again, letting in the noise of the crowd. There's another fight about to start, by the sound of it. Two guys come in with my opponent, whose arms are slung over their shoulders. His eyes are barely open.

They help him in and to a chair on the other side of the room. One of the guys blocks my view as he pays attention to his injuries.

Whatever. I should've hit him harder.

The door opens again, and Tyler leads in a pale Scarlett. My fury spikes again at the guy's words, and I know he wasn't making shit up. She wouldn't be this freaked out by me fighting.

That would imply she cared.

"I should not be back here," she says faintly. "I need to go."

"Caught her trying to get her phone back in the hall-way," Tyler supplies.

I grimace and shove myself to a stand. "Come here."

She glances uncertainly at Tyler, who returns her look with a blank stare. When he gives her nothing, she moves across the room and stops just out of my reach.

"I'm gonna go find out about your winnings," Tyler says.

"Who is he?" I ask quietly.

I'm mindful that *he* is in the corner, and she hasn't seemed to notice him yet.

The two guys fussing over the rich asshole pay us no mind.

"Who?"

I scowl. "I'm not an idiot, *Scar*."

She stiffens. "Don't call me that."

Touched a nerve. I lean in. "Did he call you that?"

Slowly, she nods.

"And?"

Her expression changes. Anger then resolve.

All at once, I don't want to know. I don't want to pry these details out of her—it doesn't matter. Beating him in the cage didn't matter. I want to strangle him *now*, simply for putting her on the defensive. For making those comments about her.

Jesus, where is this coming from?

She's my stepsister. I'm supposed to be protective, aren't I? It's like...I can mess with her, but no one else can.

Yeah, that's what we'll go with.

I deliberately turn my attention to the guy, and her gaze goes with mine. She gasps and staggers back. Her shoulder hits my chest.

Automatically, I wrap my arm around her—to steady

her or to keep her from sprinting away from me, I have no fucking idea. She trembles. Every muscle in her goes taut.

"Let me go," she whispers. "Cross—"

The guy seems to hear her. His laugh comes from behind the two guys, and he swats them away. He orders them out, and they go without a word.

To be fair, he looks like shit. His nose, which I absolutely broke, has been set straight, but it's swelling and darkening the skin under his eyes. His cheekbone might be broken, too.

"Scarlett," he breathes. "I've been searching for you."

She's no more stable than a feather in a hurricane. I tighten my grip and shift so she's partially turned away. Her hands come up to my forearm, and her nails bite my skin.

"Don't look at her," I bark.

His laugh is ice-cold. His gaze flicks to me, appraising, and I fear I'm revealing some secret weakness.

"I came so far for this sort of reception?"

"I want nothing to do with you, Nicholas." She sounds shockingly confident.

He touches the blood under his nose idly. "You used to call me *Nick*. When did that change?"

I catalog the detail, although I'm going to need a lot fucking more than his first name to bury him.

"It's no matter," Nicholas continues. "I got an upgrade after you left. She handles her liquor a bit better. She's one I can take home to my parents, you know?"

"Great," she hisses. "Then why are you here?"

"I missed you. Thought we might relive some old times before I head back to school."

There's something wrong with his head. In his brain.

He wants to, what, get her drunk and have his way with her? He traveled all the way here for *that*?

"I'm a little strapped for cash, too," he adds.

"What does that mean?" Scarlett demands. She pries my arm off of her, but she doesn't move away. She plants her hands on her hips. "I don't have money."

He rolls his eyes. "Your daddy does."

He leans to the side, where a bag is tucked partially under his chair, and pulls out a cell phone.

Even *I* don't have mine. Who the fuck didn't check his bag?

"Here."

He shows an article about her father's company going public. The headline is legible from here—probably because I wouldn't shut up about how it meant this guy was just another rich, white asshole, and I practically memorized it.

"You pay me, and I pretend you didn't file a report with the school." His eyes narrow. "You nearly got me in trouble, Scar."

"I—" She shakes her head. "I'm not asking him for money."

He glances at the phone. "I've got a nice little video I could send him. One of you in your glory days at those frat parties... Or maybe of your boyfriend cage fighting? It's a secret, isn't it? I'd hate for this to get posted."

"Boyfriend?" she questions.

Nicholas motions to me.

Ah, fuck.

He flashes a video someone must've taken discreetly— one of his goon helpers, probably. It's got my face in it.

"How much?" she asks.

My mouth dries. She must *really* not want whatever

video he has of her to get out. Not that I can blame her. God, my mind is a jumble. I think I do have a concussion.

"Hmm…" Nicholas smirks. "Twenty grand sounds reasonable."

Her jaw drops.

My gut churns.

"I don't have that," she whispers. "I can't *ask* for that."

He shrugs and pretends to pick at his nails. The phone disappears back into his bag. "I don't know, Scar. It's either that or those two videos get sent out, and I get to watch both your lives crash and burn."

"Nicholas—"

I can't hear her beg him.

"I'll pay," I blurt out.

I have twenty grand. Locked in a safe in the house. I'll have to figure out another way to pay back the Webber brothers, now that the plan for this fight has gone out the window. Now that I've failed their test. But I'd rather deal with that than *this.*

Scarlett's jaw drops, but she recovers fast. "No, Cross—"

"It's fine," I say quickly. I step forward and put myself between them. "I pay, and you disappear for good. Is that the deal?"

Nicholas rises. He puts a hand to his ribs and tries to suppress his reaction. He can't hide the flicker of pain, but it passes after a moment. He meets me in the middle and sticks out his hand.

"And you delete the videos," I add.

He pauses. His eyes gleam, but after a beat, he nods. We exchange numbers—grudgingly—and I shake his hand when all I want to do is punch him in the face until he'd need surgery to put his nose back together.

He snickers and steps away first. He turns his back like he doesn't have a care in the world about the two of us. He grabs his bag and heads to the door with a promise to see us later.

The noise rushes in when it opens, then leaves us in the devastating quiet when it slams shut again.

I look at her, and for once, I'm at a fucking loss.

CHAPTER 14
SCARLETT

CROSS GRABS A HOLD of my arm and drags me over to another door. "Let's go."

I huff and try to tug out of his grip. "Go where?"

The door opens, and instead of the noisy crowd appearing, it's a long dark hallway. Cross glares at me over his shoulder. "To get the money to pay off your *boyfriend*," he hisses.

I jerk on my arm again, but Cross keeps pulling me behind him. "He isn't my boyfriend," I stress.

He rolls his eyes. "Ex-boyfriend, then."

"He's not even an ex-boyfriend!" My voice echoes against the walls and follows us all the way out to the back parking lot.

Cross spins me around, his grip on me still tight around my arm. "Then what is he?"

My mouth clamps shut, teeth clattering. Cross raises an eyebrow. His swollen cheekbone is bruising, and there's dried blood on his lip. I move my eyes back and forth between his. He waits for me to answer, but I don't.

I *can't*.

Eventually, he rolls his eyes and continues pulling me over to his car. I try to put the brakes on, but it's no use going up against Cross.

"What about my phone?" I ask.

He opens the passenger door and pushes me inside. "I'll tell Tyler to get it."

"And what about—" The door slams in my face, and I growl.

As soon as he's settled in the driver's seat, I continue. "What about Sawyer? I came here with her. She's going to wonder where I went."

Cross floors the pedal, and we zip out of the parking lot. "Tyler will get her, too." He glances at me, and his mouth flattens. He has his phone in one hand, tapping out a message. Presumably to his best friend. "Put your seat belt on."

I do as he says, though it nearly kills me.

It takes us no time to get back to the house. I put my hand on the door handle when the car is in park, and he snaps his attention over to me so quickly the air moves.

"Stay here."

I cross my arms. "I'm not a dog!"

His eyes narrow in the dark. He gets out and slams the door again.

I'm tempted to get out and run, but after seeing Nicholas and learning that he's so close, I'm more afraid to do that than stay in this car with my broody stepbrother, whom I'll now owe twenty thousand dollars.

When Cross gets back in the car, the silence is nearly deafening. He drops a thick, padded envelope on the center console. It's folded in half and secured with a rubber band.

His hands, still wrapped around the knuckles from his

fight, grasp the steering wheel. Wordlessly, we head back the way we came.

The closer we get to the warehouse, the more nervous I am. My fingers tremble so much I'm forced to tuck them underneath my legs.

Gravel crunches beneath the wheels. Cross comes to a stop, putting the car in park, and if I wasn't here an hour prior, I never would've believed there was an elaborate fighting scheme. The warehouse is desolate now, the crowd leaving without a trace.

More silence stretches between Cross and me, and I refuse to look over at him.

I hate that he's privy to something so personal in my life and that I owe him. But there's also a small part of me that's full of gratitude, because he's willing to part ways with his money just to banish Nicholas from my life—if he sticks to his word.

I can only imagine what that video shows of me in a drunken state, drugged from something he slipped me.

My stomach churns at the thought.

I pull my hand out from beneath my lap and wrap it around my torso, slumping forward slightly to ease the nausea.

Cross shifts beside me, and I glance at him out of the corner of my eye.

That's all it takes for him to break the cold silence. "So that's your type? Rich pricks?"

He strikes a nerve, a gasp dropping from my mouth. I snap my attention to him, and as much as I want to blurt out the truth, I choose indifference instead. He knows more than enough about me at this point. He isn't getting anything else.

"Everyone is rich at Yale," I quip.

He snorts and adjusts himself again in the driver's seat. A wince digs into the shadows across his face, and for a split second, I feel bad. The fight was short-lived, but Nick got a few hits in. With every right hook to Cross's jaw, my heart had skipped a beat.

"Do you know what video he's referring to?" he asks.

My spine straightens. I bite into my bottom lip to keep it from trembling with fear, or maybe anguish? Probably both.

Nicholas took a part of me that I'll never be able to get back. As much as I don't want to let his actions ruin that zest of life that ran within, I don't know if I'll ever be able to trust another person as much as I blindly trusted him.

"You do know," Cross says quietly. "I can tell by your body language."

I look out the window while arguing, "No, you can't."

He snorts. "You're easy to read, Scar."

I jerk my head over to him, a wave of nausea cresting in my stomach.

He makes a face. "I mean…*Scarlett*."

We stare at each other until a pair of headlights comes into view. My heart races, and I bring my knees up to my chest and wrap my arms around them. Cross makes a noise that resembles a low growl before snatching the envelope full of money from the center console. He holds it tightly in his grip and opens his door.

The cool air swoops into the car, and I tremble even harder.

Loose gravel crunches under his weight, and I move to undo my seat belt, but before I can, he leans down, and we catch eyes.

"Lock the door."

I furrow my brow. "You don't want me to go with you?"

A sarcastic chuckle leaves him. "And reward him by letting him look at you again?" His sinful smile disappears. "Lock the door."

He straightens, but before he can shut the door, I blurt out, "Cross."

He lowers himself again, his face taut with impatience.

"I'll pay you back," I force out.

He stares at me intently then leaves me alone in the car. He strides across the lot with his shoulders straight. I envy his confidence in this situation.

I quickly hit the lock button, checking over my shoulder just in case. There's no one there. I swivel back. The passenger door of the other car opens. Cross hands off the envelope to someone other than Nicholas.

The coward is probably inside the car, opposite ours, with his sights on me. My skin crawls.

I slump down farther in my seat, out of view. Cross was right to have me wait here. Even the thought of Nicholas's eyes in my direction sends me into a complete spiral.

***

"Why are you so jumpy?" Sawyer asks, her eyes crinkling at the sides with suspicion.

"Me?" I play stupid. "I'm not jumpy!"

Sawyer snorts. "You've been beady-eyed since we got here."

I glance around the dining hall, bypassing several faces I saw the night of the fight. It's packed with students talking to their friends over cereal and eggs, drinking stale coffee in between rubbing the sleep from their faces. How many of them were rooting for Nicholas? How many of them know him?

"I just recognize some faces from the other night."

It's not a lie.

But it's not really the truth either.

I am beady-eyed, but I can't tell Sawyer the real reason I'm on edge. Ever since my run-in with Nicholas, I've been on alert. My body has been in fight-or-flight mode for the past several days, and I *swear* someone is following me.

As if on cue, Cross comes into the dining hall with his backpack slung over his shoulder, wearing his bruises loud and proud. We immediately lock gazes. I turn my back to him, annoyed that he keeps appearing out of thin air.

I mean, we live with each other, so passing by him in the kitchen makes sense. However, I've found him lurking outside my classes multiple times this week. Sometimes, he's with a group of his lacrosse friends, and other times, his arm is slung over some girl's shoulders.

Either way, I keep catching him in my proximity, looking in my direction.

"Come on." I gesture to Sawyer. "The coffee cart has better coffee."

I toss our to-go cups of coffee in the trash and walk in the opposite direction of Cross and his friends.

"Two coffees, one with cream and sugar, and one with only cream," I say.

Sawyer tries to step in front of me to pay, but I beat her to the punch.

"You know, I'm fine with paying for our coffees every once in a while, too." She elbows me.

I smile. "You can get the next one."

To be honest, I *should* let her get the next one—since I owe my stepbrother twenty thousand dollars.

"Oh shit," she blurts. "I'm going to be late for class."

Sawyer pushes her phone into her back pocket and gives me a quick hug. "Text me later!"

Then she's off, half running down the sidewalk toward the science building.

I laugh, until it's cut short when a deep voice rumbles behind me.

"You just want a black coffee?" the barista asks. "Nothing in it?"

"Just black," Cross repeats.

I turn and gape at him, and sure enough, he's leaning on the coffee cart with one elbow, staring directly at me.

"Are you following me?"

He doesn't answer me. Instead, he just stares, expressionless.

"Do you need something?" I pop my hip.

The barista hands him his coffee, and he takes it before giving him a nod of gratitude.

"I sent your last assignment to your email," I stress. "So I don't owe you anything. Why do you keep following me?"

Cross takes a long sip of his coffee, his throat moving with a swallow. He lowers the cup from his mouth, and my stomach slips when his tongue jolts outward to lick his bottom lip. I'm suddenly flushed. I rug my hair to the side, letting the cool air rush to my warm neck.

"You don't owe me anything?" He hums. "I disagree."

I pull my phone out of my pocket and check my email. "I swear I sent your assignment—"

"You did," he interrupts. "I got an A."

I gaze at him, and a sly smirk is waiting for me.

"You do still owe me, though." His head tilts. "Remember? Starts with a two…four zeroes following it?"

My shoulders suddenly feel heavy, like bricks are resting on top of them.

"I remember." I take a sip of my coffee, hoping it'll burn my tongue so I have an excuse not to talk to him.

Cross eyes me closely. His dark gaze drives so deeply into mine I'm afraid he can read all my thoughts. My pulse beats loudly inside my ears, and the only thing that breaks our stare-off is the clearing of a throat.

I jerk backward, my coffee spilling from the top of my cup.

Tyler is standing between us, eyeing us both with confusion. I panic and turn away from them both. I hurry off toward my next class, and I'll be checking over my shoulder *yet* again.

But I'm not sure who I'm expecting to see more: Cross or Nick.

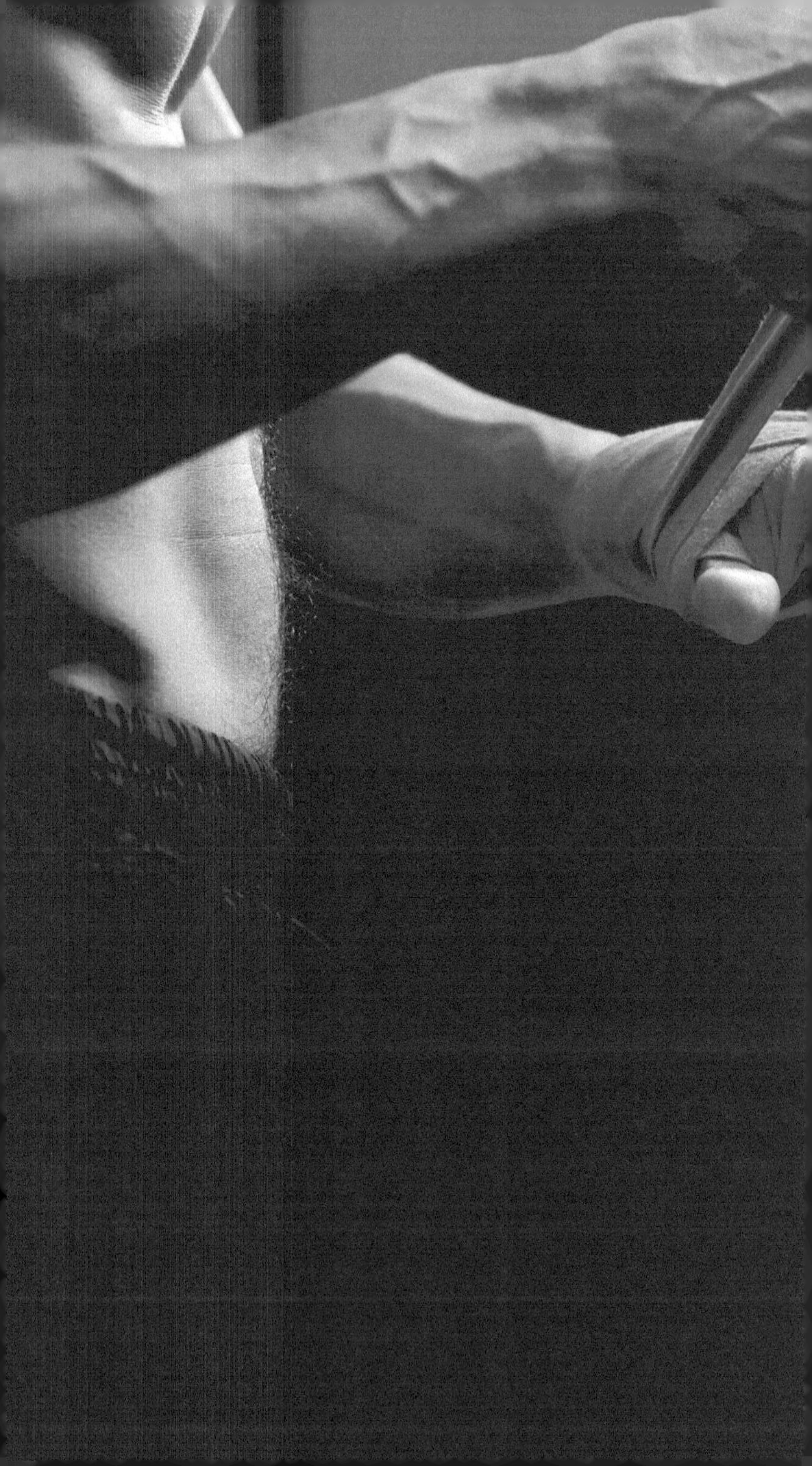

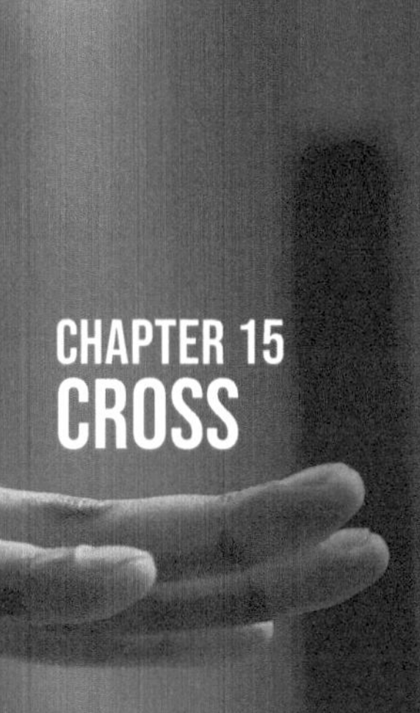

CHAPTER 15
CROSS

"THIS IS KIND OF DUMB, you know."

I glance over at Tyler and frown. "What is?"

"You."

"Well, you said *this* is kind of dumb, not *you're* kind of dumb—which I would take a little more offense to, by the way—so I assume you're referring to my actions?"

He sighs, which is essentially a yes. He's pointing fingers, but he's the one who decided to join me this morning. I was perfectly fine trailing Scarlett around campus by myself.

This morning is a particularly cold one, and a layer of fog hovers over the snow-covered ground. The figures crossing the quad are dark silhouettes, students hunched against the cold.

It's been four days since I won the fight I shouldn't have then subsequently got blackmailed into forking over so much money I get sick thinking about it. I should've spent it—that would've shown Scarlett.

What the *fuck* did I do?

"Earth to Cross." Tyler snaps his fingers in front of my face.

I jerk back and scowl.

"Where is she?"

I sigh and gesture. She's across the quad, barely visible in the mist, with Sawyer. I'm not sold on the new friend, but whatever. I feel better giving her more space—since Scarlett's been a little snotty about it—when she isn't alone.

It *is* when she's alone that I…*worry*.

And trust me, it pains me to use that word.

Tyler sighs again, louder.

"Well, no one asked you to come with me," I grumble.

"You literally said…" He opens his phone and scans our messages. "And I quote, 'Can you come take a shift watching Wallace while I run an errand?'"

"Oh, yeah." I smile at his irritation. "Thanks, by the way."

He grunts. "Where are you going?"

"I've got to face Stanley at some point. Figured I'd do it when the gym has some witnesses."

My best friend doesn't know about the mess I made—or the shit currently stuck to the bottom of my shoes. Figuratively, I mean. I didn't have the heart to tell him.

He claps his hand to my shoulder. "You rebounded so well after that loss. He's not gonna be mad."

"Yeah, well, I lost my head." I stand and point toward where Scarlett and Sawyer are now disappearing into the science building. "She's got a class on the fourth floor. Get moving."

"Jesus, you owe me one—or five."

"Listen, just don't let her out of your sight, and it'll be fine."

Tyler shakes his head. "Can you just tell me why you're so worried about it? About *her*? For months, I listened to you bitch and moan about her and her dad."

I can feel the tension raising my shoulders. I've managed to keep Tyler in the dark about my deal with the devils. And honestly, it's probably safer that he stays there. And then there's the whole issue of paying off Dickwad McGee. Who knows if that's going to stick?

I had a nightmare last night that he came back around, asking for more money.

"This doesn't feel like a protective-big-brother thing," he continues. "Are we trying to intimidate her?"

"Um…no." I cock my head. "Well, you're not. I'll do the intimidating."

"You're just worried she's gonna run away or something," he finishes. "Or start some nasty rumor about you to get back at you."

I snort. "We're not restricting who she can talk to. But the guy I beat at the fight was looking at her and making comments. You never know what those assholes are gonna do."

"Right." He doesn't quite buy it, but whatever.

"Fourth floor," I urge. "Go on."

He sighs and hunches his shoulders, heading toward the admin building. He disappears into the gloom, but I wait in silence.

I should really examine why Scarlett Wallace makes me such a headcase, but that's a problem for another day.

Instead, I head back to my car and drive the short trek over to the gym. Mid-morning, it's fairly quiet. Stanley is at one of the bags with another younger fighter, but he pauses when I arrive. He says something to the kid and motions for me to follow him upstairs.

"Stanley—"

"Just hold your horses," he snaps under his breath. His pace up the steps is quick, and he holds the door open for me at the top of the stairs. He closes it behind me. "Sit."

I do. I'd rather pace, but following his directions seems like a better way to make amends.

"The fact of the matter is, son, you're in more trouble than you think." Stanley stares me down. "It's not just the upfront money they want back. They've invested more into you that they've now lost."

My stomach knots. "Like what?"

"Listen, I'm just the messenger. Don't get testy with me." He slides a paper across his desk. "The message is this: you come up with fifty thousand dollars, or they'll start going through those closest to you and extracting repayment that way."

Fifty thousand dollars?

Twenty seemed impossible to come up with, with Nicholas whoever-the-fuck walking around that much richer. But *fifty*? That's more than double.

My palms are sweating, but I pick up the paper.

It's a printed photo…of Scarlett and me. At the coffee shop the other day. She was so angry—you can see it in her face as she looks at the back of my head. The way her lips turn down, her cute little scowl.

Ah, fuck, her scowl is *not cute*.

"What is this?" I demand. "Are they—are you threatening my stepsister?"

Stanley nods slowly. "It would appear they are, yes. You come up with the money—"

"I don't have it," I blurt out. "I don't know where to start…"

He considers me for a long moment. He's always been

rather jovial, but now the ruddy tone to his cheeks and the serious set of his lips makes him seem intimidating. It's easy to see why fighters listen to him without question.

But then he says, "You could fight more."

"I—"

"There are some other circuits," he says casually. He leans back and threads his fingers together, hands on his belly. "I didn't involve you in them because they're more violent. More potential to get hurt. And they're outside of the city limits."

"But they pay?"

"Yes."

"Sign me up."

He inclines his chin, and I get the distinct impression I'm being dismissed.

Fine by me.

Fifty fucking thousand dollars. How on earth am I going to come up with that?

And worse, how am I going to keep Scarlett safe if the Webber brothers grow too impatient to wait?

CHAPTER 16
SCARLETT

CROSS'S VOICE carries down the hall. I step off the last stair and head toward the kitchen. The flash drive I've compiled some of his finished course work onto sits heavy in my palm, and I walk quietly down the hall for no other reason than to eavesdrop.

"Did you just call me an *escuincle*? Again?" Cross's tone is playful.

I can't help but wonder who he's talking to. For once, he doesn't sound arrogant and broody. I also can't help but find his Spanish attractive.

I scrunch my nose. *Ugh.*

"I am not being impossible," he argues.

Who is he talking to?

A girlfriend?

I scoff quietly. Cross doesn't do girlfriends—from what I've heard, at least.

"I'm going to have to repay Robert, *Mamá*. I don't like handouts."

The realization hits me like a freight train. Of course

he's talking to his mother. Who else would he be using that softer tone with?

"He isn't my *papá*." Cross pauses. "I've turned out just fine with you raising me."

He huffs, and I lean forward to get an eyeful. He pinches the bridge of his nose with one hand, the other holding the phone up to his ear. Irritation etches onto his face, his jaw taking its usual hot—I mean, edgy—form.

All of a sudden, Cross loosens his fingers along his nose, and his eyes flick to mine. I jerk out of sight, my cheeks burning with humiliation from being caught.

"I've gotta go, *Mamá*," Cross's smooth voice floats down the hall to where I'm hiding. "My study partner is here."

I roll my eyes so hard I see stars. Study partner must be another word for slave.

After Cross hangs up, I gather my bearings and walk into the kitchen where he's standing with his back against the counter. As usual, he's his typical arrogant self, arms folded with his biceps on full display, the tattoos naturally catching my eye. He eyes me.

I hold out the flash drive for him to take.

"Here, study partner," I snark.

The scent of rich coffee fills the kitchen, and my mouth waters for a taste, but since Cross was the one to brew it this morning, I refuse to pour myself a cup.

Cross's mouth lifts on the side with my arm still outstretched, holding the flash drive with half of his completed course work. He moves at a snail's pace, my pulse gaining momentum with each stride. Eventually, he grabs a hold of it. Our fingers brush, and electricity zaps all the way up my arm. I yank my hand away and put my back to him so he can't see the blush spreading across my cheeks.

It's the tattoos. They're distracting.

"And this is?" He draws out his words, his voice lingering in our quiet kitchen.

"Three weeks' worth of your course work done," I clip.

He snorts. "Tell me you don't have a life without telling me."

I spin around in a fury, my hair skimming past my face to show him how irritated I am. "What does that say about you, then?" My arms fold against my chest defensively. "You've been following me around like some sort of babysitter, so does that mean you don't have a life either?"

Cross's eyebrows dip for a brief second before he smooths his face. "If you didn't act like such a baby when you ran into Nicholas, then maybe I wouldn't have to babysit you."

His words light a fire inside me.

My teeth grind. "I did not act like a baby."

Cross pushes the flash drive into his pocket lazily and shrugs. "You were shaking like a leaf, Scar."

I gasp at the nickname and take a step away.

Cross's eyebrow hitches with the tilt of his head.

Shit. I hate it when he's right.

A frustrated noise leaves me, and I spin around and stalk down the hallway.

He calls after me, "And where are you going?"

"None of your business!" I yell over my shoulder.

The metal doorknob does nothing to cool the burn of embarrassment on my skin. I forcibly open the door and step onto the porch, then come to a complete halt. My heart drops, and I instinctively take a step backward into something hard.

Cross's arm winds around my waist, and he steadies me against his chest.

"Watch it," he bites out.

My spine locks. I stare at the black SUV parked across the road.

That's three times in the last two days that I've seen it.

I grab on to Cross's arm holding me upright. My nails dig into his skin. I should shove him away, but instead, I stand immobile.

"What is with you?" Cross asks, his voice muffled by the pounding inside my ears.

I swallow my thick spit. "I keep seeing that SUV."

He shifts behind me, my nails still digging into his skin. I'm half hopeful I'll leave painful marks behind, but that would just remind him how I held on to him like he is a lifeline.

"And you think it's Nick?" he asks, already knowing the answer.

"He has one like it." I'd know—since he got handsy in the backseat once.

A gust of morning wind brushes past us, and I inhale deeply. My eyes widen, the air lodged inside my lungs. The window on the SUV begins to roll down…only to reveal someone other than Nicholas.

My chest deflates. "It's not him," I say with relief.

The tight grip I have on Cross's arm lessens, my nails removing themselves from his warm skin. Except, to my shock, he doesn't let me go.

Instead, his grip tightens.

He tugs me backward through the door and slams it shut.

"What are you—" My sentence stays on the tip of my tongue.

Cross spins me around hastily, his eyes wild with something I can't name. He pushes me against the wall with his hand glued to my hip while the other fiddles with the alarm system right beside my head.

He sets the alarm, the faint beeping noises mixing in with my heart rate, and then slices his fierce, dark eyes over to me. "A black SUV has been following you?"

I open my mouth and croak out a noise. His eyes bounce back and forth between mine, waiting patiently for me to answer him.

"Yes—no." I shake my head and glance away. "I don't know. I mean, I thought Nicholas was, b-but…" Cross's free hand grips my chin firmly. He forces me to look at him again, and my stomach twists with something other than irritation.

"But what?" he snaps.

"But it's not him. I'm just being…"

The hold Cross has on my hip gets stronger. His fingers brush the sliver of skin peeking from below the bundling of my shirt, and I'm suddenly at a loss for words. His tongue slips out of his mouth to wet his lip, and my entire body grows warm.

What the fuck.

"I'm just being paranoid," I blurt.

I try to push off from the wall, but Cross doesn't move an inch. I'm trapped. I can't even turn my face away with the tight grip he has on my chin.

"What exactly did he do to you?"

The question draws out of his mouth with slow curiosity. He surveys my expression. His gaze trails down my rapidly rising chest, only to snap back up once more.

I lie, my cheeks giving me away immediately. "Nothing."

Cross's eyes narrow. The brown color that was once warm moments ago turns dark. "You need to learn self-defense."

I gape at him, a scoff coming next. "I'm fine. Like I said, it's not Nicholas."

His jaw flexes. "But it's someone."

Okay, now *he's* being paranoid.

Does he have a point? Yes.

It would at least make me feel better if I had some way to defend myself if, God forbid, I find myself alone with Nicholas, or someone like him, but I'm *not* agreeing with Cross.

"Fighting is your thing, not mine," I argue.

I push on Cross's arm, and to my surprise, he lets me go. I round the stairs, rushing to escape into my bedroom, but his voice follows me.

"Get dressed for the gym. We leave in ten."

I stop mid-step and grab the hand railing. I peer down the flight of stairs at Cross, who is staring up at me with an expression that should scare me. Instead, it does the opposite. For a brief second, I let down my guard and allow that hot glare to do what my body wants it to do, but I regret it almost immediately when heat washes over me.

I quickly put my back to him. "Or what?" I snap, irritated at him and his stupid glare.

"Or I'll come up there and dress you," he threatens. "Ten minutes, Scarlett."

I run up the stairs and rush toward my bedroom to get dressed, but little does he know, I'm actually running from him.

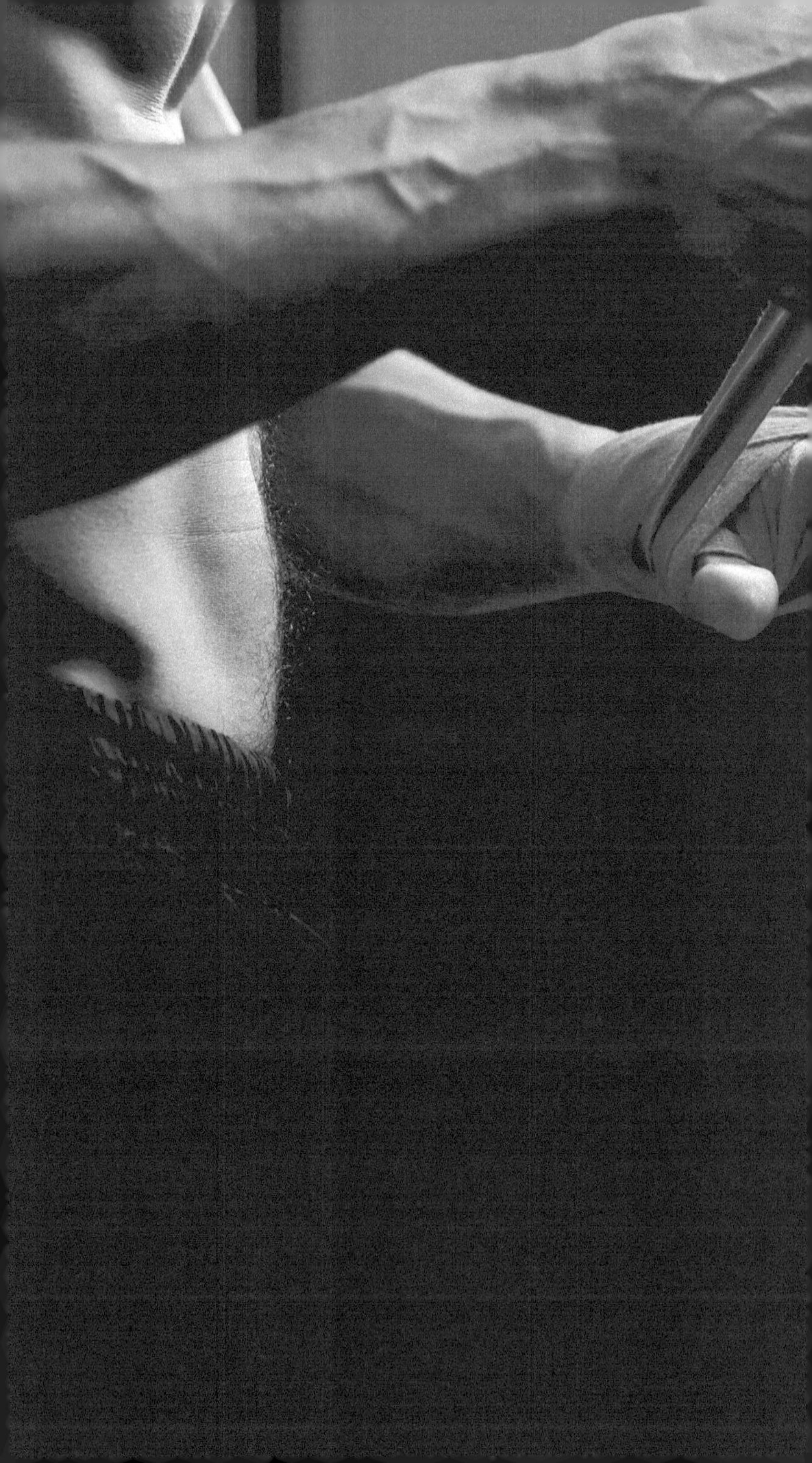

CHAPTER 17

CROSS

I DON'T KNOW why I'm fucking panicking about Scarlett not knowing how to defend herself, but seeing that SUV—and her split second of fear that then dissipated when she realized it wasn't that bag of dicks—twisted me up. And then *I* saw who was in the driver's seat, and I was back in Stanley's office while he fucking threatened to harm her.

Because of my idiocy.

Damn it, Tyler was right. I *am* a dumbass.

"Where are we going?"

I glance over at Scarlett sitting shotgun in the car I used fighting money to buy last year. I had saved up for, like, fourteen months to pay cash. And then my mother marries a guy who would've bought this for me without batting an eye—or notice the missing cash from his bank account.

In reality, I should've told my mother the truth when she called. I should've thrown Scarlett under the bus. *Instead*, I said I wanted to upgrade my car and asked if Robert could front me some cash.

Lie. But how the fuck am I going to come up with fifty

thousand otherwise? Scarlett thinks I only owe twenty. Stanley has already texted me details about the fight in the next town over. It's not cage fighting. It's more like scrapping with no rules. Like the movie *Fight Club*. It's no wonder I hadn't heard about this ring. First rule of fight club, after all…

The money is decent if you win, but Stanley made some vague claims about it being damn hard to actually win. The fighters are bigger. They're full-blown adults who will not take kindly to a college kid walking in and trying to claim their prize money.

Whatever.

"Cross." Scarlett's tone is impatient.

I smirk. "Yes, dear?"

She tenses. "I asked—"

"You should recognize this route." I make the final turn, and the abandoned warehouse comes into view. "You drove it once with Sawyer, and again with me."

"Fucking hell." She eyes me. "I don't want to be here. I thought you said we'd go to the gym."

"It's better no one knows," I reason. "If they suspect you have some knowledge of self-defense, they're going to come at you differently."

"You haven't said *who*." Her eyes widen. "Are you talking about Nick?"

I grimace. "No. Well, sure. Maybe."

I throw the car into park and hop out. The side door is still unlocked—I'm shocked it's even closed all the way, honestly—and the hinges squeal when I shove it open. The bottom scrapes across the dirty concrete.

"I don't like this place," she says softly, right behind me.

Jesus, maybe being a ghost could be one of her talents.

I motion for her to go into the dark, objectively creepy hallway first. Her phone's flashlight comes on, and she steps ahead of me.

I follow and slam the door shut behind me, enveloping us in darkness.

"What's your plan? Tackle me in the dark?" Her voice quivers. Her flashlight is pointed down, illuminating her shoes.

"You're not very big. I think it would be rather easy."

She scoffs.

I move around her then lunge at her back. I grab her shoulders.

She lets out a yelp and swings at me. The bright light flashes across my face. I pry her phone out of her hand and dance away, a laugh bursting out. She raises her hand to block it when I shine it at her face.

"Come on, then." I turn and saunter away, the flashlight arcing across the floor in front of me. She'll just have to follow in my shadow. I leave her in the dust and find the breaker. There's a switch for the generator outside, which is how they lit this place up for the fight.

The hum of electricity makes the building seem to come alive around me, and I round the corner to find Scarlett standing in the center of the huge main room. She's climbed up into the cage and spins in a slow circle.

"Intimidating, isn't it?" I hop the steps and snag the door with my fingers, swinging it shut behind us.

She jumps. "A little."

I smirk.

"Okay." She rubs her hands together. "Let's get this over with."

"Faster we do it, faster you get to go home?"

She nods emphatically.

I laugh. It's not true. I'm going to keep her here until I'm satisfied she won't be a worm on a hook for the people coming after her, whether we jump right into it or have a little foreplay first.

Instead of revealing that, though, I appraise her. She's wearing a long beige coat, a fuzzy scarf tucked into it, tight jeans, and fashion ankle boots with a low heel. Her hair is loose around her shoulders. Before we left the house, I made her switch out her glasses for contacts, but still.

Tactically, this is all shit that will get her killed.

I could wrap her easy-to-catch hair in my fingers and yank her toward me, strangle her with the scarf wrapped around her pretty throat, or get her all tangled up in that coat and trap her arms or pin her thighs...

"Strip."

Her eyes grow wide.

Another thought occurs to me: her panic was visceral when she was facing the douche canoe who shall not be named. She was shaking and frozen.

I need to figure out what else will make her freeze. Or throw her into *flight* mode. And then, I suppose, teach her how to fight through it.

Ugh.

I tap my foot on the mat. It's weird to be standing here in shoes, but I have a feeling Scar—*I should not call her that* —would resort to foot stomping, especially when I come at her from behind.

"Are you going to follow my directions or just stare at me?"

"I'm cold," the liar says.

"Your cheeks are flushed."

"I'm just nervous."

I burst into motion, crossing the cage and getting in her

space in an instant. I catch her oversized coat, bunching the fabric in my hands. It's easy to corral her sleeves without holding on to her wrists, and I pin them behind her back with one hand. With my other hand, I grasp her scarf and twist just a little, allowing the fabric to tighten around her neck.

She gasps.

"See that?" I get in her face. "You're a walking victim, Scar."

She flinches.

"I'm trying to fix that." I twist more.

Her face reddens, and her mouth opens and closes.

"Go on. Get out of my hold."

Her body jerks in my grasp, to no avail. I've got her arms trapped, her head and neck. Our chests are nearly touching. But she doesn't raise her knee to get me in the balls. She just trembles like there's an earthquake inside her.

I wait until her eyes roll back and her legs buckle. I release the scarf and catch her waist, guiding her to the floor. She comes back to life a second later, and her shock morphs into anger.

She slaps me. Her palm cracks against my cheek, but there isn't enough force behind it to turn my head—or make me do anything but grin.

"Strip," I repeat. "Or do you want to find out how else your coat and scarf are hazards?"

"Bastard." She picks herself up and tears off her scarf then unbuttons the coat. She throws both to the side and glares at me. Without the scarf and jacket, she's in a simple long-sleeve black sweater and jeans. "Was that necessary?"

"Apparently. Next time I say jump, do it instead of questioning me."

Her scowl deepens.

"Take a breath. Relax."

"Why?"

I tsk. She just can't fucking help herself, can she? When I cock my head, she blows out a long, slow breath. It seems to physically pain her, though, and after a long moment, she shakes out her arms.

Slight progress.

But in reality, an attack will come as a surprise to her. She's probably not going to see it coming. I circle around her. Her hair is still down, but I'm not quite ready to latch on to that weakness yet.

I want to see what will make her clam up—or worse, completely shut down.

When I'm behind her, she stiffens ever so slightly. Her shoulders rise. I pause in her blind spot, but she doesn't turn around.

Okay. Fine.

I wrap her in a bear hug, my grip strong but not too tight. I haul her back, lifting until she's on her toes.

"Get out of my hold," I say in her ear.

"This is awful," she mutters, thrashing. "Jesus."

"Nope, it's just me." I grin.

She smells good—probably the floral shit she uses in her hair, which is now stuck to the stubble on my jaw. Unfortunately, she's really bad at attempting to defend herself. She kicks out, but she doesn't make contact. Her elbow grazes my side and does literally no damage.

I think a kitten could hold her hostage, and she'd let it.

"You're not trying." I squeeze her. "You're not going to hurt me."

"I don't like your methods."

"I don't like that I spent twenty thousand dollars

making your ex-boy toy go away," I growl. "And yet, we all make sacrifices. This is yours."

She grunts. Her heel connects with my shin, and I loosen a fraction of an inch. She kicks again, sensing a weakness. Then, she stomps.

"Fucking finally." I release her.

She stumbles away from me and whirls around. "What was that?"

"Use what you've got." I come at her again, from the front.

She sees me looming and backpedals. I catch her shoulders and shove her against the cage then pin her with my hips. My knee parts her thighs.

This position wakes up the *other* side of my brain—the side more often reserved for the girls I use to distract myself. It's not my fault Scarlett is pretty.

She pushes at my chest. The cage wall rattles. This isn't freaking her out enough. She's just too timid.

"Maybe I should hold you down and pour alcohol down your throat," I goad. "Let's see if your ex was all talk, or full of—*oof*."

She punched me in the throat? I cough, but inside, I'm proud. At least she's angry.

Good girl.

She ducks under my arm and puts distance between us. Her chest heaves. "That was uncalled for, Cross."

I pull the flask from my back pocket. "So is that a no?"

Her face pales.

I shake it, letting her hear the slosh of liquid.

"Cross—"

I've found the trigger. One of them. She stares at me with huge eyes, and her feet stop moving.

Bad idea.

I approach slowly. Carefully. I drop my arm, but she still seems too caught up in the fact that I have a flask to notice I'm getting closer. The cage is a circle—there's no corner to box her in. But her fear is a cage all its own, and I seem to have locked her inside it with one simple action.

She doesn't notice I'm right in front of her until my hand is in her hair.

Her lips part, her breath ragged, and the flinch that rolls through her body is wicked. I tug her head back, and her gaze flicks to mine.

"Drink it, and we'll have a little fun," I say.

My stomach rolls at the insinuation. It was very fucking clear what that douche said in the cage, but Scarlett hasn't admitted anything beyond *he isn't an ex*. Get her drunk, and what, she'll open her legs?

Or she'll pass out and not know what he's doing?

One or the other.

Slut or victim.

I touch the cap of the flask—*closed*—to her lips, and she shuts down. I watch the light vanish from her expression like a candle being blown out.

Does she really think so little of me?

Probably, you dick.

How the fuck are we going to work around this fear? I release her hair, but she doesn't move. Some part of her has taken over and pushed her into survival mode.

That makes me fucking livid.

I toss the flask and grasp her jaw lightly. Her nostrils flare, and her gaze slides to mine then away.

"Don't do that, Scarlett," I say in a low voice. Concern prickles at me. "Come back."

Nothing.

I shake her head.

Nothing.

I can't tell if I'm angrier at her or myself. I didn't think it would cause *this* much of a reaction.

And…well, shit. That means the situation with what's-his-face was probably eighteen times worse than anything I'd imagined. I should probably try to remember his name so I can find him and fucking kill him later.

Can I murder someone and get away with it?

Maybe…

Tyler would probably have to help me.

Fuck, I'm in over my head.

"Scarlett." I tap her cheek. "Wallace."

I walk her backward and let her lean against the cage. I put my hand on her waist, and she doesn't cringe or shove me off. She just tips her head back and closes her eyes.

Honestly, I can only think of one thing to do. One thing that will *really* piss her off. But pain might be just the thing to get her to snap out of it. Slapping her across the face is a low I'm not willing to stoop to—not to mention, my mother would fry me alive if she ever found out.

So, it's option B.

I lean in and down. My lips touch her throat, and I inhale her scent again.

And then, like a fucking savage, I open my mouth and bite her neck.

CHAPTER 18
SCARLETT

PAIN SEARS MY NECK, and I gasp. There's a heavy weight on my waist. The cage digs into my back. *What the—?*

I blink to clear my vision.

It only takes half a second to remember where I am and who I'm with. The other half of that second is me teetering between being turned on and angry.

"What the fuck, Cross?" I push on his hard chest, and he willingly moves backward.

His smirk fuels the anger simmering on the inside to boil over completely. My gaze drops to the flask on the mat beneath our feet, and I shake with fury. "What is wrong with you?" My voice vibrates.

"The real question is, what's wrong with *you*, Scarlett?"

My forehead furrows, and I fold my arms. "Nothing is wrong with me!"

Cross leisurely walks over to the flask and swoops it into his palm, then walks closer to me. The metal catches a glare from the light when he shakes it in front of my face like a tease.

"You're sick," I seethe. "Why would you say that to me? Why—why…would you—" I stutter and try to find the correct words. "Why would you fuck with me like that?"

Cross's gaze darkens. His eyes narrow into slits. He leers at me from no more than a foot away. "Who said I'm fucking with you?"

Fear wraps around my throat like a vise grip.

My heart beats a mile a minute, and I press against the cage. Only, there's nowhere to escape to. I couldn't run with Nick, and I can't run with Cross.

He quickly erases the space between us, our breath dancing in front of one another. Short gasps escape from my rising chest, and his gaze falls to the rapid movement. He quickly pinches my chin between his fingers, squeezing just enough to get my attention. "Open your mouth."

I clench my jaw. "No." My refusal slips out between my tight teeth.

Something shifts across his expression, and weirdly enough, it looks like pride.

"Don't you trust me?" he asks.

I stare at him for far too long. His brown eyes are no longer filled with anger but, instead, curiosity.

Being this close to him should scare me, and it does to a certain extent, but not for the reason it should. It scares me because the little voice in the back of my head is telling me to say that I do trust him.

But I *don't*.

Right?

Cross squeezes my chin again, this time my lips pursing.

I reach up out of instinct and grip his wrist. It's strong and sturdy, just like he is.

"I trusted *him*," I admit, referencing Nick. "So excuse me for not trusting you."

With one hand still holding me hostage, the other messes with the flask. My pulse thrums when Cross lifts the opened container and positions it above my closed mouth. I squeeze my eyes shut and wait for the bite of alcohol to touch my lips. Except, it never does.

My eyes fly open when the liquid flows onto my tongue.

"It's water," he says. "I just wanted to see how you'd react."

I unclench my jaw. "Why?"

Cross's gaze shifts languidly between mine, like he's trying to learn every one of my secrets.

He stares at me for a brief second.

"Is this what he did to you?" he questions.

He tips his head back to let the water inside the flask pour into his own mouth. His throat moves smoothly with each swallow, until he tosses the container off to the side. The sound of it hitting the mat echoes around us, but all I can think about is how that same flask was just touching my lips a moment ago.

"Did he get you drunk so he was able to do this..." Cross quickly drops my chin, and both of his hands end up around my waist.

I arch my back, and a sharp breath of air leaves me. I push myself onto the cage again, the metal rattling around us. The temperature seems to kicks up a degree. Cross's knee makes its way between my legs, spreading them open just enough to get me thinking all sorts of things I *shouldn't* be when it comes to him.

What is wrong with me?

This is wrong, on so many levels.

One second, I'm ready to murder him, and the next, a flush is working itself up my neck.

Not to mention, we're *stepsiblings.*

Cross's warm breath coats the side of my neck, and I exhale shakily. His nose graces the delicate skin, and it puts me in a daze. My head falls to the side, and I swear I hear him chuckle.

"Or..." The warm embrace from Cross's closeness vanishes. He moves quickly, his nose skimming my skin. He positions his face in front of me. "Did he slip something in your drink so he didn't have to face your rejection?"

Like he pulling the trigger of a gun, I look away, unable to face the question.

Cross tugs me toward him, the cage behind my back no longer there to support me. Instead, it's him and his hold on my waist.

"Answer me." His low voice is more of a command than anything, and I could lie, deny his accusation. I could pretend it never happened and that Nick was just some lousy ex-boyfriend.

But for some reason, I find myself opening my mouth and doing the complete opposite.

Maybe it's because of our close proximity or the way his brown eyes soften. He waits for my reply. Either way, my voice croaks when I give him exactly what he wants: the truth.

"The latter," I say quietly.

Cross's eye twitches. "He spiked your drink?"

I flare my nostrils in an attempt to keep myself from showing him how ashamed I am. My throat grows tight, and the longer I stare into his waiting eyes, the more twisted I become.

"It's not that uncommon." I chalk it up to something much less severe than what it is. "Girls get drugged all the time."

The muscles at Cross's temples flex, and the grinding of his teeth is louder than my pounding heart. "I'm going to let that slide," he forces out. "Now tell me more."

I bite the inside of my cheek, then give in. "We were seeing each other. Nothing serious." My voice quivers, so I look away, staring out into the dark gym. "We kissed a few times, and then he invited me to a party. We danced throughout the night…and he was the perfect gentleman. I'd heard nothing but good things about him, but…" I shrug. "I guess I wasn't putting out quick enough."

Cross steps away from me. His back is the only thing I see. He storms across the cage. I exhale loud enough for him to peer at me over his shoulder, and when our eyes connect, he's spinning back around and heading for me again.

"That fucking bastard," he growls, his hands sliding across my waist again. "When he made the comment about you, I didn't think—"

Shock flickers throughout. "What comment?"

"He told me to get you drunk so you'd open up your legs for me."

My vision blurs. "That fucking asshole," I mutter. "I hate him."

"Good," he bites out. "Use that fire I see in your eyes, and take it out on me. We're not leaving this gym until I feel that you're capa—"

Suddenly, my lips are on his.

Something dangerously intoxicating explodes, and I'm

doing exactly what he said to do: I'm using the fire burning from the inside out, and I'm taking it out on him. My tongue dives past his lips, moving against his with an urgency. The grasp he has around my waist tightens, and my breasts press to his hard chest, my heart beating a million miles a minute, like it's going to charge right out of my chest.

He deepens the kiss as my back slams against the cage, his taste blinding me from everything. I've never felt this wild before. My entire body is in a frenzy. The way his mouth seals over mine is life-changing. It's like he's trying to suck the soul right out of my body, and I'm willingly letting him.

One hand disappears from my hip, only to grab my wandering hands. He pins them above my head, the metal cage biting into my skin.

God, this is hot.

Pleasure rushes to my breasts, my nipples pleading for him to take my shirt off.

Cross tears his mouth away. "What the fuck—"

My eyes open as soon as he steps away. I exhale sharply and try to steady myself on shaky legs. Cross's face is filled with horror, and he wipes the back of his hand over his glistening lips.

We stare at each other for a few seconds, but a thousand thoughts flicker across his face.

I shouldn't have kissed him.

His regret is painfully obvious, and I should be feeling the same way.

What was I thinking?

"I…" I shake my head. "I—"

"Save it," he snaps. "We're done for the day."

Cross strides across the cage and hops on agile feet to

the floor. I follow after him quietly, the guilt and embarrassment haunting me like a shadow.

I can't believe I kissed him.

It was like something came over me, and I couldn't be stopped.

I climb inside his car, and right then, I decide it's best to just pretend it never happened. I refuse to look in his direction. Instead, I stare out the window at the blurring yellow lines until we pull up in front of the house.

I'm out of the car before he even manages to turn the engine off, and I don't fully breathe again until I'm tucked away safely in my bedroom.

I flop onto my desk chair and fiddle with my protractor. I stare at myself in the mirror with disappointment. I tuck a piece of hair behind my ear and quickly do a double-take.

"What the hell—" I turn my head to the side, and my jaw falls.

My hand instinctively flies up to my neck to cover a red-and-purplish mark that resembles a bite. Heat bursts across my cheeks with the faint memory of Cross's lips on my throat.

I clench my eyes shut to rid the thought from my brain.

Shit.

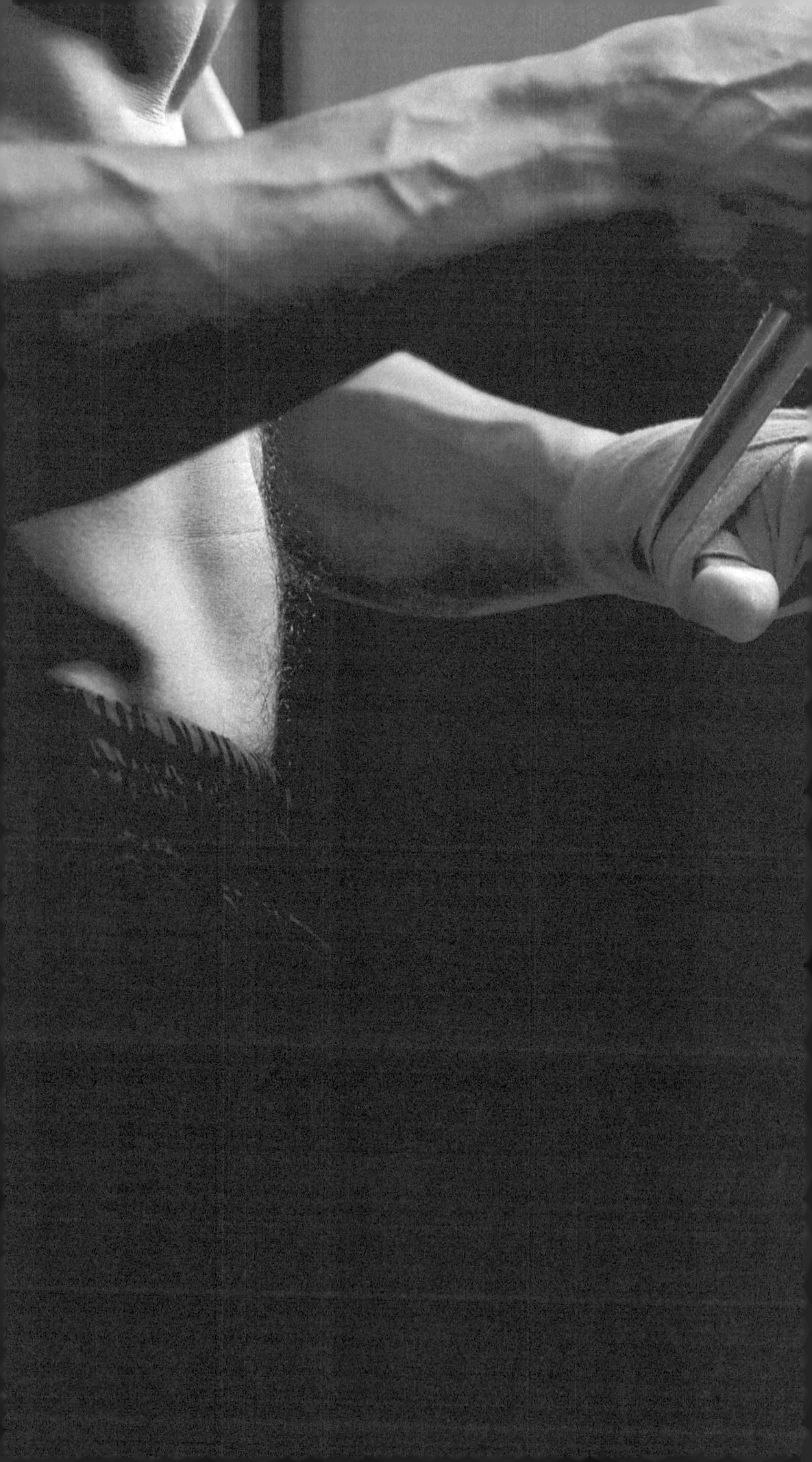

I CAN'T STOP THINKING about that damn fucking kiss.

She took me by surprise. The *last* thing I expected was for her to rise on her toes and press her lips to mine. And, yeah, I lost myself for a moment. I allowed myself to treat her like someone I can kiss anytime I want—as someone I *want* to kiss whenever I want.

Then, naturally, it got fucking awkward. Scarlett was embarrassed at her impulse.

I was just trying to get my dick to stop throbbing.

I was also pissed at myself for indulging in that.

Has there always been some underlying lust toward her? Now that I think about it…*yes*. But what's a guy to do? Force himself onto his stepsister who loathed him from the moment she saw him? That's something her dickbag ex would do. Not me.

No, instead you bully her into doing your homework.

I run my hand over my face.

The crazy thing is that I want to kiss her again, and I don't want to stop. I picture it, the slide of her lips on mine, and the little whimpers she'd let out, and my dick stiffens. I ball my hands in my sheets, refusing to touch myself.

Fuck, this is stupid.

I've been trying to sleep for ages, but all I've managed to do is replay that kiss while staring at my ceiling.

That's it. I'm done. The best way to get rid of a song stuck in your head is to just play it, so that's what I'm going to do.

I push the blankets off and swing my legs over. The cold floor wakes me up even more. I slip out of my room and across the hall, not even pausing to consider Scarlett's shut door. If she really wanted me out, she'd lock it. Probably.

We're about to find out.

It opens on silent hinges, and I step in. Her room is darker than mine—I think she's hung up blackout shades —but an old-school digital alarm clock on her nightstand gives off a red glow and faintly illuminates her silhouette.

I cross to the side of her bed and let my eyes adjust. Her hair is in two braids, and she's sleeping on her back. Her lips are slightly parted.

This is a wicked temptation.

I reach out and touch her lower lip.

"Scarlett," I whisper.

She shifts a little.

"Scarlett."

Her eyes flutter open, and I withdraw my finger before she notices I was touching her. My heart squeezes and picks up speed when she registers me and doesn't immediately panic.

"What are you doing?" she asks, her voice groggy.

I tug at the blanket covering her, and she automatically

shifts aside. Not one to waste a perfectly good silent invite, I climb into the bed and get close to her. I want her to be awake. I need her alert for this moment, because I'd feel like scum if I kissed her when she was sleepwalking or some shit.

"I'm gonna kiss you," I tell her.

She slow-blinks. When I don't move, she sucks her lower lip between her teeth.

"Okay?"

She nods.

Anything to get you out of my head, Wallace.

The air seems to thicken when I inch closer. I run my hand up her arm, and goosebumps break out across her skin. Her hand finds my waist, and she grips my shirt—to push me away at a moment's notice, perhaps.

I press my lips to hers softly, once, then I withdraw. Her huge eyes fill my vision. Ah, fuck. She leans forward, and suddenly, we're kissing again. Her fingers graze my ribs, my shirt fully in her grasp. Our mouths naturally part, and my tongue slides along hers.

This is infinitely better than the first.

I taste her, but she fights back. Someone, somewhere, taught her how to *kiss*. The thought makes me irrationally angry, and my teeth score her bottom lip.

She moans.

My dick wakes up. Her palms are flat against my bare chest, but all it does is send lightning bolts through me. I shift, rising onto my elbows. I hover over her, guiding her flat on her back.

I tear my lips from hers and drag my mouth down her jaw to her neck. Her scent fills my nose, and I nip and kiss my way down to where I bit her earlier. With any luck, it'll be recognizable for what it is in the light of day.

She pulls at my waist, but I freeze.

It takes all my fucking willpower not to grind my dick on her leg—or worse, between them. She's my *stepsister*. I'm going to have to look at her across the dining table at family functions for the rest of my life. She's never going to disappear, not like the girls I date and then dump when I grow bored of them.

It's like ice water crashing over my head, and I practically throw myself off her. I'm on my feet and out of the room before my brain can catch up. My heart hammers. I flick the light on in my room then dig out sweatpants, socks, sneakers. My sweatshirt is slung over the back of my chair, and I've got a hat somewhere.

Scarlett is a temptation I can't afford.

Both literally and mentally.

She's standing in the doorway of her room when I reemerge dressed for a run. I spare her a glance, getting an eyeful of her mussed hair and swollen lips.

"Fuck," I growl.

I pivot and beeline for her. I catch the back of her neck and lean down. This kiss is rough. She bites my lip, and the metallic taste of blood blooms across my tongue. I *like* it. I want more of it. I want her teeth on me—and that's precisely the problem.

Tonight's memories will have to be enough.

I step away, taking in her half-lidded eyes and rather pleased expression, and I sear that into my memory, too.

Because I have a feeling from here on out, it'll be only scowls.

CHAPTER 20
SCARLETT

I DIDN'T SLEEP A WINK.

Every time I think about last night, my body grows warm and my heart beats harder.

After Cross left, I lay awake in bed for hours. It was nearly three in the morning when I heard him stomping up the stairs again. I pretended to be asleep because I wasn't sure what else to do, but I felt his presence in the doorway.

He stood there for so long I finally peeked one eye open, only to see his backside disappear down the hall to his own room.

Now, here I am, in our kitchen, pouring myself a cup of coffee with a shaky hand.

What were we thinking?

Better yet…why can't I stop?

He's my stepbrother. Our parents are married, and to most people, marriage is forever. That means Cross will always be in my life, one way or another.

I sip on my coffee and scroll my phone, wondering if maybe I should try to hook up with someone else—on my terms, of course. Someone who I trust. Someone who won't spike my drink, and take advantage of me, and listen if I say no.

Someone who *isn't* Cross.

I jump at a raspy clearing of a throat. Coffee splashes out from the top of my mug, scalding my hand before landing on the counter.

"Shit," I curse.

Cross moves to stand beside me and peers down at my mess. He says nothing. Instead, he reaches past me for the coffee pot, our arms nearly skimming.

Goosebumps race to my arms from the mere breeze. My cup clanks to the counter when I place it beside the spill, and I take the opportunity to move across the kitchen for something to clean the mess with.

Mid-cleanup, I glance at him. My hand freezes with the soaked paper towels in my grip. Cross, in low-hanging sweats and a half-unzipped jacket, sans shirt, stands with his back against the counter, the coffee pot up to his mouth.

He gulps down the hot coffee with ease before flicking his eyes to mine.

I can't move. I can't breathe.

"Did you finish that last assignment?" he asks, casual as ever.

I blink. *What?*

One of his eyebrows hitches. He waits for my answer, the impatience obvious.

Is he just going to pretend last night didn't happen?

Was I dreaming?

My gaze shifts to his mouth.

My lips tingle at the sight of his.

It most definitely wasn't a dream.

His gaze slowly slips to my neck. A flush begins to work its way across my chest. He puts the coffee pot back up to his mouth, but I see the slight twitch of his lips.

I quickly reach up and pull my hair forward to hide the bite mark he left behind. I shift on my feet because I'm choosing not to acknowledge the pulse between my legs.

"I'll have it done this afternoon." I put my back to him because *fuck him.*

My hackles rise at the sound of his slow and steady strides back to where I'm standing. He reaches across me to put the empty coffee pot back in its rightful place, and his hot breath coats the side of my cheek. *God, this is bad.*

"Good," he clips out. "You can bring it to the gym when you're finished."

I turn abruptly, our faces close. "The gym? Again?"

"That's right."

My eyes flutter closed with his breathy response. He pushes my hair past my shoulder, showing off the bite mark he left me with no less than twenty-four hours ago.

I open my eyes, and he glares.

"But try to keep your mouth to yourself this time, *sis.*"

My lips part with shock. Cross turns and puts his back to me while lifting his hood up onto his head. He stalks down the hall to round the stairs.

He jogs up the steps, and I'm left standing in the kitchen feeling even more turned on than I did last night.

And I hate myself for it.

With Cross's paper clutched tightly in my hand, I stumble into the gym with Tyler following after me. Apparently, my dearest stepbrother forgot to mention that I was going to have a handler all day long in addition to completing *his* homework.

"I think I can manage the rest of the way," I bite out. "Thank you very much."

Tyler chuckles from beside me. "Cross told me not to trust you, so I'm walking you all the way over to him until he takes you."

I roll my eyes and exhale loudly. I tighten my fingers, stomping across the gym floor toward the raised fighter's ring. The paper in my hand crumples even more.

It's empty. Our echoing footsteps blend in with the punches Cross throws toward a mat that some guy holds up in front of him.

The man barks, "Again!"

Cross does as he says, his muscles rippling. He works his body in ways that only a true fighter could do. He dances around on light feet, and I can't help but stare.

My lips part the longer I watch. Sweat droplets roll against Cross's skin, the tattoos on his arm appearing wet and glossy.

"Fuck. Okay, I'm done," Cross wheezes.

He turns and locks on to Tyler first then immediately drops his eyes to me.

Just to prove a point, I glance away and turn my chin up in his direction.

Tyler chuckles again, but this time, he tries to cover it with a clearing of his throat.

"Delivery!" he calls out, referring to me.

I plant my hands on my hips. "I'm not a fucking package."

"More like a gift," someone muses.

Tyler sucks in air from beside me at the same time someone wheezes. I peer up at the cage, and the trainer who Cross was working with is bent over at the waist, cradling his stomach.

"What…the…*fuck*, Cross?"

Cross puts his back to the trainer and stalks toward the door. He calls over his shoulder, "Don't talk about her like that."

My mouth falls open.

Cross hops down onto the floor in front of Tyler and me, and I glare at him. A sweat droplet hangs off the end of his nose, falling in between us. He grips my chin between his fingers. He closes my mouth and stares down at me.

"Don't mistake my chivalry for something other than it is. I'm just sticking up for my sister."

Embarrassment hits my stomach.

I bite down on my tongue, the taste of metal filling my mouth.

"Oh, and I'll take this." He pulls the paper out of my hand with ease.

I'm too angry and confused to bite back some type of insult. I take a step backward and run into something hard.

"Whoa." Tyler's hands fall to my waist from behind. "Careful, Scar."

My spine goes rigid, a breath lodging in my throat.

Cross moves quickly. He puts himself between me and Tyler, half shielding me from his friend. "Don't call her that."

I exhale and quickly shake myself out of it.

"My bad," Tyler says slowly, clearly confused. "Don't call her a gift. Don't call her any sort of nickname. Got it. Anything else?"

Cross just grunts.

I roll my eyes, but then an idea strikes. I head toward the raised platform where his trainer is still shaking off Cross's cheap shot. I glance over my shoulder to where my stepbrother stands, shirtless, with the paper I wrote for him clutched in his tight grip.

This will show him. I carefully unzip my jacket, aware that Cross's attention tracks my every move, and toss it toward him. I duck under the ropes and face the trainer.

My smile is shy. *Coy.* "Can I train with you?"

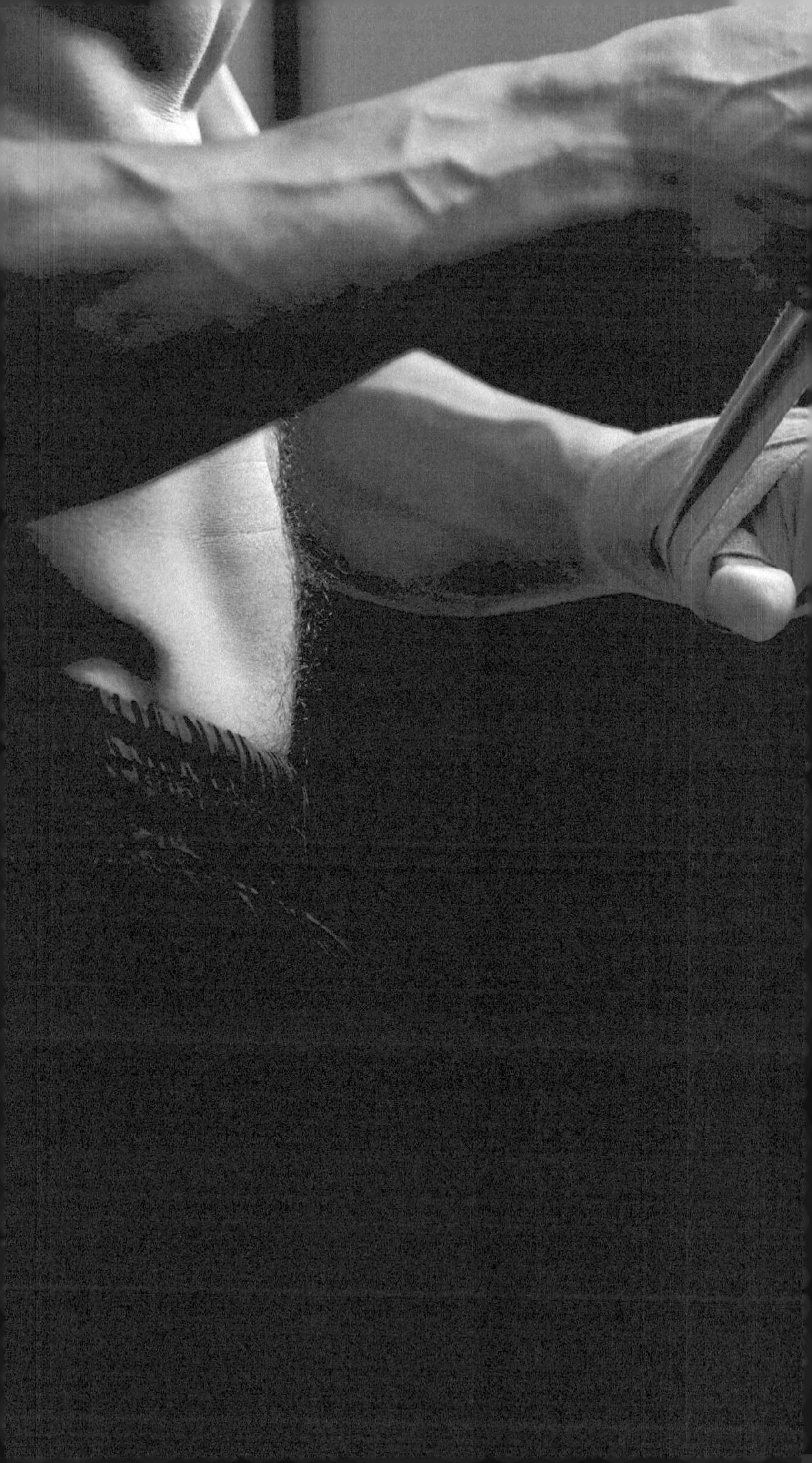

CHAPTER 21
CROSS

OH. Hell. No.

I feel like I'm on fucking drugs. I start forward, and Tyler grabs my arm. He yanks me back, giving me a look like I'm the crazy one.

Yeah, I'm unhinged. No one's surprised.

The one thing I promised never to do, though, was hurt my best friend. As much as he's a pain in the ass, I'd never risk injuring him based on some hot-headed moment. But that is *really* put to the test the moment he holds me back from jumping up there.

"*Look,*" Tyler says in my ear. "We have an audience."

He tips his head toward Stanley's office, and my heart stops. He's at the top of the staircase, glowering down at us—not surprising, that's a common occurrence—but someone is with him.

One of the Webber brothers.

I haven't told Tyler the truth—should've, but didn't. It was easier to lie and say that I was asking him to babysit Scarlett all day because I was worried about her horseshit ex coming back. I should probably tell him the whole truth

—about throwing a fight, *not* throwing another fight, the secret twenty grand going into the pocket of a rapist, and my fifty-thousand-dollar bill.

And how the Webber brothers are threatening to collect by any means necessary if I don't cough up some coin.

That just seems like a headache in the making, though, and I'm over it.

That, and my mother keeps calling me. She's kind of superstitious, and I think she's picking up some vibes that I'm in trouble. I'm not superstitious—more like a *little* stitious, if we're honest—but I take her concerns seriously. When she tells me to smudge my room with sage, I do it. I don't want beef with bad spirits.

Anyway.

Tyler releases my arm, and I face him. "Get her."

His eyebrows rise. "Excuse me?"

"Get her and take her the fuck out of here." I'm speaking through a clenched jaw. My instincts say, rush up there, punch the dude in the face, and throw her over my shoulder like a caveman. But for the first time, I don't trust myself to act.

Tyler makes a show of sighing, and we both check the ring. I wouldn't call Jim a *trainer*. He's more of a workout partner who makes sure my form stays solid. But right now, he's showing Scarlett how to throw a punch and holding up the blocker on his hand for her to hit.

I watch her wimpy hit, and Jim smiles encouragingly.

That wouldn't stop a toddler.

I elbow Tyler, and he finally goes into action. He hops up and ducks under the ropes, approaching them. He waves off Jim and approaches Scarlett. I shove my free hand in my pocket to hide my balled fist. I turn away. I don't need to see her look at me and glare some more.

I *know.*

I feel the heat of it on my back, but I walk away. I go to the locker room at the back of the building and tuck the printed assignment into my backpack. The door opens behind me. I finish closing my bag and turn around, only to come face to face with Webber.

Alex or Jason…I've got a fifty-fifty shot.

He raises an eyebrow. Today, this one is in a black button-down shirt, black slacks, and black loafers. A gold chain peeks out from under his shirt collar. If he's not in the fucking mob, he's doing a hell of a job cosplaying.

"Where's our money, Cross?" he asks.

I straighten. "Like I told Stanley, I'll pay you back."

His expression reminds me of a seasoned fighter's: dead inside. They're there for a paycheck, but they've learned to shut off the emotion. Adrenaline is good, but excitement, fear? Not so much. I can't tell what's going through his head.

"You spent it before you earned it," he says.

It's not a question, so I say nothing. My mouth has dried out anyway.

He nods slowly. "Okay, Cross. I understand. It's a lot of money to suddenly come into, to think that you have the right to spend. And, well, you *would've* been able to spend it with a clear conscience if you had followed through."

I stare at him. There's got to be a point, right? A threat he'll make then leave, and it'll give me time to figure out what the fuck I'm going to do. That other circuit is holding an event soon, I hope. Stanley gave me limited options, and…I don't fucking know.

"That girl out there is mighty pretty," Webber states. "She's wearing some expensive stuff. Like she comes from money or something."

"Leave her out of it."

He smiles. I immediately wipe the scowl off my face, disappointed in myself for dropping my guard. A split second or an eternity—it doesn't matter. I opened my mouth, and now he knows she's important.

"She doesn't have money," I lie. "Just some shit she inherited from a dead grandma."

"Sure," he says easily. "Scarlett Wallace is poor, and I'm just a fucking car salesman."

I bite my cheek. My face heats at his blatant display of knowledge. Of course he knows her name. He probably knows everything about me.

He's blocking the door. I could go through him, but that might just add to my bill. And so far, they haven't done anything but threaten.

He pulls his hand from his pocket and holds out a folded piece of paper.

I tense. "What's that?"

"It's not a bomb."

When I don't move, he tosses it at my feet.

"It's an offer," he says.

I stay where I am. "I think I'm done doing deals with the devil."

The barest hint of a smile flickers across his lips. "Is that so?"

When I don't reply, he turns on his heel and leaves as fast as he came. The instant I'm alone, I dive for the paper. I unfold it, scanning the "offer" from the Webber brothers. It's not just another fight. It lists my opponent, too.

Nicholas Thomson.

Well, I've done my best to not name the guy who's no better than ballsack sweat, and now his full name is staring at me in Webber's blocky handwriting. They want me to fight him again—and lose.

My stomach twists. It doesn't say my debt would be cleared, the bill erased, with this fight. And I have a hunch that this wouldn't be a one-and-done situation.

I crumple the paper and shove it in my pocket. I collect my bag and exit the locker room. I need to get out of here.

Outside, the cold air blasts through my thin shirt. My jacket is in the car.

"Come on. Let me drive you," Tyler's voice floats through the frozen air.

I tilt my head and follow it around the corner to the parking lot on the side of the building. Scarlett appears to be the warmest dressed of the three of us in a puffy coat and scarf tucked into it.

Exactly what I told her not to wear.

"I'm going to walk," she informs him.

He groans. "If you walk, then *I* have to walk."

"You can just…"—she makes a vague motion—"drive along beside me."

I shake my head and stride toward her. She doesn't see me—too focused on Tyler in front of her—and therefore can't escape when I finally give in to that base instinct and grab her hips. I haul her over my shoulder, her body weight an easy lift, and she screeches like a banshee. The noise cuts off when she folds in half, and her fingers dig into my back.

"I've got it," I tell Tyler.

He snickers. "Good luck."

She kicks out, and I quickly band my arm across her calves. It puts her feet in close proximity to my groin, but hopefully it won't come to that. I go to my car on the street and contemplate letting her sit in the front seat.

But that's a little too generous, seeing as how she's still struggling like I'm kidnapping her.

Wait. Am I kidnapping her?

I pop the trunk and consider that then smile to myself. Yeah, I suppose I am.

I unceremoniously drop her into the trunk, only pausing to make sure her limbs are all folded inside. She seems shocked, looking up at me with her hair in her face.

That's the last expression I see before I close the trunk with her in it.

CHAPTER 22
SCARLETT

IT'S OFFICIAL.

I *hate* him.

The top of my head hits the side of Cross's trunk for the fifth time, and I'm beginning to think he's taking these turns sharply on purpose. The sound of tires on asphalt echo around me, blending in with my fast breathing, and I groan again.

Who the hell sticks someone in their trunk, besides a serial killer?

Is Cross a serial killer? Because I'm beginning to think he is!

"Cross!" I shout. "Let me out of here, you psycho!"

With my hands pressed flat above my head, I take the heels of my boots and kick the inside of the trunk. I do this over and over again until my muscles burn with agony.

"Cross!" I yell again, my throat scratchy and dry. "If you don't let me out of here—" My body slams against the hard surface. "*Oof.*" The cutting motion knocks the wind completely out of me.

I wheeze as my lungs beg for air. I press my hands to

my chest, as if I can force the oxygen into them by the simple act.

"Cr—" I inhale sharply. "*Cross!*"

My eyes spring open at the sound of his door slamming. A bleak darkness surrounds me, and I'm mad with impatience. I already have a plan in place. As soon as the trunk opens, I'm going to claw his fucking eyes out.

"I know you're out there." I force myself to speak through the sharp pain in my chest. "Open the fucking trunk."

A knocking noise comes from above.

"Say please."

I sink my teeth into my bottom lip. *Fine.* I'll play his game.

"Please."

The trunk unlatches, and cool air filters inside the stuffy space. I quickly glance around, having no idea where we are. Tall, looming trees border the desolate road he's pulled off onto, but none of that matters because I'm wild with anger and pent-up hostility. Even more so when I see Cross's smug face staring back down at me with a pleased glimmer in his eye.

He may dominate in the cage, where he can use his fists on opponents, but out here, all alone with me? He has another thing coming.

"Did you enjoy your trip?" He chuckles with the question, the shadows playing with the sharp curves of his face to show off that stupid smirk of his.

I smile coyly. "Not as much as I'm going to enjoy this."

With one hand on the edge of the trunk, I swing my legs onto the ground and stand firmly on two feet and slam it shut. Before I can back down, I quickly lift my hand

and smack him clean across the face. The noise is as jarring as the stinging in my palm.

I stare at the side of Cross's face, and the tiniest hint of red spreads across his cheek. He focuses out on the forest. His jaw, as sharp as a knife, wiggles back and forth before he turns slowly and locks eyes with me.

"Was that for putting you in the trunk or for leaving you with an achy cunt last night?"

My lips part, but I don't let the shock of his words last long. "You think I didn't finish what you started?"

Aha.

Cross's eye twitches, and it fills me with satisfaction. He can play tough all he wants, but I remember the way he kissed me last night. It was a hungry kiss, with passion and urgency, one that went all the way to my toes.

He wants to pretend like it never happened—that much was made painfully obvious this morning—but after stuffing me in his trunk, I'm not letting him off the hook.

"What?" My voice drips of sugar. "Jealous you didn't get to watch?"

Cross says nothing, but I see the way he sizes me up and down.

I bat my eyelashes and curve my lips into a sweet smile. "As soon as you left the house, I crawled back into my bed and let my hand wander down my body until it landed between my legs..."

I back up to Cross's car and rest my elbows on the top of the trunk. He watches me closely, his mouth set in a firm line, shoulders straight with his arms folded over his chest.

"Then..." The word lingers between us. "I slipped my panties down past my thighs...then my knees...until they were finally all the way off, leaving me *bare.*"

The faintest growl slips from Cross's mouth, his chest moving up and down much faster than it should for the athleticism he yields.

Reaching up, I undo my hair from my high pony and let my locks fall gracefully past my shoulders. I shake the waves out and tip my head back to gaze at the stars. I'd undo my scarf, but then he'd see that lovely little bite mark he left behind that I've desperately tried to cover since last night.

"After my panties were in a pile on the floor…I spread my legs wide and let my fingers slip inside to give me the release that you were too afraid to witness."

I bite my lower lip and tip my chin down to peek at Cross. His glare appears so much more dangerous with the nightly shadows skipping across his face, but knowing that my words are affecting him fills me with delicious anticipation. In fact, I've nearly forgotten all about him stuffing me in his trunk like the savage he is.

"Something wrong?" I ask teasingly. "You're flushed, Cross."

His head tilts in a predatory way, and I *hate* that it excites me. After what I went through with Nick, you'd think I'd be terrified to be alone with Cross, but instead, I'm eager.

Cross takes one step toward me, and my heart races.

"You're playing a dangerous game, Scarlett."

"What game?" I toy with my scarf, seemingly uninterested.

"The one where you think you can fucking win," he growls.

I huff. "By the looks of you, I think I already have."

Cross charges me, his glare hot with need.

The need to win? Or the need for something else? I'm

not entirely sure. And he's right. I *am* playing a dangerous game. Yet, for some reason, I can't seem to stop. He irritates me but excites me…and that's the real dangerous thing at play.

Before he gets too close, I spin and slip out of reach. The gravel crunches under my feet. Finally, we both stop in place, nothing but a few feet separating us. Cross chuckles and shakes his head back and forth. "You're no match for me, Scarlett. Stop fucking around and get in the car."

I raise an eyebrow. *Mmm, I don't think I'm done playing yet.*

"You think you can stuff me in your trunk, then expect that I'll bow down at your feet and abide by your demands?" My laugh is sarcastic. "Yeah, I don't think so."

"Oh?" Cross mimics my stance and raises an eyebrow. "And what's your plan? Touch yourself in front of me to get me all riled up? Is that your grand plan to show me *who's* boss?" He snickers with a roll of his eyes. "Seducing your stepbrother?"

I purse my lips, as if I'm thinking, but the truth is, I already have my plan locked and loaded. I shrug. "Maybe."

Cross sighs loudly and pinches the bridge of his nose. "Get in the car, Scarlett."

I bite the inside of my cheek to keep my smile at bay. "Fine."

His eyes snap to mine with surprise, and that's when I let my lips curve.

"But you're going to have to catch me first."

And with that, I spin and take off through the trees.

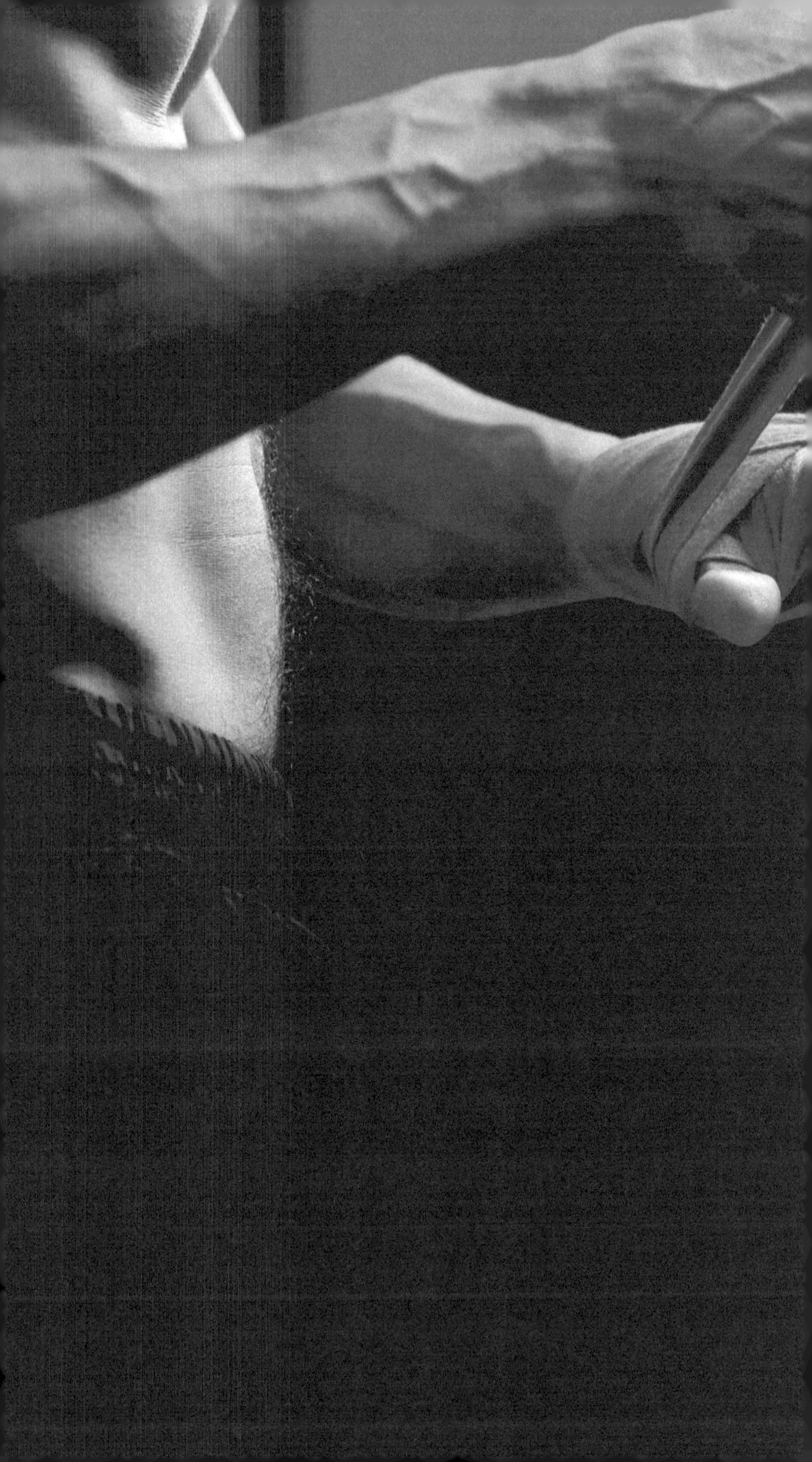

CHAPTER 23
CROSS

SHE DISAPPEARS INTO THE TREES, and I spare only a moment to shrug out of my sweatshirt. I toss it on the trunk of the car, crack my neck, then take off after her.

There's a hint of a path through the underbrush. My feet slide on damp leaves and snow, which is nowhere near as thick under the cover of the forest. The branches overhead seem to lean in, blocking the little light we have left in the day.

I spot a flash of movement ahead and pick up speed.

What will I do when I catch her?

Adrenaline bursts through me, lending power to my sore muscles. She's fast, but she's no match for my long stride. She glances back at the sound of my footsteps and shoots forward.

I laugh. I can't help it. I come so close I could grab her, but all I do is reach out and let my fingers graze the back of her neck.

She screams and swerves through the trees, losing me for a moment when I go around a thick trunk.

Okay, enough.

I sprint forward and reach. I grasp her coat, slowing her enough to spin her around. I propel her into a tree, and she lets out an *oof* when her back hits the bark. She glares up at me, but I'm right there.

Nowhere to go.

And, unfortunately, my dick is hard.

Goddamn it, why is she so alluring? Why can I not get her out of my head? And worse...why is she tempting me like this?

"What's wrong, Cross?" she breathes. "Can't handle the heat?"

I lean down and kiss her. My teeth catch her lower lip, and she moans. The sound goes straight through me, and I rock my hips into her. She can feel what she does to me—she can't miss it.

But the thought of some asshole touching her without consent, taking that away from her, makes me hesitate.

I pull back an inch. My lips hover over hers, but I open my eyes and wait until she does the same.

"I can take you back to the car...or you can say yes to what happens next."

She swallows, and a myriad of emotions flutters across her face. Her jaw sets, and she nods firmly. "I'm saying yes, Cross."

She shifts her weight, and her knee suddenly connects with my inner thigh. I let out a hiss, my hold on her weakening.

In a flash, she slips free. "But you'll have to try harder!"

I groan. That was *too close* for comfort. She almost rendered me unable to speak. Still, the contact gives me a wicked Charlie horse, and I take a few staggered steps before I can actually pick up a jog.

Then a run.

I catch up to her and grab at her coat again, but she's ready. It slips off her easily, and I drop it. Her laugh coasts on the air between us. She unwinds her scarf and lets it fall, too. Her arms pump, and we fly through the forest.

Is her heart beating as fast as mine?

She reaches out and catches a tree, using it to swing her body in a sharp turn. She leaps over a fallen branch, but her breathing sounds strained even over our pounding footsteps. I follow her path and lengthen my stride.

And then I leap.

I tackle her, rolling mid-air to prevent her from falling face-first into the dirt. We land on our sides, and she immediately kicks at me. I catch her arms behind her back and crawl over her, using my weight to keep her pinned to the ground. She flattens out on her belly, her exhale moving strands of hair out of her face. Snow and leaves catch in her loose hair fanned around her head, and the dampness soaks into my knees where I straddle her thighs.

One-handed, I tug her pants down. She squirms, but as soon as the cold air touches her bare ass, she lets out a whimper.

A good one?

I lean back and get her shoe off, pulling her leggings fully off the one side to get better access. Once that's done, I reach between her legs. She's slick with arousal and heat. She's practically throbbing with it. I push my sweatpants down and release her hands to grasp her hips. I lift her ass up slightly and run my cock head along her sensitive center.

"God, you're ready for it, aren't you?" I murmur.

My heart pounds, and my ribs scream at the exertion, but I would not trade anything for this moment. She makes a noise of affirmation, and that's all I need. I guide my dick to her entrance and slowly push in, but the agony of drawing it out is unbearable.

I lean forward and thrust into her. Her pussy squeezes me. I find her hands, covering them with mine and inter-twining our fingers into the dirt. Both of us will walk out of here dirty—there's no denying that.

I fuck her without restraint, like a fucking madman chasing a high. But it isn't enough. I pull out and lean to the side, giving her room to roll over. And then I'm between her legs, sliding back home. Her gaze bores into mine.

"Touch yourself," I breathe.

I shove her shirt up and take a handful of her breast. I roll her nipple between my fingers. I'm inside her, and I'm not close enough. And yet, I watch as she slides her hand between us and plays with her clit.

"Better than last night?" I goad.

"Fuck, Cross." She hooks her free arm around my neck. "Kiss me."

With pleasure.

I claim her mouth again. Her tongue wars against mine, and her legs come up on either side of my hips. Her heels dig into my ass, and suddenly, her nails cut into my shoulder. She scratches along my neck. Heat races down my spine.

One fuck is not going to be enough to get her out of my system.

Such a number might not exist.

And that's how I know I'm in trouble.

I drag my mouth from hers, down her jaw, to her neck. She makes another noise, her pussy tensing, and I smile. I lightly nip her skin. Her whole body jerks.

"That *hurt*," she snaps. "Before."

"Don't disassociate when I'm inside you, and we'll be fine," I say in her ear.

"Ass."

"I'll take that next, if you're offering."

She pinches my shoulder.

I bite her, not as hard as earlier but enough to make her go still, except her pussy is *definitely* wetter.

She likes a chase, and she likes a bit of pain—my kinky girl. I chuckle.

A buzzing sound makes me pause. I draw back to look at Scarlett, whose expression seems caught between lust and confusion. She seems to register the noise before me, and she fumbles for her phone, trapped in the pocket of her leggings.

She flashes me the screen. "It's my dad. I already ducked his call once today—" Her thumb hovers over the red button to decline the call.

Where's the fun in that?

I pull out and slowly thrust back into her. It takes everything in me to stop.

"Answer it," I say in a low voice.

She clenches involuntarily around me and seems to debate it. But when I stay still, she makes a face and accepts the call.

"Hi, Dad," she greets him. Her eyes focus on my face but not in the haze of pleasure and lust like before. This time a bit more...reserved. Sharp. "Yeah, Cross and I are getting along okay."

I smirk and grasp her hips. I shift, sliding the tiniest fraction deeper into her.

Her eyes widen. "...uh-huh. No, the classes are different to Yale, but—"

I draw out and push back in slowly. My muscles tremble, but it's Scarlett's legs around me that tense and shake. Her heels press into the backs of my thighs, and she puts her hand on my chest. Her arm straightens, as if that would keep me away from her.

"You're coming to Shadow Valley?"

I ignore her arm and run my hand up under her shirt. My fingers find her bralette—nothing more than scraps of lace, from the feel of it. I pinch her nipple through the fabric. Her back arches, her lips parting, but her glare only eggs me on.

"W-when?"

I move a little faster. My hips, my hand exploring under her shirt. She shoves at my arm, but I just silently laugh at her. I pull out and slam into her hard enough that she slides in the leaves. She's going to be picking out bits of leaves and dirt from her hair for ages when we get back. The rough-and-tumble lifestyle will do that to a girl.

"Of course we'd go to d-dinner," her voice wobbles. "No, I'm fine, just on the treadmill."

I snicker. That's a great euphemism for our *run*.

I withdraw my hand from her shirt and spread her legs open wider. I rock back and look down at us. My dick spears her open. She's so fucking wet I could drown down there.

Instead, I touch her clit. Her body tenses, and she tries to snap her knees closed, but I block her legs. I run my finger over the sensitive button, tuning out her conversation. The words still flow—or stutter—out of her, but I want to make her come.

Preferably in the next thirty seconds.

I redouble my efforts, my fingers now moving faster

and harder on her clit. Her pussy is throbbing around my cock, but we're not *there*.

"I gotta go, Dad," she bites out. "Yes, we'll see you tomorrow."

She hangs up and throws the phone aside right as her orgasm hits her. She squirms under me, her eyes squeezing shut. I am going to memorize this expression and replay it when I need a dose of serotonin. Her tightness and the way she reacts tips me over the edge. I pick up speed, pounding into her, and chase my own high.

My balls tighten, and I come. Tingling bliss zips up my spine, and I bow forward over her. I stay still, the silent knowledge that my cum now fills her pussy—that we didn't use protection—radiates through me along with the caveman instinct to stay still to keep it inside her.

Finally, Scarlett's eyes open, and the realization of what I did dawns on her.

"You asshole," she bites out.

"Obviously. But an asshole who can make you come." I lean over her. "Did you see stars?"

She grimaces.

"That's that, then."

"Get off." She pushes at my shoulder.

"I just did, thanks."

She pauses and rolls her eyes.

With a sigh, I withdraw and rock back on my heels. I stare down at her open legs another moment longer then hop to my feet and drag my sweatpants back into place. Then, to occupy myself, I go find her missing shoe. When I return, she's balanced on one foot, her leggings back on.

"Your coat and scarf are a ways back," I tell her.

I hand her the shoe and hold her elbow while she slips it on. Her arms come around her waist.

"Good," she murmurs. "I'm freezing."

I dip my head. She leads the way back through the forest.

"So, interesting phone call?"

She elbows me, and I can't stop the smile that spreads across my face. Guess I'll find out tomorrow at dinner.

CHAPTER 24
SCARLETT

IT'S torture looking at him.

Every time our gazes skate past one another, my cheeks fill with heat and my body tingles in all the wrong places.

Or the right places, depending on who you ask.

It's been almost twenty-four hours since he was buried inside me, and I still can't stop thinking about it…or him.

Now, we're stuck at an awkward dinner with our parents, pretending that we're one big happy family. I've contemplated taking the fork and stabbing myself in the eye, just to get out of it, but alas.

"So, lacrosse?" my dad questions. He focuses directly at my nemesis. "How is that going?"

Cross, in a crisp button-down, shifts his weight. His lips press together tightly, and he reaches for his glass of water. "It's good. Season hasn't started just yet. We're practicing every day, though. With a few scrimmages in between."

My dad turns toward me. "Have you been to any of the scrimmages?"

I open my mouth to answer, but Cross beats me to it. "She's been to one."

My dad chuckles. "Yeah, sports aren't really her thing."

"I don't know…" Cross leans back, his legs spreading wide underneath the table to graze the side of my thigh. "She likes to run. Maybe track is your thing?"

I clench my teeth together and give Cross my attention. My tight-lipped smile is laced with venom, but fuck my heart for beating right out of my chest when our gazes collide. He keeps his face unmoving, stoic almost, but there's a wild challenge in his gaze that fuels me like nothing ever has before.

"I'd rather be in the library than anywhere else on campus." I slide my attention to our parents and give them a soft smile.

Cross snorts and tries to cover it up with a cough.

My hackles rise, and I snap my head over to him. "Do you know what a library is? The place where you study? I know you're not too keen on the idea…given your grades."

Cross narrows his gaze, but the way his mouth twitches tells me he likes our little sparring game. Knowing him, it's probably a turn-on.

Sofia laughs quietly, my dad smiling beside her.

Cross and I break our stare-off, and I see my dad reach for Sofia's hand. They're smiling at one another and then at us.

"What?" I ask my father.

"You two are like true siblings," he muses. He turns and smiles at Cross's mom. "Aren't they?"

"Arguing like cats and dogs." She shakes her head, another soft laugh leaving her.

Siblings?

Last night, he had his dick inside me.

We are *not* siblings.

My spine straightens with the faint skim of Cross's jeans rubbing my bare leg again. My attention flies beneath the table, where he inches a little closer, unbeknownst to everyone around us.

What is he doing?

"Step-siblings," Cross corrects, as if the word *step* is going to excuse what we did the previous night.

"Right." My dad nods to the waiter, a young college student, if I had to guess, who comes by with a pitcher of water.

He tops off my father's and then Sofia's. His eyes dip past Sofia's face to her cleavage, and I roll my eyes. Just when I think I'm the only one who notices, Cross's leg presses tightly against mine, his entire body stiffening.

I shift my eyes from his clenched jaw to my father, who is seemingly glaring at the waiter.

I offer the waiter a polite smile after he pours water into my cup. "Thank you."

He grins at me, his lip lifting on the side, and then just like he did with Sofia, his lazy gaze moves downward to get an eyeful of my breasts.

My father clears his throat.

Cross growls quietly.

My stomach twists, the slightest tinge of apprehension hitting the back of my throat. Before, when a guy would make a pass at me or let his gaze wander below my chin, I'd take it as a compliment.

But after Nick, I've come to fear it.

I don't exhale again until Cross's palm lands on my thigh. I instantly settle, my shoulders relaxing, my lungs loosening.

"That's enough," Cross bites out.

"I agree," my father says.

An awkward silence fills the table. The waiter scurries away. Cross doesn't let up on my thigh, but his attention is halfway across the restaurant, glaring in the direction of the kitchen where the waiter disappeared to.

The tension is rising. His shoulders are squared, the sound of his teeth grinding loud enough for our parents to hear. So I do what I shouldn't and send him a lifeline. I gradually slip my hand into his, and he eagerly laces our fingers together.

He's showing all his cards, and if he's not careful, someone will start to read them.

I squeeze his hand gently, silently pleading with him to chill.

Breathe, Cross.

To my surprise, he follows my lead. A slow breath leaves his mouth, and he squeezes my hand back. Not once, but twice.

My dad's faint chuckle brings me back to the present. I pull on my hand, but Cross doesn't let up. He keeps his fingers clamped onto mine.

"Your mom was right," my dad says.

Cross appears cool, calm, and collected now. "About?"

"She said that Scarlett would be safe with you. That's why, when I heard about the housing situation, I was more than eager for you to move in with her."

The slightest bit of annoyance slips in at the idea of anyone thinking I can't fend for myself, but the truth is…I can't.

Not yet anyway.

"Of course." Cross's lip hitches into a half-smile, but

it's more arrogant than anything. "My little sis is most definitely safe with me."

I try to jerk my hand away without moving too hastily beneath the table, but naturally, he holds on tighter.

"Little sis?" I repeat with disgust.

A different waiter, much older than our previous, comes by to lay the check down, but it does nothing to break the rising friction between Cross and me.

"Would you prefer rugrat instead?" he asks, tipping his chin toward me and hitching his eyebrow.

I glare at him, and he continues listing names.

"Pest? Brat? Gremlin?"

"*Escuincle*," his mother warns from across the table.

Cross smiles wider. "Good one, *Mamá*."

"I was referring to you," she retorts.

Cross shrugs, and I take the opportunity to pull away again, but it doesn't work. Cross laughs under his breath, my dad too busy with the check and his mom boxing her meal to pay any attention.

"Let go of my hand," I whisper, seething.

"Make me," Cross says under his breath.

I dig my nails into the top of his hand, and his mouth twitches with amusement. Annoyance shoots from my palm all the way to my shoulder, so I bite down on my cheek and decide to go another route.

I turn slightly, my long hair shielding the side of my face so our parents can't hear my whisper. "You asked for it."

Cross's eyebrows dip for a split second before he smooths his face and engages in another conversation with my father about lacrosse.

Apparently, Cross is the son he never got, considering I didn't play a single sport growing up. Instead, I was too busy building with blocks and sketching designs for tall, extravagant buildings in my spare time.

With Cross distracted by giving an in-depth explanation of lacrosse and his position, I extract my fingernails from his skin and rub the pad of my finger faintly over the tiny indents. I do this a few more times, all while pressing my thigh a little closer to his, opening my legs just enough for him to feel the warmth from in between.

I allow a quiet, lustful sigh to fall from my lips—something I know only he'll notice—and gradually guide our pressed hands to his lap instead of mine. Cross glances at me briefly, his eyes curious and wondering before slipping back into the conversation with our parents.

The new waiter comes by to take my father's credit card, and I pick up the pace, knowing we'll be leaving soon. Gradually, but with force, I steer Cross's palm up his leg until it's close to his zipper.

I scoot forward in my seat to hide my movement of pressing down onto his cock, and I rub it just enough to get his attention. He coughs, his fingers clamping on mine even tighter to stop me.

I told you that you asked for it.

As if it's magic, a bulge forms behind his zipper, and I smile to myself.

Last night, he fucked me while I was on the phone with my father, and today, he insults me in front of them at dinner. There's no way he's getting away with either one of those things.

I'm only half listening to the conversation at the table, and I barely notice the waiter when he comes back with my father's card. I'm more focused on the way Cross's dick grows beneath our combined hands and how his breathing picks up the pace as the seconds pass.

Just when I think he's going to let go of my fingers, like I asked him to several minutes ago, he joins in on my torture and angles the heel of his palm so it's pressing down even harder.

Somehow, my payback stunt turned into me squirming in my seat, too.

How did *that* happen?

"I think we're good to go," Sofia announces, smiling at both Cross and me.

"Great!" I say, a little too eagerly.

Cross reluctantly releases my fingers, but our eyes snag in the midst of scooting our chairs backward. His gaze, wild and hungry, narrows briefly. With a quick roll of my eyes, I round the table to lead both my dad and his mom to the exit so he can figure out how to hide his hardened dick.

It doesn't take long for him to join us at the entrance, and now that the cool night air surrounds us, I'm back on even ground with rational thinking.

What am I doing?

What are we doing?

If I thought last night was crossing the line, what would I call tonight? I just purposefully teased him and made him all hot and bothered *right* in front of our parents, as if we aren't actually stepsiblings.

I've lost my ever-loving mind.

Yet, as soon as our parents leave with the promise to come back in a few weeks for another *family* dinner, I find myself locking eyes with Cross and bubbling over with anticipation from the hazy, lust-filled look in his eye.

His hand wraps around my wrist, and even though I know I should put up a fight, I let him tug me through the restaurant until we end up at the bathrooms.

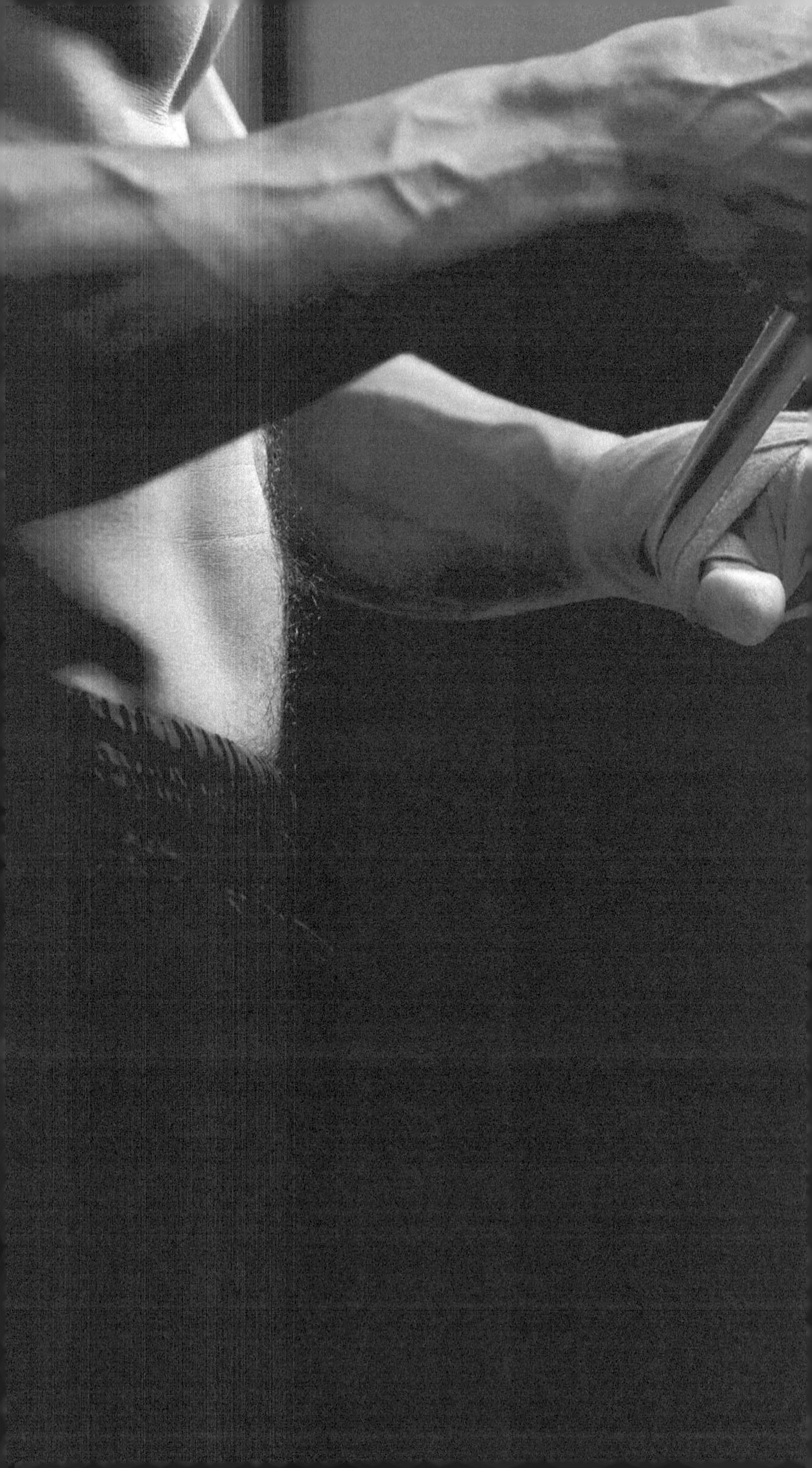

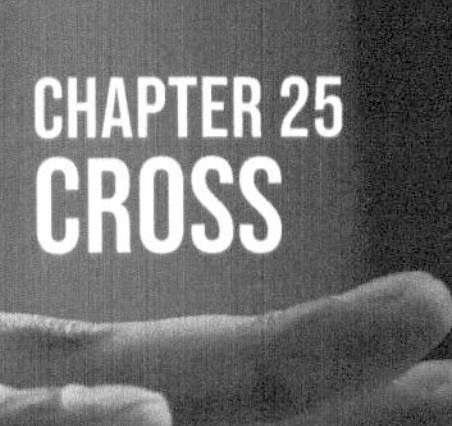

CROSS

IT'S OFFICIAL: I've gone crazy, my brain has taken a leave of absence, and my dick is in charge. Surely that's the reason I pull Scarlett through the dimly lit hallway and into one of the single-stall bathrooms.

I flick the lock behind us, but she's on me before I can take a step. She pulls at my shirt, untucking it from my slacks, and slides her hands under it. Her fingers graze my abdomen, my stomach, then drop back down to my waistband.

"Scar—"

She shakes her head the slightest bit. Her lower lip is caught in her teeth. She doesn't slow down, though, undoing my belt and the button. The zipper.

My mouth opens and shuts.

She pushes me back against the door, and I let it happen. I watch her guide my cock free, but my eyes widen when she drops to her knees.

"Didn't realize we were both so turned on," I mutter.

"Shut up." Her big eyes flick up to my face.

She's *right* there, her lips inches from my dick. Her

warm breath hits me when she speaks, and it twitches in the open air. Her attention swings back to the, uh… *elephant* in the room. Her expression seems uncertain.

"Have you done this before?" I ask.

"Shut *up*, Cross," she growls.

Her hand wraps around my length, pumping once before taking me into her mouth. I let out a low groan. She seems to be figuring it out but also an expert? Or maybe it's just that it's her.

I can't take my eyes off her.

After a moment, she seems to shake off any nerves or hesitation and gets into a rhythm. The head of my cock bumps the back of her throat, and I clench my fists to keep from surging forward, down her throat. It would probably freak her out.

But…

Her slow speed is going to get us caught.

I reach out and catch a lock of her hair between my fingers. I tug. She hums, and I smirk. I palm the back of her head and guide her deeper.

Her free hand lands on my thigh, her nails digging in.

"That's it," I coax. "Relax and let me fuck your throat like a good little stepsister."

Her eyes roll.

"That sass is going to get you into trouble," I warn.

But *fuck*, it feels good. She curls her tongue and flicks at the sensitive spot under the tip then hollows her cheeks when I push back in. I move my hips, using pressure on her head to control the speed…and slowly increase it.

Tears fill her eyes, but she doesn't try to pull away. Her lipstick smears across my erection—*gonna keep that there as long as possible*—and I can taste the glimmer of my orgasm in the distance. I chase it, using her mouth. She gags around me, but her teeth never so much as brush my skin.

Aw, she does care.

She twists her hand and squeezes, adding to the sensations ricocheting through my dick and up my spine. My balls tighten, and I can't help but let my head fall back on the door.

"Gonna come," I manage to get out.

She doesn't pull away as I expect. I groan and it barrels through me. My cock pulses in her mouth.

Someone knocks on the door.

Fucking hell.

Her throat works as she swallows, and her gaze finds mine. Carefully, she releases me and wipes her mouth with the back of her hand.

"Goddamn," I whisper.

The knocking comes again, along with a jiggling of the handle.

"Occupied!" Scarlett calls, her voice steady.

I shake my head. "You did not just do that."

"Quiet." She smiles.

I offer my hand, which she takes, and I help her to her feet. The person outside is going to see both of us exit. There's no way around it.

May as well make them wait, right?

I guide Scarlett back toward the counter and lift her onto it. She gasps and clutches at my shoulders, but I just spread her legs. I push her skirt up and get an eyeful of the lacy black panties. They hide her sweet pussy from me, but not for long.

"Hope you're not too attached to these," I say a split second before I tear the thin fabric.

"Those were my favorite pair," she hisses.

I pull the torn lace away and shove it in my pocket. "I'll make it up to you."

Now it's my turn to go on my knees. I run my mouth up the side of Scarlett's leg, starting at her knee and tracing a direct line up her inner thigh. I reach the apex of her legs, and she leans back. I bury my face in her cunt.

It's official—I could die happy here. Especially when her nails scratch the back of my head, pressing similarly to how I directed her movements just moments ago. I taste her. Kiss her. Get to know her pussy by the way her muscles tremble and her breathing changes.

Another knock comes at the door, but we both ignore it. She's lost in short gasps above me, and I'm drowning in her arousal.

My teeth graze her clit and she makes a noise. I take it in my mouth, sucking the sensitive bud, and slide my index finger inside her. Her hips roll when I add a second finger and curve them.

Her legs squeeze then tremble, but I coax her orgasm out slowly and keep going until she grips my hair and pulls my face away. Her upper body rests on the mirror, and she looks at me through half-lidded eyes like she can't believe I just did that.

I lick my lips.

"We can continue this at home," I say in a low voice. Because…well, shit. That line's been crossed. How can we un-cross it?

She straightens her skirt and hops down. "You're…"

"Impressive?" I finish. "A dream come true?"

"Insufferable," she mutters.

I grin.

I make sure my clothing is back in place while she fixes her hair and makeup, swiping away the bleeding dark streaks from her running mascara. I exit first, scanning the hallway. There's a kitchen entrance at the far end, and I eye it when it swings open.

But Scarlett is already coming out behind me, sliding her coat on, and I lock eyes with the waiter who was getting a little too much of an eyeful earlier.

I spin and push Scarlett against the wall, one finger under her chin, lifting her gaze to me. I kiss her hard, my tongue exploring her mouth. We taste like each other's arousal, and my dick wakes up again at the thought of her tasting herself on my lips.

"Shit, I thought you were siblings," the waiter mutters as he sweeps past us.

Scarlett shoves my chest, her lips puffy and eyes narrowed. "Asshole."

I throw my arm around her shoulders and grin. I can't contain it. He deserved to know that she's taken. "Guilty as charged, *sis*."

CHAPTER 26

SCARLETT

I CAN'T FOCUS.

The library is quiet, my peers studying with their headphones on, scribbling in their notebooks or working out some complicated math equation on a piece of scrap paper, and yet I stare at the same paragraph discussing architectural theory and how it explores the ethical foundations of design.

I can't stop thinking about Cross—*my freaking stepbrother*.

I can't stop thinking about how I don't care that he *is* my stepbrother.

This morning, I talked Sawyer into going to his lacrosse scrimmage, blaming it on the fact that I promised his mom I'd take videos of him playing so I could send them to her.

It was a total lie. I wanted to go to his scrimmage so I could watch him play, like some little fangirl.

Ugh.

He totally noticed me, too, all the way from across the field in the brisk, cold morning fog. His dark gaze snagged on to me leaning across the chain-link fence. His lip curved, and his cheeks, rosy from the cool air, hitched upward to show his amusement—or worse: his satisfaction.

I made sure to dodge him afterward, and I've been hiding out in the library most of the day, unsure of what I'll do if I'm alone in the house with him.

I clearly can't be trusted, and if fucking me while my father was on the phone has anything to say about it, Cross doesn't really care.

I'm in the middle of reading the same sentence I've tried comprehending three times now when my phone buzzes on top of the table. I grab a hold of it quickly, the vibrating pulling a few eyes in my direction.

CROSS

Where are you?

Energy surges to my fingertips, and I immediately suck my lip into my mouth, my teeth clamping down so I don't smile like a fool.

ME

Training with Jim.

I'm only trying to piss him off so maybe he'll be the one to put distance between us, because, again, I can't be trusted.

CROSS

If that were true, he'd never walk again.

Try again. Where are you, Scar?

Scar.

I don't know if he's calling me that to gain the upper hand in our argument or if he's doing it to desensitize me.

It should be concerning that I'm sort of okay with him calling me Scar, just like I should be concerned with the fact that I like him wanting to know where I am.

Does he want to know because he's still cagey about the SUV following me around? Or does he want to know because he can't stop thinking about me, too?

I sigh and type something neutral.

ME

I'm safe and sound, studying.

I'm not telling him where I am.

If he wants to find me, he will. If he's just concerned about my safety, then I've reassured him.

I click my phone off and toss it into my bag in an attempt to clear my thoughts so I can actually absorb the words I've been reading for an hour. I scribble a few notes and then flip the page, only for the book to close directly on my hand.

A sharp gasp leaves me. I spot the familiar black ink tattoos on the hand holding the book shut. I glare up at Cross, who leans over me, and pray he can't read between the lines.

"I told you I was safe and sound," I say with a roll of my eyes. "No need to show up to check on me."

Cross slowly pushes the book toward the middle of the table, and my hand slips out from the brittle pages. Cross hooks his finger around my hair, pushing the strands back behind my shoulder.

"I'm not here to check on you," he admits in my ear.

I lift my chin to meet his gaze. "Then why are you here?"

His attention falls to my mouth. Something hot spreads

to my chest, and my stomach twists with that same familiar ache I only feel with him.

Cross says nothing, but he doesn't have to.

His face says it all. The warm color of brown in his eye shifts into something darker, something *hotter*, and before I can convince myself otherwise, I slip my glasses off, scoot my chair back, and stand.

I glance around to make sure no one is eyeing us. We hurry toward the back of the library, our elbows grazing just enough to send my arm hairs standing up. I keep walking, Cross taking my lead, until we end up at the farthest aisle where mostly unused books are stored.

It's darker back here, quieter. There aren't any listening ears or wandering eyes.

"So, why are you here—"

Cross's hands come around my waist. He presses me against a bookshelf and peers down at me with a hooded gaze, his perfect lips slightly ajar. His hands disappear from my hips, and he grips the sturdy shelf beside my head, trapping me in place.

I peer up at him. "Cross."

He shuts his eyes, his jaw flexing. "Don't say my name like that."

"Like what?" I ask quietly.

He pins me in my spot with a hot glare. "With conviction. Like you're warning me."

My heart is beating out of my chest, my pulse thrumming, eager for something neither one of us should really be partaking in.

"I probably should warn you…" My back arches, and I push my chest onto his. "But that depends on why you're here."

I suck in a sharp breath. He cups my face with force,

his fingers tangling within my hair. One slight pull against the strands and my mouth would be on his.

"You know why I'm here," he says.

A neediness digs into my bones. "Say it."

The bookshelf creaks from Cross's firm grip beside my ear. I watch in awe as his tongue slips out to wet his bottom lip.

"I'm here because I'm fucking desperate." He bounces his gaze back and forth feverishly.

"For what?" I whisper.

His eyes narrow, his mouth a breath away from mine. "For you, Scar. I'm desperate for *you*."

There's need in his tone. It's quiet but prominent, and although I know I should deny him, I do the opposite. I lean forward, and he takes the bait. Our lips collide, a quiet moan slipping off my tongue as he ambushes my mouth. The kiss is deep, his tongue halfway down my throat, like he's afraid I'm going to pull away.

I'm not.

I'm letting him have his way with me because there's a charge in the air that tells me he needs this. That he needs me.

He breaks our kiss and moves his mouth to hover over my ear while pressing his hips into me. "Let me have you," he groans.

I nod once, just barely, but he catches it.

He quickly flips me around and pulls my pants down to mid-thigh.

"Grip the shelf."

I do as he says, my legs trembling with need.

Cross centers himself between my legs from behind and angles my hips for access. He rubs against me a couple of times before easily slipping inside. He catches my gasp with his mouth, and we're back to kissing again.

I can't believe I'm doing this.

In the library.

With my stepbrother.

It's so hot.

"God, you're soaked," he murmurs against my mouth. "Is indecent exposure your thing?"

"I've…" Cross's hand winds around my stomach to dip below my navel. I bite my lip, the words disappearing. "I've never…"

He groans and pulls out of me slowly while rubbing fast circles on my clit. *Fuck.*

"You've never done this before? Is that what you're trying to say?"

I whimper and nod.

Cross hisses behind me, his thrusts getting faster. "Wrong thing to tell me because *fuck,* the thought of being your first makes me lose my mind."

His teeth sink onto my ear, and he pulls on the lobe. His hot noises fill my head, sending my body haywire with a powerful orgasm.

"Cross." His name is more of a gasp, and thankfully, he slaps his hand over my mouth to drown out my cries.

It only takes a few more thrusts for him to still, pressing into me deeply.

We only stay like that for a few seconds before he pulls away, leaving me wet and messy. He spins me around, a hazy gleam driven into his eye while he kneels to tug my panties and pants back to their rightful spot.

I bite my swollen lip to keep myself from smiling, but I know he notices.

He takes his hand, the same one that was in between

my legs, and frees my lip. It plops out from behind my bite, and he winks at me, then turns and stalks out of the library. He leaves me with wicked thoughts and a sated body.

My cheeks are still warm to the touch thirty minutes later. I pack up my belongings. I linger on the book Cross shut on my hand and shake my head, trying to hide a smile. *Damn him.* His taste lingers, and the hungry way his hands skimmed my skin left behind a touch of rebellion I never knew I needed.

I couldn't concentrate earlier, and I surely can't concentrate now.

I hurriedly push through the library doors, eager to get home just to see if he's there.

The elevator dings, and I step forward, a smile playing against my lips at the thought of later. I turn and press L, then gaze at myself in the reflection.

God, look at me.

My wavy hair is a wild mess, framing my pink-stained cheeks and puffy lips. I glance away with a giggle on the edge of my tongue when someone stops the elevator with a black-gloved hand, keeping the doors apart.

I straighten my spine and act nonchalant, as if they're going to know the dirty things I did in the library with my stepbrother thirty minutes prior.

"No need to hide that pretty face from me."

I jerk my chin upward, my teeth clacking. My eyebrows furrow. I eye a man dressed in cheap clothing with an even cheaper gold chain hanging below his thick neck. Once he sees that he has my attention, he smiles smugly at me to reveal his yellowing teeth.

"Care to go watch your boyfriend get the shit beat out of him?" He hits the *close door* button of the elevator, and from the width of his body, there's no chance I can reach the emergency button.

"Boyfriend?" I repeat, playing coy.

Who the hell is this?

Did Nicholas send him? Is Nicholas telling people I'm his girlfriend?

"Don't play stupid with me, Scarlett Wallace."

The way he says my name sends me spiraling. My throat closes with anxiety, my heart racing behind my tight chest. I suck in air when his grimy hand wraps around the strap of my bag, but I'm quick to pull on it to let him know that I'm *not* okay with the manhandling.

"Let go of me," I hiss.

The elevator dings, and I pray someone is waiting on the other side of the door.

"Not until we get to the fight. Your little boyfriend..." The man pauses to chuckle. "I mean, *stepbrother*...owes us a fight, and let's just say that you're *collateral*."

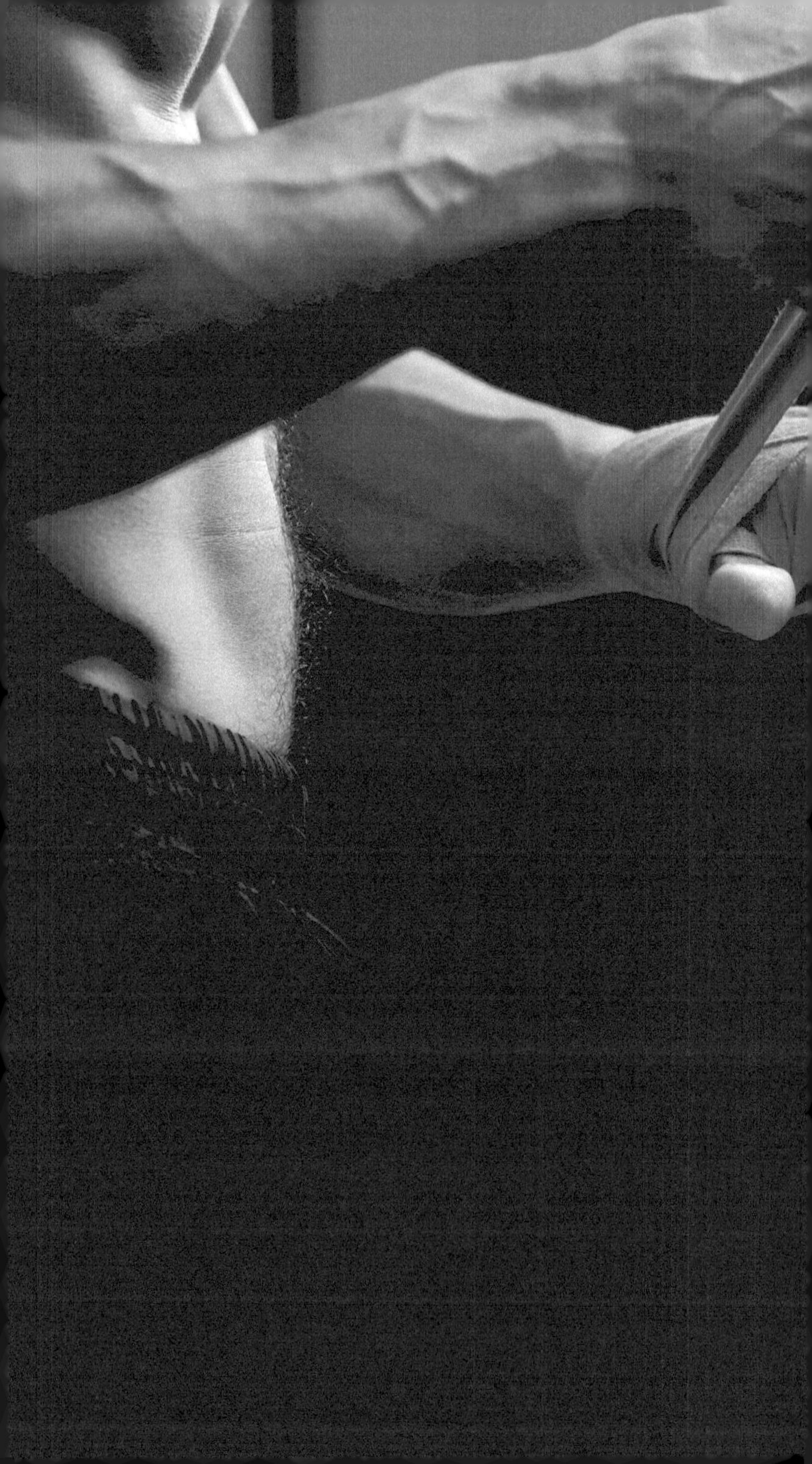

CHAPTER 27
CROSS

LOSE.

I have to lose.

I have to lose to the guy who got Scarlett drunk and drugged her, then forced himself on her.

In her.

I've been in her—I was allowed. I was *welcomed*. I got to hear the sweet noises she made when she was surprised, and turned on, and so fucking willing she was soaked between her legs.

He wasn't allowed. He hurt her.

And here I am, letting him punch me in the face.

I catch myself on the mat by my hands and knees. The room—this time a basement of some factory—tilts. My vision tunnels, and I swallow hard a few times. I shouldn't let him hit me in the face anymore, but I literally walked right into that one.

Some part of me just wants this to be over.

Stanley is here.

One of the Webber brothers is here.

They both came into the makeshift dressing room

before my fight, one—Stanley—with a pep talk, and the other with some threatening glares. I guess there's more money on this fight. The audience is older, and there's a bookie set up taking bets. There are skimpily dressed girls wandering around with drinks.

This is *not* the sort of place I've ever been invited to. This circuit seems more serious. I should know just by the fighting order—the douche nozzle and I are the appetizers. The first fight on a list of six shows.

"Had enough, Lopez?"

I shove myself back to my feet and dodge his foot. If that had connected with my stomach, it would've been brutal. I probably would've lost my lunch.

He's still huge, still tough, but it's instinct to see an opening and go for it. I get in three hits, then I remember: *lose, goddamn it!*

He shoves me off him and comes back with a fury. I protect my head, but pain radiates down my arms, my ribs, with every punch. He gets me against the cage, and I just have to fucking wait it out.

My muscles cramp. My body is on the verge of revolting.

And then, he gets me in the side of the head. I don't know how it happened. My arm dropped for a split second? My shoulder spasmed?

Either way, I see fucking stars. I stumble away, pushing to put space between us and take a few deep breaths, and that's when I see her.

It's like my attention is unable to see anything else. It's her.

I didn't think she would come… I didn't tell her about the fight. How the fuck could I tell her? *Hey, I'm a little more in debt than that twenty grand I used to pay off pube face.*

Actually, it's more like fifty because I was supposed to let him kick my ass. Because I'm an idiot and agreed to throw a fight.

And now I'm throwing another one.

But *fuck*, she's right next to the other Webber brother. That bastard brought her here on purpose.

"Had enough?" the monster behind me rasps.

I focus my narrowing vision on him. I probably have two more hits left in me before I'm toast. I'm not sure how I'm still on my feet.

Pure stubbornness, probably.

And then I glance over and see the utter horror on Scarlett's face.

Anger surges through me, blotting out my pain. I've done a good job so far keeping this fight on even footing, when all I wanted was for it to be a massacre. *His* massacre.

But now, I see red.

I don't remember what happens next. I move forward, my steps suddenly light. It's like everything that happened prior to this moment evaporates, leaving me fresh. And pissed.

I go on the attack, striking faster than I ever have.

And in a matter of seconds, he's out cold.

…I was *not* supposed to do that.

CHAPTER 28
SCARLETT

"WHAT THE HELL are you doing here?" Tyler's gaze dances all around, worry etched in the line between his eyebrows.

I flutter my eyelashes at him, confusion, worry, and anger hitting me all at once. I jerk my attention to the hand on my arm, the pressure of my handler's grip tightening to the brink of pain.

"Fight's over," I stress. "Let go of me."

I'm shaking, my legs like Jell-O, even with Tyler standing beside me. He doesn't stand a chance against whomever this man is.

"So much for collateral," he hisses under his breath. "He blew the fucking fight."

Cross won the fight. How the hell did he blow it?

Someone grabs the man's attention over the buzzing crowd, a much different vibe from the last fight I found myself at, and he curses.

My lip is raw from my nervous chewing, and I can't stop staring in the direction that Cross exited through, right before Nicholas was carried out, still unconscious.

Did he know he was fighting Nick again?

Is that why he didn't tell me anything?

Tyler's arm begins to slide across my lower back, and we make eye contact. He inches his head, as if to say *let's make a run for it*, but to my relief, my arm is dropped, and only a tiny bite of pain is left behind from the man's grimy fingers.

"This is a fucking mess," he mutters before disappearing in the thick of screaming fans, eager for the next fight.

Tyler grabs my wrist and quashes the space between us. "Let's go."

He weaves us in and out of the crowd toward a dingy door and an even dingier hallway. Must and mildew trail us as our shoes stomp against the damp floor, and then he pushes through a doorway to reveal a sight that makes my heart stop.

Cross.

Before my brain can catch up with my feet, I rush across the room and squeeze between a red-faced, angry man and the guy who *apparently* means more to me than I'm willing to admit.

"You're hurt," I whisper.

My eyes water, panic working through my head. I take in every last wound and swelling knot.

Cross's gaze bounces between my eyes, his own worry cutting through. "Did they touch you?"

"Jesus Christ, Cross!" the man snaps. "That should be the least of your concerns!"

"Fuck you, Stanley." Cross grips my arms and scans me, then flicks his attention to Tyler. "Did they?

"He had her arm, but other than that…"

Cross shifts back to me. "What arm?"

"I'm fine!" I shout. "You're the one who is hurt!"

Cross, unwilling to bend, pushes my sleeve up past my elbow on my left arm, inspecting it closely. Once he's satisfied with it, he does the same to my right. I hold my breath and watch the color drain from his face. He exhales deeply, his temples flexing with the grinding of his jaw.

"I want to see them. Right. Fucking. *Now.*" He glares at Stanley. "Bringing her here and then *this?*"

I glance at my arm. Tiny bruises are left behind from the man's grip, but I have to agree with Stanley on this one. The marks on my arm are nothing compared to the condition Cross is in.

"Just…" Stanley runs a hand through his hair while briefly looking at me. "For fuck's sake. You guys go home while I try to smooth things over. I can fix this."

"Fix what?" I stare at Stanley with a furrowed brow. "What is going on?"

"I kind of would like to know the same," Tyler says.

Stanley's gaze moves from me and Tyler to Cross.

It's evident that there is something going on here that neither Tyler nor I am privy to.

"Go!" Stanley urges. "I already know they're angry, and if they get a hold of you…"

He shakes his head, and a wave of nausea hits me.

"If they get a hold of me?" Cross roars, face hot with anger. "They don't want me to get a hold of them!"

Tyler steps forward. "Dude, that's the adrenaline talking. You're swelling like you've been stung by a thousand bees. Stanley is right. We need to go."

Stanley interjects again. "You need to fucking go. Now!"

What the hell is going on?

First, I'm hijacked from the library by some disgusting

wannabe gangster with a fake gold chain, brought to a rundown building with half-dressed women and rowdy men, put in the vicinity of Nicholas again, and now this?

Cross's hand falls into mine, our fingers interlocking immediately, seizing my thoughts.

"Fine." He spits out the word, then winces.

His hand instinctively flies up to his bruised ribs, and strangely enough, it's like *I'm* the one in pain.

Our steps are quick over the damp concrete, Cross's sharp breaths cutting through the stomping. Tyler pushes on a cracked door, the cool night air swallowing us whole. We step into the packed makeshift parking lot.

"Fuck." Cross wraps his free hand around his bare torso.

His ribs, sunken with short gasps, are honed to the point that I can see every last muscle flexing with pain.

"Tyler, come help me."

His best friend obliges. Tyler's arm wraps around Cross's lower back, and Cross uses him like a crutch. I tug on my hand, but it goes absolutely nowhere because Cross's fingers clamp tightly against mine, like he refuses to let me go.

"As soon as we're in the car," Tyler groans, holding most of Cross's weight, "you're fucking explaining yourself."

A curt nod is the only response Cross gives.

Silence fills the kitchen.

Tyler pinches the bridge of his nose, his head hung low.

I'm a silent participant, too swept up in my own thoughts to utter a single noise.

I press the cool rag to Cross's knuckles, bruised and red from hitting Nicholas.

"I can't believe you agreed to throw the fight in the first place." Tyler's voice breaks the quiet. "And then to let him get in your head, so you knocked him out? Then to do it all over again tonight? This doesn't sound like you at all."

Cross inhales, his abs tightening.

I stop pressing the towel onto his knuckles, my fingers pausing from the weight of Tyler's words.

"It's because of me," I whisper. "Isn't it?"

"What?" Tyler asks.

"No," Cross rushes out. "It's because of him. Not you."

"But—"

He grips my chin with tender force and angles my face toward his. "*No.*"

I sink my teeth into my bottom lip to hide my emotions, and thankfully, Tyler interrupts the moment by putting two and two together.

"Clearly Nicholas did something to Scarlett," he mumbles, talking to himself more than us. "And I don't even want to know what, because then it'll give me a reason to justify your behavior, and fuck…" Tyler paces behind me, Cross following his quick steps with his eyes. "Someone has to think rationally in this situation."

"Stanley will take care of it." Cross throws his head back.

I dab alcohol onto one of the scrapes against his stomach and his shoulders tense. He hisses under his breath, and I wince. I know it has to sting.

Tyler stops walking. His fast steps halt. "And if he doesn't?"

Cross slowly levels his chin and stares over my head at his best friend.

Heavy silence cuts through our quiet kitchen again, each of us tense with the unknown.

After a few long seconds, Tyler curses from behind me. Swiping the keys off the table.

"I'm going to the gas station to get you bags of ice."

Cross slowly sits up a little taller and shouts after Tyler, "You know the house code?"

"I've got it," he says over his shoulder. "Scarlett, don't let him go upstairs without me. He's too fucked up to climb the steps."

"Okay," I say quietly, then go back to tending to Cross's injuries.

"WHY DIDN'T YOU TELL ME?" I focus on taking care of Cross versus looking him in the eye.

"Tell you what?" he grits, teeth clenched in pain. "There are a lot of things I haven't told you."

I peek at him from kneeling on the kitchen floor, a damp rag pressed to his hand. "Like?"

Cross's face relaxes, the lines of pain smooth, his sharp inhale slowly releasing. "I only started playing lacrosse so my mom wouldn't question my bruises from fighting. Violence isn't her thing, given my father."

Confusion hits me, and it doesn't take him long to realize.

"He's in prison. Used to beat her." He shrugs, as if it's no big deal.

I slowly stand, and for once, I'm the one with the height advantage. With the cool rag in my hand, I step closer to him and touch it against the side of his jaw where a faint bruise is forming.

My whisper cuts through the quiet kitchen. "What else?"

Cross shrugs again, a wince following it. "I think that's why it bothered me so much when you told me about Nick. Men who abuse women don't deserve to breathe, in my opinion."

I pause my movements and let the cool rag linger in front of Cross's jaw. Our gazes bounce back and forth, both of us attempting to get a good read on the other.

"Is that why you knocked him out tonight?" I ask hesitantly. "You think what he did to me is worse than you owing those men money? That's in the past—"

Cross's hands fly to my hips, and he grips me hard. He pulls me between his legs, the rag in my hand falling to the floor with a splat. He angles his chin so he's peering at me with a fierce glint in his eye, and I gulp.

"It doesn't matter if it's in the past. If I could kill him and get away with it, I would," he whispers.

A swallow works down my throat, and my heart pounds painfully hard behind my ribs.

Cross's tongue wets his bloodstained lips. "Seeing you in the crowd did something to me, Scar. That's why I did what I did."

My stomach dips, but this time, it isn't because he used the nickname Nicholas gave me.

I place my hands on top of his shoulders, the warmth of his skin seeping into my own. "What did it do?"

Cross pauses, his heavy brow line creasing. His lips part. The kitchen becomes even quieter. We stare at one another, and just when I think he isn't going to answer, his hands tighten around my waist and his voice fills the gap between my racing heartbeats.

"It made me realize that you mean a lot more to me than a stepsister should."

My stomach dips.

I repeat the words in my head a few times, Cross's gaze bouncing back and forth between mine, and before I can stop myself, I lean down and gingerly touch my lips to his.

Cross opens his mouth and kisses me back with silent passion, like he's trying to tell me something without using words, and I feel him consume my body like he's a part of me. I press closer and deepen the kiss, my tongue eagerly exploring his mouth to find out all of his sweet spots.

What started out as a soft gesture quickly switches to something fueled with desperation and yearning.

I climb onto his lap, my legs falling open on both sides of his thighs. My breasts press against his chest, and a whimper slips out from in between our kissing.

"Fuck, Scar," he breathes my name into my mouth, his hands traveling up my spine to unhook my bra.

He quickly pulls it from my body, slipping it out from beneath my shirt. He pushes the cotton up to press his mouth to the tight bud. I throw my head back with a hot gasp, and he grows even harder beneath me.

Instead of letting him explore my body with his mouth, I put my hands on his shoulders and scoot off his lap. There's a crease between his eyebrows, disconcertment moving over his expression from the sudden space between us, but then his attention drops to my hands, and a fiery glint takes over his expression.

I slip the button of my jeans through its hole and shimmy out of the denim, leaving them in a heaping pile on the kitchen floor. Cross adjusts himself in the chair, his long legs spreading out wide in front of him as I hook my thumbs through the delicate lace of my panties.

"What are you doing?" he asks lazily, a hot smirk curling onto his lips.

I lick my own and step back between his legs. "Taking care of you."

Cross's jaw flexes, and suddenly, he's lifting and pulling himself free from his pants. He grips himself, already hard and ready. I settle over his lap and sit slowly, the feeling of him widening me euphoric.

The tug on my hair is delicious, and his grasp sends my head flying backward with a moan. Cross peppers my neck with hot kisses, pulling me farther away from thinking this thing between us is totally and irrevocably wrong.

I move above him, refusing to let him do anything that could hurt him more, and work my body in ways it's never been worked before. My hips curve, and I grind over him, his fingers digging into my torso to send me into a frenzy.

"So good," I whisper through a moan.

"The best." His voice is strained, and just the sound of it has me picking up the pace.

An orgasm takes me by surprise. He holds my face in his hands and kisses me with blinding passion. I dig my nails into Cross's shoulders and fall over the edge of pleasure, every single nerve ending tingling. Cross flexes his hips upward, stretching me even wider, until he stills.

A hot groan vibrates out of his chest. I collapse onto him. My sweaty forehead lands on his shoulder, our chests both heaving for oxygen, or maybe just a grip on reality.

Minutes pass, or maybe hours, before I scramble off of his lap at the sound of the door opening.

"I'm back—" Tyler shouts, bags of ice crinkling with his every step down the hallway.

Cross's deep voice travels throughout the house. "Stop where you are."

The rubbing noise of plastic stops abruptly.

I quickly tug my panties and jeans back on, hopping on one foot until they're righted on my hips and buttoned back up, as if we'd done nothing out of sorts while his best friend was gone.

"No use in hiding it." Cross slowly pushes himself up from the chair. Even hunching over in pain, he towers above me. His warm hand grips my chin, the pad of his thumb rubbing against my swollen bottom lip. "Tyler sees the way I look at you."

Tyler, from somewhere down the hall, interrupts the rare, soft moment between us. "Everyone sees the way you look at her..." He comes around the corner and shakes his head. "And it's becoming dangerous."

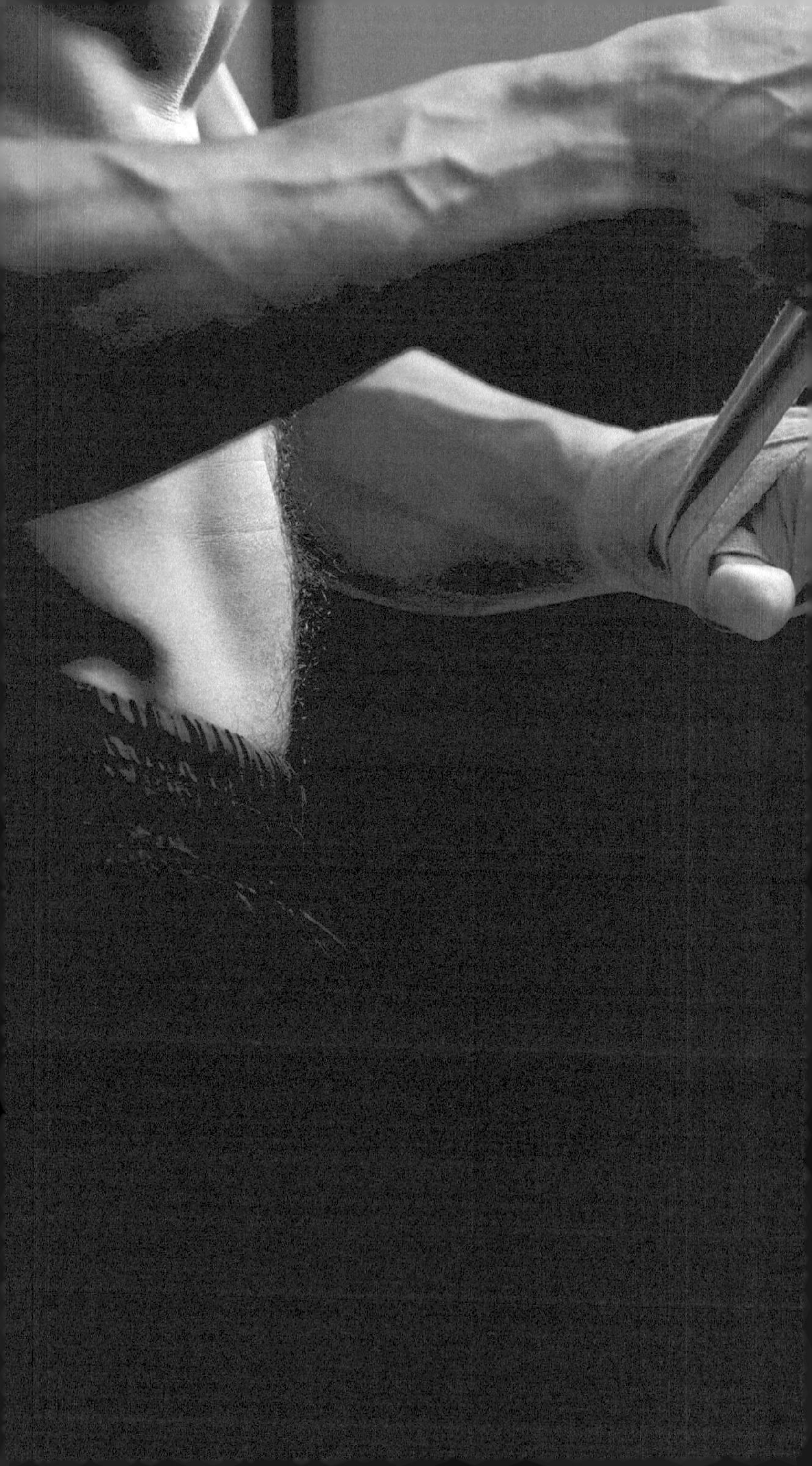

CHAPTER 30

CROSS

"HEY." I kiss Scarlett's cheek. "Wake up."

She groans and rolls into me, tucking her face in the crook of my neck.

I suppress my chuckle and run my finger down her jaw. "I've got to go run an errand. Tyler is coming over to, uh…hang out while I'm gone."

"Babysitting duty?" she murmurs.

I smile. "Yeah. Sorry."

"Be careful."

"Of course." I extract myself from her embrace and slip out of bed. I go to my room and get dressed then meet Tyler at the front door.

He eyes me, taking stock of my injuries. My face is bruised and swollen, and every muscle screamed when I slid out of bed. I'm sure I look like shit, but I open the door wider and let him into the foyer.

"Don't," I warn.

"Who, me?" Tyler raises his hands. "The day after you get the snot kicked out of you—*again*—I would never tell you what a fucking dumbass you are."

I sigh. "Yeah. Thanks."

"I'd *never* say that you're the biggest moron I've ever met. And no wonder you've been getting beat up more than usual lately. You've been warring with yourself over whether or not to *lose* these fights." He sets his phone down on the table and crosses his arms. "You lunatic."

"Jeez, thanks." I roll my eyes. "It was supposed to be easy. But then my opponent started talking about Scarlett. He—" I shake my head in disgust. "He's going to get what's coming to him after the hell he put her through."

My friend pinches the bridge of his nose. "So noble of you."

"Shut up."

"Oh, I'm Cross Lopez. I got twenty thousand dollars to lose, and I couldn't do it because the guy wasn't holier-than-thou."

"Seriously, fuck off."

"You could've lost then beaten the shit out of him another day," Tyler reasons. "You could've followed him home and cut off his dick. Instead—"

"I *know*." I grab my keys. "Which is why I'm going to go plead with Stanley. I think he can help…"

I'm pretty sure he can't help. I caught a glimpse of one of the Webber brothers right before he stormed away, and it promised retribution.

Which is why I need to move fast, and Tyler is going to watch Scarlett.

Thank God for the alarm system her dad had installed. That should give us some warning if anyone targets the house. But even at the gym, the school's main address is listed for my mail and shit. Tyler is my emergency contact. There's no connection here…

Minus that time we spotted one of the Webbers in an SUV out front.

My apprehension rises. "When she wakes up, you should take her to her dad's place."

"Cross—"

"Just till this blows over, you know?" I shrug. "I don't know what they're gonna do. Because my tab ran up a little more than the twenty grand they originally gave me."

I glance over my shoulder. I didn't mention that to Scarlett, and I'd rather not have her hear it by eaves-dropping.

"Excuse me?"

"Scar thinks it's just the twenty grand. I gave it to"—I make a face—"the prick when he tried to insinuate that he missed her or whatever. But then the Webber brothers basically said I had run up a tab, and I owed more like fifty."

"Fifty thousand dollars," Tyler repeats slowly. "Fuck me sideways."

"You're not my type."

He groans. "Now's not the time for jokes."

"Jokes are the only thing holding me together." My mirth drops, leaving me cold. "How the fuck am I going to get out of this in one piece? Stanley had suggested fighting —earning back money."

"They never should've bet on you to lose." He gestures. "Get out of here."

I point to the security system panel on the wall. "Set that right after I leave."

The whole way to the gym, my stomach is a mess of nerves. I try listening to music then go without. I can't decide which is worse: the upbeat tunes grating on me or the silence drilling holes in my ears.

The gym parking lot is relatively full. Most of the guys with memberships come before work—or, in my case, school. It isn't out of the norm to find me and Tyler meeting here at dawn either. It feels, for a split second, like this is just a regular day.

But then I park, and my stomach flops, reminding me that *nope*, this is going to be painful.

I pocket my keys and phone then enter the gym. Some guys cast looks my way, and a few congratulate me on the recent win. Not many know about it, and I give the ones who acknowledge it tight smiles.

My gaze goes up to the second-floor office. Stanley's massive frame is silhouetted through the windows, and I have to think he's spotted me.

When I make it upstairs—slowly, every muscle protesting—the door is already open.

"Come in, Cross," his voice booms out from within.

I enter, glancing around to make sure we're alone.

He sits behind his desk, glasses perched on his nose, typing on a laptop he makes seem tiny. He plucks at the keys with his index fingers, and it isn't until the door has shut and I'm seated in front of him for a solid thirty seconds that he finally pauses and looks up.

"So."

I spread my palms out on my thighs. "I need your help."

"I think you need a lot more than that, son." He closes the laptop with a *snick*. "I tried to help you, and you threw dirt in my face. How do you think that makes me look?"

I frown. "Bad, I'm guessing."

"Correct. I have a relationship with the Webbers that I

work hard to maintain. Having someone I recommended to them go rogue—not once but *twice*?" He slaps his desk. "I'm of a mind to throw you out and be done with you."

Fuck. "I was hoping we could come to some sort of agreement. Maybe if they just knew the circumstances, they'd understand—"

"Ain't no understanding." Anger flashes across his expression. "But fine. Explain it to me."

"The guy I was fighting..." I swallow and drop my gaze. "He raped my stepsister, sir. And he took the opportunity before the first fight to throw that in my face."

"And you couldn't control yourself," he finishes.

My mouth gapes. Tyler had said the same thing.

Is this really so fucking hard to understand? My mother married a guy who beat the shit out of her. I'm glad I didn't get stuck with his last name—*Martin*—or anything else to do with him. But it did instill in me a need to protect my mother from anything else that could hurt her. As soon as I was big enough...

And I have protected her.

It was instinct to not let the guy who hurt Scarlett get away with anything, especially with her watching.

"Consequences, Cross," Stanley says slowly.

"Why did they need me to lose so badly?" I force myself to meet his gaze. "Why couldn't I have won a fight?"

"Because you're the favorite. Anywhere you go. You have a reputation for winning—and clearly, it's well deserved. But you weren't supposed to win, and that's why you're in this mess."

"Please, Stanley, tell me how to get out of it."

He sighs and settles his weight back in his chair. He folds his hands across his belly and seems to contemplate me. "I'll make some calls and see what I can do. But the Webbers are loose cannons. I have no leash when it comes to them. We're acquaintances in this business and nothing more, understand?"

I rise. What I understand is that even a promise of a phone call is throwing me a bone. And at this rate, I'll take any scrap.

"Yes, sir. Thank you."

On my way to the car, my phone goes off like a siren. I pull it out and scan the screen, and my heart fucking stops.

Security System Activated.

I jerk like I've been electrocuted and burst into a run. I get into my car and fumble the keys to start it, barely checking my mirrors to see if the way is clear. I peel out onto the street and press the pedal to the floor. It's quiet at this time of morning—no super-early commuters in Shadow Valley—which makes speeding home easy.

Halfway home, my phone chirps.

Security System Deactivated.

Okay. Maybe it was a false alarm. Maybe Tyler took Scarlett out, like I suggested, and they forgot to turn off the system.

My skin crawls. I'm pretty sure I'm just lying to myself at this point.

I slam the car into park in front of the house and rush to the front door.

My stomach immediately turns.

The door is ajar, but it appears to have been kicked in, not opened normally. The frame is splintered, the deadbolt still sticking out from the door in the locked position. Pieces of wood litter the floor.

I check the street behind me, but it's empty and quiet. I toe the door open, wishing for a weapon. Oh, wait. I quickly double back to my car and find the crowbar in my trunk then return to the house. I step in quietly.

I've never cleared a house before. I channel all those cop shows I used to watch in high school and hoist the crowbar over my shoulder. I'm ready to whack someone at a moment's notice.

My imagination runs away with me, picturing a man with a gun poised to burst around the corner any second.

But the house is silent.

I make it to the kitchen and go still. It seems like something happened in here—the items previously stacked on the counter are scattered across the floor, shattered glass. And then I spot the legs.

"Fuck." I rush forward and round the island, nearly falling onto Tyler.

He's flat out, and blood pools around his head in a halo.

"No, no, no." I drop to my knees and press my fingers to his neck. His pulse is there. Solid. A little slow, perhaps. But he's alive. "Okay. Wake up, Tyler."

I shake his shoulder, and nothing happens.

Where is Scarlett?

I rise and continue my search, making sure the downstairs is totally empty before I rush upstairs.

Her door is wide open, and there's blood on the frame. It's a bit lower than hip height, but it looks like a decent spray of droplets.

"Scarlett?" I call.

I go into her room. Her blankets are on the floor along with everything that had been on her nightstand: lamp, glass of water—it soaks the rug—plus her glasses and her phone.

She wouldn't leave without her phone…and she really wouldn't leave her glasses behind.

A chill sweeps up my spine.

They came and took her. I know it. I just can't prove it.

My phone goes off. I scan the incoming text with no small amount of apprehension, expecting it to be a threat from the Webber brothers.

It's arguably worse than that.

SCARLETT'S DAD

Cross—call me ASAP. Where is my daughter?

CHAPTER 31
SCARLETT

I PULL the covers up higher after Cross kisses me goodbye and inhale. His scent is all over my bed, and I *love* it. I know this thing between us teeters on the line between right and wrong, yet I can't help but indulge in it.

The painful wound from what Nick did to me is more like a scar now, and as much as I hate to admit it, I think Cross is the reason. He pushes me to the brink of insanity, but I crave it. His hot glances and possessive touches evoke something in me that I thought was lost forever. Being in his grasp is like a burnt-out wick catching aflame again, especially when he let the truth bleed out last night: *You mean a lot more to me than a stepsister should.*

Butterflies swarm my lower belly as I drift in and out of sleep, a faint smile slipping onto my parted lips until I'm jerked awake from a loud crashing downstairs.

I sit up quickly, my hair falling past my shoulders. I reach for my glasses on instinct and stare at my bedroom door.

What was that?

On quiet feet, I tiptoe over to the window and peer down onto the foggy street.

I let out a relieved breath when all I see is Tyler's car. I'm being paranoid—not that anyone could blame me—but Tyler probably dropped something, and it startled me awake in my half-sleep state.

I reach for my phone, only to drop it a moment later when there's another loud noise echoing throughout the house.

My pulse thrums. I scramble for something in my room for a way to defend myself when my door slowly swings open.

I freeze, mid-step toward my desk. "*You.*"

The burly man from the previous night grins. "Oh, *Alexxxx,*" he singsongs loudly over his shoulder. "I've found her."

Silence slips between us.

My stomach knots.

Blood whooshes through my ears.

And then he pounces.

His large hand reaches for me, but I duck, just like Cross taught me to do in the cage. That seems like so long ago. I slap my palm onto my desk, in desperate search of my compass from the plans I'd drawn up for class, and my glasses fly off my face. My fingers feel for the compass, and as soon as it's in my grip, I swing it around and slice the air with the pointy end.

"Ow! You bitch!"

My teeth clank from a swift hit to my chin, and I crumple to the floor only to be met with a kick to my stomach. I gasp from the pain, my breathing labored.

Black starts to creep into my vision, but I try to crawl away.

Except, there's nowhere to go.

This place is familiar.

As is the apprehension pooling in my stomach.

"Fucking cunt," spits one of the men responsible for my early morning field trip to the same empty factory basement they brought me to the night prior.

A trickle of blood drips on the dirty floor from the puncture wound I'd given him from our scramble, and if they'd take the tape off my mouth, they'd see me smile at the thought.

The only thing I feel bad about is that my protractor is now broken.

I should have stabbed it into his neck.

Another man, similar in size and looks—who I assume to be Alex—throws him a dirty rag with a roll of his eyes. "It's not that bad. Quit being a bitch, Jason."

My victim snaps his beady eyes over to me. "She's the bitch."

"A rich bitch." Alex chuckles. "But not for long."

I tug on my wrists, and the zip ties dig into my flesh. They have to be bleeding from the sting left behind, but I refuse to be a sitting duck. I've already mapped out an escape and spotted several objects through my fuzzy vision and pounding temples that could be used as weapons on my way. I know Cross taught me how to hit, but I'm truly no match to these men. They're bigger and much stronger than me.

Obviously.

That doesn't mean I'm going to let them have their way

with me, though. Or allow them to rob my father because Cross lost a fight and owes them.

They've already sent a ransom text to my father, who is no doubt losing his mind right now, right along with Cross.

Then there's Tyler.

I pray he's okay. While in and out of consciousness, I caught a blurry glimpse of him on the kitchen floor with blood seeping from his head.

A text tone cuts through my thoughts, and my gaze flies in the direction of it. I pull on my wrists again, the chair creaking beneath my weight. Jason glances in my direction with a smirk, while the other hungrily scans the phone.

I try to focus, my vision too strained without my contacts or glasses—which broke in our scuffle—but the gleam of his teeth tells me he's smiling.

"Didn't you say that your daddy wouldn't fall for our ransom?"

My heart stops.

I bite the inside of my cheek because, with the tape over my mouth, I can't do anything else.

Footsteps shuffle on the floor, and the bright light of his phone is inches from my face. I scan the text quickly, and a wave of nausea rolls inside my stomach.

It's from Cross.

Send me the location. I have the money.

I'm relieved but terrified.

These aren't your typical men. Who is to say they won't kill him on the spot after Cross hands over the money? Who is to say they won't turn on him and then claim me as their prize, like they've been threatening to do since being alone with them in this empty, musty building?

I clench my eyes shut and turn my head away from him.

It isn't until the creaky hinges of the door swinging opened that I come back to reality. Except, it isn't what I hoped for at all.

There are no sirens blaring in the distance or men in SWAT suits with their guns pointed at my captors.

Instead, it's Cross. And he's all alone.

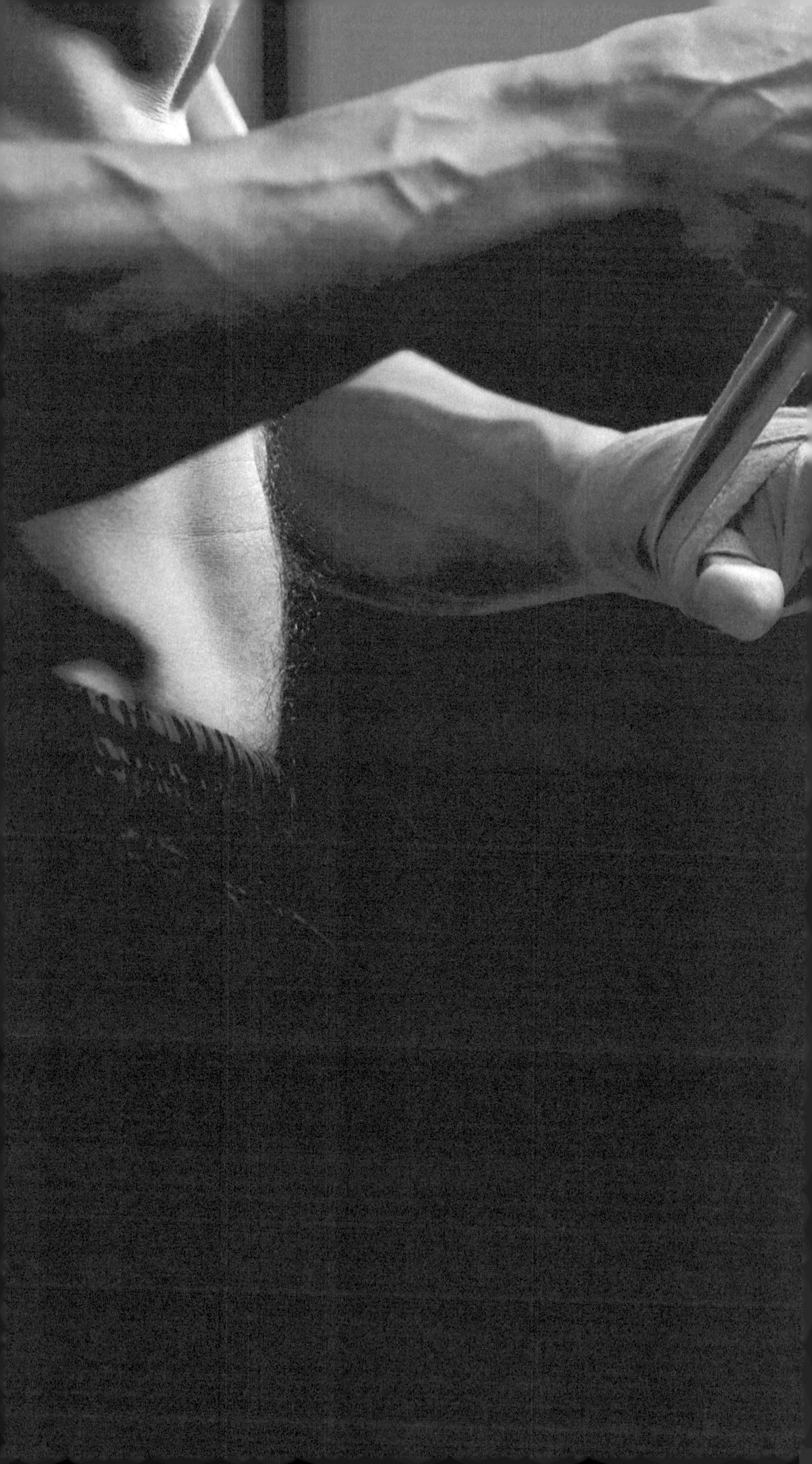

CHAPTER 32

CROSS

MY MOM and Scarlett's dad meet me at the edge of Shadow Valley an hour after his text comes through. In that time, I brought Tyler to the emergency room—he woke up shortly after I came back downstairs, but he seemed too disoriented for my liking—and told Scar's dad that we had to meet.

I spare a moment to hug my mother, whose concern is etched all over her face. Beyond that, she looks good. Her hair is shinier than I've ever seen it, and she has little gold hoops in her ears. She's wrapped in a thick puffy jacket lined with faux fur, and her gloved hands take mine.

I face Scarlett's dad. I still can't think of him as my *step*father. It doesn't seem real. I haven't spent enough time with the man to even consider him family.

But he's *her* family.

And I've never seen the emotions controlling his expression right now. A mix of worry and anger. He thrusts his phone out, the message from a private number on the screen.

UNKNOWN

We have your daughter. A hundred grand for her life. You have until 5PM. Police = no deal, and you'll never see her again.

[IMAGE]

A hundred thousand dollars? I blanch. The photo is of Scarlett—fiery, glaring—sitting on an old rickety chair. Her hands are bound behind her back.

There's a newspaper leaned against her shins.

"That's the headline from today," he says in a low voice. "What the hell is going on, Cross?"

I swallow and meet his gaze. "I did something bad. This is all on me."

"Cross," my mother gently pleads, looking at my bruised face. "Just be honest with us."

I close my eyes and tell them the story. It starts with my fighting.

"Fighting," Scarlett's dad repeats.

"I train at a reputable gym in town, but the owner got me into some fights for extra money." I glance at Mom. "I needed every penny I could earn to stay in school."

"You had a lacrosse scholarship—"

"It didn't cover everything, *Mamá*. It didn't cover food and books and..." I shrug. "General cost of living. I couldn't burden you with it."

Tears fill her eyes.

"Focus," Scarlett's dad murmurs. "Please."

I suck in a deep breath. "Stanley, the gym owner, set up a meeting with these guys. They had twenty thousand in cash. They gave it to me to lose a fight. And I swear, I was just going to do it once. That kind of money would be life-changing."

I see it in his eyes that he disapproves.

"My opponent saw Scarlett and me talking before the fight."

"You brought her—"

"She found her own way there," I interrupt. "And the guy…he was from Yale. He was telling me horrible things about w-what he did to her."

I'm sick at the memory of it.

"In that moment, I snapped. I couldn't let her see me lose to someone like that. But more than that…"

"Cross," my mother cries. "God, I never wanted your future to be so clouded by what your father did to us."

"I know."

Scarlett's dad's face is red. "What did he do to her?"

I shake my head slowly. "That's her story to tell. He demanded money, and I used the twenty grand to make him go away. But the point is, those decisions cost me. The brothers who paid me to throw the fight came back and said I owed them more than what they paid me. That I had run up a debt."

I explain the rest—how there was another fight, another opportunity to wipe the slate clean, but my opponent was the same. And I saw red.

By the time I'm done, I hang my head. "It was never a hundred thousand that I owed. I don't—I don't know why they want that much."

"Because they know I'll pay it." He reaches out and puts his hand on my shoulder. "These men are predators, Cross. They targeted you, and now they're targeting our family."

My guilt is going to choke me.

"I have the money," he says suddenly. "I didn't file a

report with the police, but I will be as soon as you tell them you'll deliver it to them."

"What?"

He pushes his phone at me. "Keep that. We're going to the police, and your mother will keep your location tracked through my phone. With any luck, we'll be able to follow you and get these guys."

Their car beeps, and the trunk opens. He grabs a duffel bag and holds it out to me. I shoulder it, knowing more money than I can fathom is inside it.

He's trusting me to get his baby back in one piece.

I let out a long, slow breath. "One more thing."

They both look at me.

"I'm in love with her."

They exchange a look, and my mother chuckles. "Called it."

My jaw drops.

She urges me toward my car. "Go. We'll discuss this more when Scarlett is safe."

HIS EYES IMMEDIATELY FIND MINE, and my heart skips a beat.

Cross strides farther into the old factory, seemingly as casual as if he were strolling through campus. A duffel bag hangs in his hand, and I bet if I listen hard enough, I'll hear bundles of my father's cash shuffling around inside.

"'Bout time," Alex says, coming to stand in front of me.

"Yeah, 'bout time," the other one repeats.

My pulse is in my stomach, and the closer Cross gets to us, the more my eyes water.

"Let her go." His tone is eerily calm.

I cling on to it like his voice is my protection.

I peek past the men and their broad shoulders at the door, wondering if the police are going to come. Or maybe my father. But there's nothing except a vast area with dormant factory machines and a dirty concrete floor.

"We will let her go when you hand over the money you owe us," Jason sneers.

"This is more than I owe you," Cross says. "What's the other fifty thousand for?"

Jason's shoulders tense. "For pain and suffering. Your bitch of a girlfriend stabbed me in the leg."

I lean to the left and catch a glimpse of Cross. His jaw is clenched tight, and he hoists the duffel bag higher in his grip.

"Have something to say, boy?" Alex asks. "Or can we get this over with?"

Cross glances at me, his brown eyes full of an apology. He tosses the bag across the room, and it lands with a thud. Dust kicks up between them. Cross attempts to get to me, only he stops abruptly, his shoes slipping against the dusty floor.

Alex pushes something onto his chest. "Not so fast."

Cross's arms immediately go up in surrender.

My eyes widen.

I catch sight of a gun, the barrel long and shiny. I plead through the duct tape on my mouth and pull on my wrists again.

Cross focuses on me instead of the man pointing the gun at him. Time stops. A tear slips over my cheek. Cross's neck bobs with a swallow, his cheeks hollow with worry, his hands remaining in their upright position.

"Count it," Alex barks.

Jason quickly unzips the bag and mutters numbers.

The longer it takes for him to finish the task, the more impatient Alex seems to become. I stare at the barrel pressed against Cross's chest, and my heart thumps so quickly I think it's trying to reach his.

"Hurry up." Alex digs the gun into Cross's chest even harder.

I clench my eyes together, too sick with worry to stare any longer.

It's fine. It's fine. They're going to take the money and run.

"It's all here," Jason announces.

I open my eyes at the sound of the zipper and watch Alex slowly lower the gun away from Cross.

Oh, thank God.

Cross finally shifts his gaze from mine and looks at both men. "This settles my debt."

It isn't a question. Instead, it's a statement.

Alex chuckles darkly. "You've got the confidence of someone who already knows how this ends."

Cross's eyebrows crease, and he has the same expression as when I told him about Nicholas. "That's because I do."

Jason shifts the duffel bag to the other hand and smirks. "He's got the confidence of someone who isn't looking down the barrel of a gun."

Alex shrugs and then raises the gun in Cross's direction.

I scream, though it's muffled. My wrists burn, but I tug on them again and again, the chair creaking beneath my weight.

"Your little girlfriend seems distressed." Alex turns and pointing the gun at me.

I stop moving immediately and stare at Alex's hand wrapped around the gun. His finger hovers over the trigger.

"If you shoot her, you'll be in the pen for a lot longer." Cross's words come out tight.

"The pen?" Jason laughs. "Unless you get the cops involved—"

Alex and Jason share a look, and suddenly their fun is

cut short. They make a run for it. Alex shoves the gun into the back of his jeans, and Jason holds the duffel close to his chest. They both sprinting toward the door.

Cross reaches me in record time, and his shaky fingers work quickly to take the tape off my mouth. I wince at the pain, and as soon as my mouth is freed, I burst out into a sob.

"It's okay, it's okay. I've got you." Cross kisses my forehead and disappears behind me. "Oh my God," he murmurs quietly, faintly touching my wrists. "Fuck, I need something sharp."

Sirens echo in the distance, and I gasp with relief.

I thought it was just a trick to get them to leave.

The police are actually coming? They know?

Cross runs to one of the machines in the center of the factory, his movements jerky. Random objects clamor to the floor, but before I know it, Cross is back over to me with what looks like a rusty utility knife.

"Stay still, baby," he says in a hushed voice.

The zip ties snap, the edges cutting into my skin, then they slip to the floor.

I'm cradled in Cross's arms before I even take a breath.

"I've got you," he whispers into my hair. "I'm so sorry. I'm so fucking sorry."

I keep my bloody hands still but press myself close to Cross. His heart pounds against my ear as I bury my face into his shirt. His grip on me tightens, and he carries me toward the door.

"You're shaking," he mutters. "You're in shock."

I shake my head without lifting it from his chest. "I'm —I'm not in shock."

After a moment, I pull away from him. Fresh air hits

my tearstained face. I glance into his face. His jaw, always sturdy and hardened, hangs loose with worry.

"I'm shaking from relief." My lip wobbles. "I thought they were going to kill you."

Cross creases his brow. "Weren't you afraid they were going to kill you?"

I think for a moment.

Cross Lopez.

My stepbrother.

The bane of my existence.

The guy I've found myself in love with.

"No," I whisper. "I was only worried about you."

His lip twitches. "And I was only worried about you."

"Scarlett!" I turn at the sound of my father and stiffen at the scene unfolding.

Red and blue lights flash in the background, and both of our parents run toward us. Several officers stand over both Alex and Jason, who have cuffs on their wrists, with the duffel and gun on top of one of the patrol cars.

"I love you," Cross whispers into my ear, his warm breath sending goosebumps over every inch of my skin.

I snap my attention to him, and suddenly the chaos is gone. Another tear slips over my cheek to land on my parted lips. "I love you, too," I whisper.

My father takes me from Cross's arms, his racing heart matching his stepson's. The mayhem ensues as I'm carried to a nearby ambulance while Cross's mom remains by his side, checking him over for injuries.

"I'm so glad you're okay," my dad chokes out.

I peer up at him, his blue eyes a perfect match to mine. "And Cross?" I ask hesitantly.

His hand rests on my knee, and a paramedic wraps gauze around my wrist. "Both of you."

I exhale deeply and flop backward onto the stretcher. "Good," I say wearily. "Because I'm in love with him."

I don't know if it's the exhaustion, or the shock of the last twelve hours, or maybe it's the high I'm riding because Cross admitted that he loves me, too, but I let the truth slide out effortlessly to my father, knowing very well that being in love with my stepbrother is completely unorthodox.

To my surprise, he chuckles.

I peer at him with confusion, and he shakes his head, half smiling. "I know, sweetheart."

He does?

How?

"He said the same thing to us before he came to get you." He rubs the back of his neck, where I know most of his tension sits. "We'll figure this out later. For now, let's get you fixed up."

I nod and give my other wrist to the paramedic.

"But sweetheart?"

I glance at my dad again.

His jaw clenches for a split second. "I want to know what that boy did to you at Yale."

My stomach turns. I immediately look elsewhere.

He pats my knee gently. "Not now. But when you're ready."

I let out a shaky breath and nod.

"Sir, can I take her vitals?"

"Oh, right. Yes, of course."

My dad hops up to move out of the way and tells me he's going to go check on Cross. Before I can even say the words, he looks at me over his shoulder and says, "And then I'll send him over, okay?"

I try to hide my smile.

But in the end, I can't.

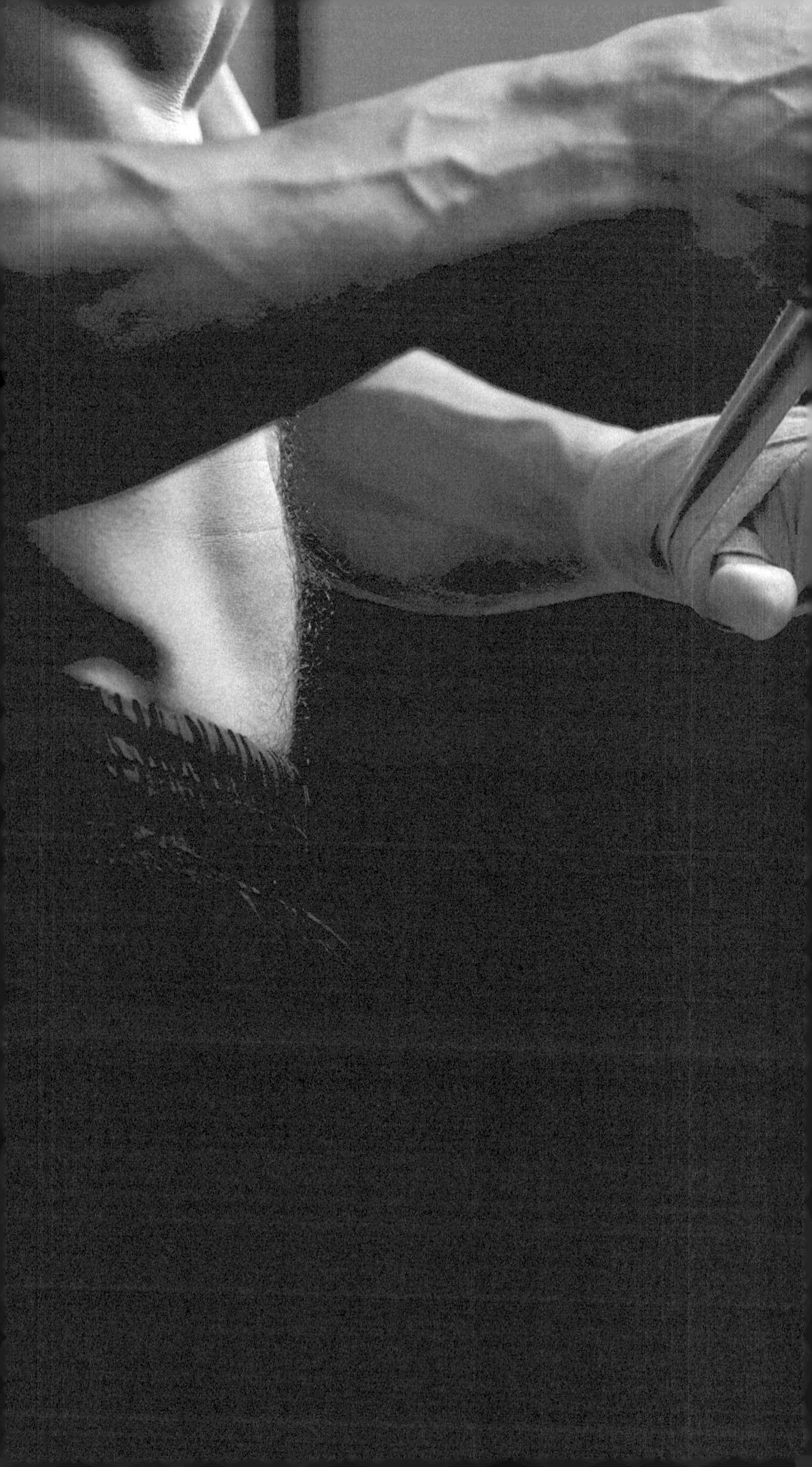

CHAPTER 34

CROSS

THREE MONTHS LATER

"THIS IS PROBABLY A LITTLE SICK," Tyler says.

I roll my eyes. "I gave you the option to bow out."

"You said, 'Don't make me do this alone. I'll probably fuck it up.' And then you gave me fucking puppy-dog eyes."

"And *then*, I said, 'But you don't have to if you don't want to.'"

"Who could resist that half-hearted offer?" He sighs. "It's fine. We're here. Let's just do this."

I look down at the crowbar across my lap then back at the house. It's dark. The whole street is silent at this time of night. We saw him enter almost an hour ago, and the lights in the upstairs window went out.

"So, we're sticking to the plan, right?"

I nod firmly. "Of course."

"No seeing red and going off track…"

"Would I do that?"

He snorts. "You're insufferable."

He gets out of the car and heads up the walkway. He seems so chill that I don't think anyone would suspect we're up to no good—if anyone is awake to peek out their windows anyway. He looks around the porch, crouches to peek under the mat, then expands his search. He finds a fake rock—I'm assuming—and holds something up.

I get out of the car, stride across the street, and join him on the porch.

He lets us into the house, and we both click on our flashlights. We make quick work scouring the first floor for signs of life then head upstairs.

From the bedroom comes loud snoring. The sort that probably would require medical intervention. I adjust my grip on the crowbar and approach the bed. Tyler shines his light on it, illuminating the sleeping pube face. And the light catches his eyes flying open a split second before I bring the crowbar down on his stomach.

He doubles up, and I hit him again for the hell of it. While he's wheezing, Tyler and I grab him and throw him onto the floor. I grasp his wrists, yanking them to the small of his back.

"Tape?" I grunt.

Tyler kneels and winds duct tape around his wrists. By the time he blinks away the delirium of sleep, he's bound, and we're out of kicking range.

"What the *fuck*?" he roars.

I motion to Tyler, who flicks on the overhead light. The dick-for-brains cranes his head around and gets a glimpse of me, and his mouth gapes open. Closed. Open. Like a fish out of water. He kind of flops around like one, too.

The bedroom is pretty sparse. There's a dresser, the bed, and a closet. Nightstands on either side. His sheets are black, and there's the faintest smell of sour sweat in the air.

"Maybe you should open a window once in a while," I comment. My nose wrinkles. "Or wash your sheets."

"Focus," Tyler admonishes.

"Can you find us a chair?"

My best friend eyes me. I hold up my hands in surrender until he's out of the room, then I crouch and grab Nicholas Thomson by the hair. I wrench his head back until he meets my eyes.

"Do you know why we're here?"

"F-for the money?" He struggles, but he has no leverage. "Some sick prank?"

"For Scarlett," I say softly. "I'm your fucking reckoning."

He pales.

Tyler's footsteps thump on the stairs, and I release him just as he reappears. Together, we haul the slimy bastard up and force him into the chair. We tape his ankles to the front legs of the kitchen chair, then I take a seat on the edge of the bed.

Tyler withdraws his phone, and he nods at me when he starts recording.

"Let's go over what happened last year," I say. "You want to tell us the truth, don't you, Nick?"

The guy doesn't seem very convinced. Or scared. Yes, he's tied up, but he probably doesn't think we're going to do anything seriously harmful.

I get up and scan the few photos on top of his dresser. One seems to be his high school graduation with his parents, complete with a dark-blue cap and gown. Another is him in football gear.

"You play?" I hold up the photo. "For Yale?"

He makes a face. "Yeah. Why?"

"And what else do you do for fun?"

"I'm in a fraternity—and those guys will find you and tear you down if you don't cut the shit."

I sigh. "Right. Of course. They probably know about that night with Scarlett. Your buddies might've even heard your plan beforehand and had a laugh over it?"

"I—"

"No lies," I interrupt. "I'm so fucking sick of your voice, but I want to hear what you did. And then maybe you'll walk out of here. Or *maybe*, your precious Yale will find out about the fighting. Do you think they'd take you off the football team? Would the frat have no choice but to kick you out?"

"My life will be just fine," he snaps.

I smile, but all I feel is an icy rage. "Will it?"

He sees something in my expression and sits up straighter. "Listen. I didn't do anything with the cash yet. It's in my closet. You can have it—"

"Yeah, we'll be taking that on our way out. But *first*..."

I come closer and press the pointed edge of the crowbar under his chin. The cold metal digs into his skin, and fear widens his eyes.

"Tell us about that night. You had no problem telling me in the cage."

His gaze flicks to the phone in Tyler's hand then back to me.

I lower the crowbar and take a seat again.

"Fine," he says on a sigh. "Scarlett loved to play hard to get. She rebuked me a few times, but she would always come to the parties with her friends. So, yeah, I thought I might give her a little something extra to help me win her over."

"And..."

"And when she finished the drink, her eyes could barely open. I helped her upstairs. And nature took over."

"Nature," I repeat. "With…an unconscious girl."

He frowns. "She wasn't passed out."

"No, you drugged her to bring her right to that edge of oblivion."

"Exactly!" He pauses. "But she wanted it. She was moaning."

My stomach twists, because I've heard her *moan*, and I bet it was nothing like what came out of her mouth that night.

"I've heard enough." I stand. "Tyler, shut it down."

He pockets his phone, his eyebrows raised.

This is the part where things go off the rails.

"I hope every step is painful for the rest of your life," I say quietly. "I hope the agony can't be fixed, and you're constantly reminded that this is because you made a strong woman vulnerable. You ripped away her ability to feel safe around men."

"I—"

I bring the crowbar down on his knee.

His plea, whatever it was going to be, is cut off in a howl of pain. I take my anger out on his leg until there's no fucking doubt that I've shattered something. Bone or joint—I don't care. He screams, over and over, until Tyler catches the crowbar and yanks it out of my hand.

Tyler darts forward and punches him, *hard*, in the temple.

It's an easy lights out.

His head drops onto his chest, and we're left staring at the bloody mess of his leg. It doesn't even really look like a limb anymore.

"That was not in the playbook," Tyler says slowly.

I shrug. "He crossed the line first."

"We should get out of here." Tyler pulls me back then methodically cuts our captive free. He unravels the tape and stuffs it in his pocket then pauses. "What he said was disgusting."

I nod.

He shoves him, and the big guy crashes to the floor.

"Okay. I feel better." Tyler leads the way outside. "Now what?"

"Now, we let Scar decide." I tip my head. "Eh, plus a little extra."

He groans. "Great. Improvising again."

"You love it."

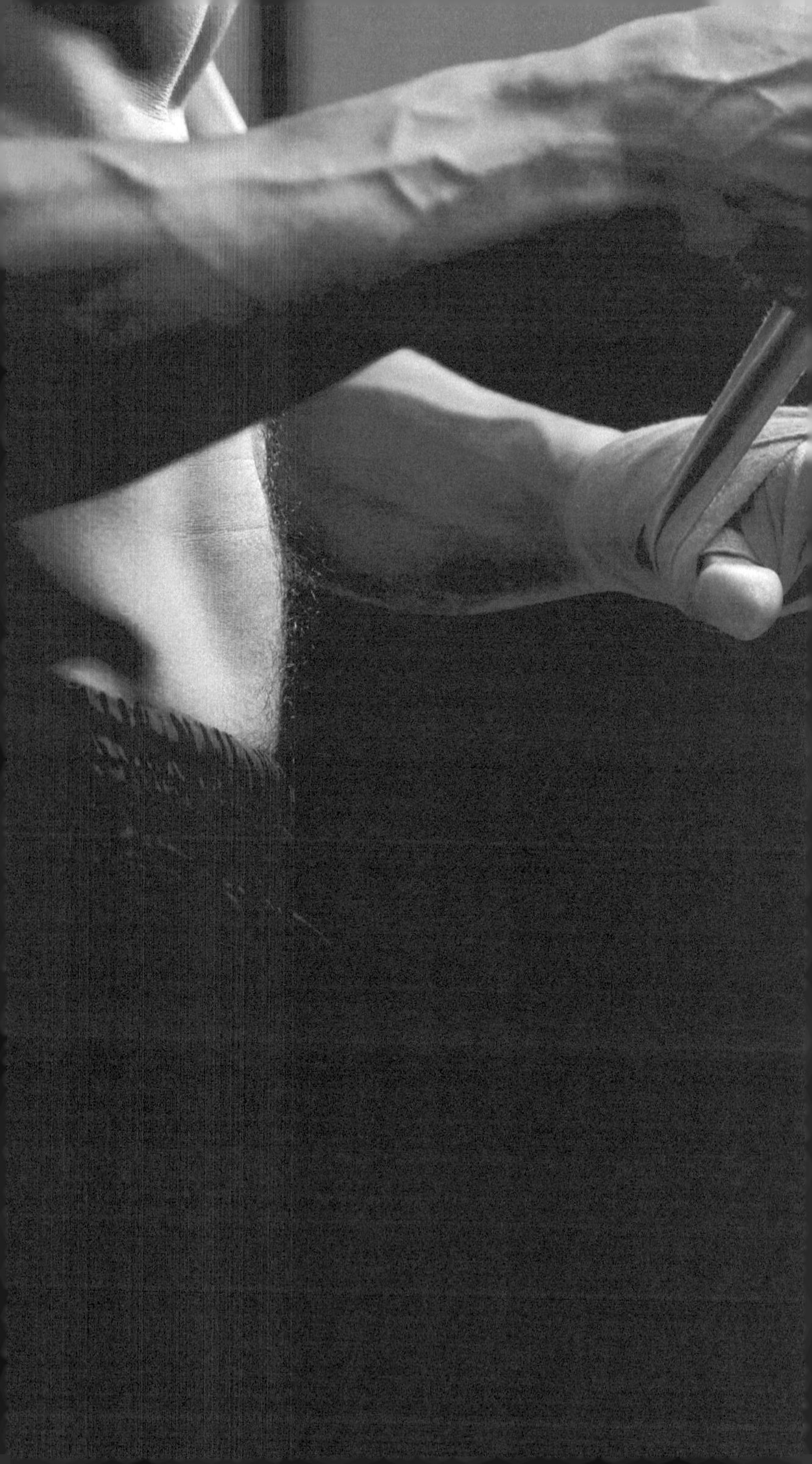

CHAPTER 35

CROSS

"CROSS," Scarlett hisses. "Where are we going?"

"You're being very pessimistic." I glance at her then sling my arm around her shoulders. "Are you cold?"

"Do I seem cold?"

"Some people shiver when they're nervous," I reason. "And I did wake you up in the middle of the night so you could experience this."

She scoffs. "I'm not *nervous*."

"After everything that's happened?" I raise my eyebrow. "No post-traumatic stress? No anxiety? How's the therapy going?"

Her cheeks redden. "It's going."

Once we got back home after the kidnapping incident—as I'm kindly referring to it as—Scar and her dad had a heart-to-heart about why she left Yale. The family decision was therapy. I went a few times, but I think it wasn't a good fit. She, on the other hand, seems to like her therapist.

Anyway. We finished out the spring semester at

Shadow Valley U, and we're home for the summer before going back for our final year.

Our parents have grudgingly accepted that we're... dating.

This has included some rearranging of the house, and I've been relegated to the in-law suite above the garage. It has a kitchenette and bathroom, so they don't feel bad about locking me out at night.

It's an effort to keep us separated at night. But, little do they know, Scarlett is just as corrupt as me. She sneaks up to sleep with me most nights then creeps back to her room before the sun comes up.

In the fall, we won't have to hide it. We'll be back in *our* place.

"This middle-of-the-night shit is for people with regulated nervous systems," she mutters. "It would help if you could tell me where we are and what we're doing."

My attention narrows back in on her, and I lean down to kiss the top of her head. "Patience, grasshopper."

"This isn't another teaching moment, is it?"

I shake my head. "Shh."

"Cross—"

"Hey!" Tyler slams his car door and hops out. "There you are."

I smirk. "She hasn't figured it out yet."

He brightens. "No? Did she try guessing?"

"Aren't our parents going to question why you brought me back to Shadow Valley for the night?"

"No." I glance over our shoulders, but the coast is clear on the sidewalk. The street is empty, just as it was a few hours ago. "Because we're not in Shadow Valley."

She does a double-take. "You told me—"

"I didn't really say anything when you made the assumption." I grin. "Sorry. Your fault for falling asleep on the ride here, maybe?"

She looks around more, seeming to confirm her suspicions. We're a few blocks away from the main strip of New Haven, Connecticut. Home of Yale University. I can see how she would confuse it for Shadow Valley—sometimes, in the dark, all the New England towns look alike.

"I recognize this…"

Tyler, ahead of us, whirls around to walk backward. "Do you?"

She elbows me, but a thread of fear seems to travel up her back. Her shoulders tense, like someone's going to jump out and grab her.

"I went to school here for two and a half years. Why the hell are we back in Connecticut?"

"I think it's this one." I pull her to a stop and turn her to face a house. It appears rather boring, the grass trimmed short, everything tidy. It's a *big* house, though, and usually there would be many people inside. But during the summer, it's vacant.

Tyler double-checked while I went to get Scar.

She clutches my arm. "Cross, this isn't funny."

"You recognize it?"

"Of course I do," she snaps. "Home of my worst nightmare."

I brighten. "Great! Then you won't be opposed to some light vandalism."

She eyes me.

Tyler hauls some red containers from where he had stashed them in the bushes. He hands one to me and another to her. She takes it woodenly, not seeming to understand what I'm saying.

"What is this?"

"Gasoline."

Her jaw drops. "I—"

"Therapy can't get you *this* satisfaction, can it?" I smirk. "Come on. Live a little. Burn down this ugly, stupid frat house with me."

Tyler bounds up the steps and kicks in the door. He disappears inside, and I wait until she nods firmly. We head in together, and her shoulders creep higher up her neck. She has a death grip on the handle.

"Douse anything and everything," I advise.

"Is this— Are we going to get in trouble?"

Questionable.

"I think your dad can get us a good lawyer if anything comes up."

She huffs on a laugh then goes to the huge L-shaped couch and splashes gas on it. It soaks into the cushions and drips onto the floor. I follow her lead. We go upstairs, and she seems to be in a trance when she leads me down the hall, past many other doors, to one near the end.

"Here?" I ask quietly.

She nods once.

My throat closes, but she doesn't back down. She enters and stops in the middle of the room. It's empty minus some bare furnishings. A twin mattress on a standard school-issued frame, a desk and chair, a dresser.

All wood.

All easy to burn.

She dumps the rest of her gasoline on the mattress. "I hate you," she says to the room. "I fucking hate this place."

"Let's destroy it, then."

She turns to face me. "But the people—"

"They'll pay, too."

She darts forward and catches the back of my neck, dragging me down to kiss me hard. Our mouths open, our tongues feuding for space. I love the taste of her.

The gas fumes are getting to me, though.

I pick her up and carry her out, tearing my lips from hers so I don't run us into a wall. I let my canister make a trail from that room out and down the hall, down the stairs. It won't be long before the whole place is engulfed.

I hope anyway. I'm really not an arsonist.

We meet up with Tyler at the front door, and he produces a matchbook.

"You want to do the honors?" he asks Scarlett.

She slides down my body and plucks it from his fingers. With shaking hands, she sets a match ablaze and tosses it.

It sputters out mid-fall.

"Kind of anticlimactic," I murmur.

"Oops." She grimaces. "Okay. Take two."

This time, the flame doesn't blow out. It hits the puddle of gasoline on the threshold, and a wall of heat hits us. I grab her arm, and we hurry down the steps, all the way to the sidewalk.

Truly, it's impressive how fast it goes up.

"As much as I'd love to watch this, we should get back to our cars before someone sees," Tyler says.

Right.

I hold out my hand for Scarlett. She takes it, and we jog together back to my car. The heat from the burning house pushes at our backs, even from this distance. I glance over my shoulder, eyes wide at the orange and yellow flames glowing in the upstairs windows.

Only one more stop.

Scarlett leans over and kisses me. I take a moment to savor it—*again*—then pull away.

"Come on," I say.

She follows me out. We pause and look up at another house. This one is familiar to me, but I doubt she knows where we are—or why.

Tyler withdraws a key from his pocket and skips down the walkway then up the porch steps. He opens the screen door and uses the key to unlock the front door. It swings inward silently, and I guide Scarlett inside.

"Quiet, now," I whisper in her ear.

I had sort of questioned whether she should come with us for this, but then I reasoned that if she has a hard time with what I'm planning, she'll just really get her money's worth out of therapy.

Maybe that's cruel. It could be just what the doctor ordered, though, right?

Whatever.

I release her once we're inside. She glances around, her brows furrowed. Tyler shuts us in. He flicks on a handheld flashlight. I find my way to the kitchen and locate the knives then lead the way upstairs.

She follows, with Tyler behind.

I enter the bedroom and flick on the light. Asswipe is still on the floor—I don't think he even tried to move. He lets out a low moan and hurls himself backward at the intrusion. He drags his leg with him, but the jostling makes him cry out.

He holds up his hands in front of his face. "Don't come near me!"

I scoff. "Perk up, buddy. Your judge and jury just arrived."

He slowly lifts his head and focuses on Scarlett. I have half a mind to step between them, but I take in her expression and decide against it. She seems half scared, half shocked. Her wide eyes take in the scene in front of her.

Yeah, that therapist is *definitely* going to hear about this.

"We got a video of him confessing what he did to you." I touch her arm. "But what you want to do with that—and him—is up to you."

"Cross." Her voice is low. She grabs my hand and drags me out into the hallway. "What is this?"

"He's not someone you need to be scared about anymore."

Her face softens. "I know. But you didn't need to do this when you've already made me feel safer than I have in the last six months just by being you."

Ah, hell.

"So..." My attention drifts back to the open doorway. "The leg was a bit much?"

A giggle bubbles out of her. She slaps her hand over her mouth. I smile in return.

"What's the plan?" I ask her. "Perfect scenario?"

"He never sleeps with another person ever again."

I raise my eyebrow. "Ruthless, but we can arrange that..."

She makes a face. "No. You're right. I just want him to go away forever."

"Our justice system doesn't really work like that, does it? Not for rich white guys like him."

"It doesn't."

"Plan A, then? Cut off his dick?"

"Cross." She comes forward and wraps her arms around me.

"Chemical castration?" I suggest. "We could poison him slowly. Tamper with his coffee or something so he drinks arsenic for the next three months."

"*Cross.*"

"Hey." I put my finger under her chin, lifting so she meets my gaze. "I would do anything for you. Just say the word."

Her eyes fill with tears. "What about blackmail?"

I pause. "Oh. Yeah, that's an option." My mind goes back to the first things he said— "Shit, Scar, we can get that video. We can erase it from the face of the earth."

"Yes," she breathes.

"On it. You can stay out here or…not."

She nods. I duck back into the room and go to his nightstand, where his phone is still plugged in. The dumbass probably didn't think about calling himself an ambulance, not after his recorded confession, which is fine by me.

It requires a face ID. Tyler hoists him into a seated position on the floor and keeps his head still. I shove the screen in his face until it unlocks, then I go to his camera roll. There's a locked, private album.

"Passcode," I demand.

He licks his lips.

"Or we break your other leg," Tyler warns.

"One-three-seven-two."

I type it in, and the album unlocks. My stomach knots.

There's not just one video—there's a dozen.

I click on one, and he lets out a whimper. It's a fucking home video, but he starts recording when the girl is carried in by two other guys. They drop her on the edge of the bed, and she immediately slides to her knees on the floor. She catches herself, her head bobbing like she can't hold it up.

It isn't Scarlett.

Then *he* moves into the frame, his hands going to his jeans. He flicks open the button, and there's very clearly the motion of him jerking himself, and he grabs the girl by the hair. She wobbles, but her eyes are closed. The only thing keeping her upright is the way he tugs at her scalp.

"Open up, baby."

I swipe to the next one. Girl on bed, her arm hanging off. He climbs on her—

"You fucker." I close the phone and lunge for him, punching him in the face. His nose breaks under my fist, and the spray of blood does nothing but make me want to keep hitting him. I get in two more strikes before Scarlett calls my name.

I freeze.

"Send those videos to the police," she says.

I look over at her, stricken. My heart is in my damn throat. "You heard?"

She nods slowly. "I thought we had an easy way out. But he kept that freaking memorabilia, Cross. And it wasn't just me, was it?"

"No."

Tyler squeezes his eyes shut. He remains very, very still, and I know my best friend is close to losing his shit, too.

I crouch and grab the rapist's jaw. "You ready, Nick? You're going to be a prison bitch. I hope your asshole is ready for overtime."

With that, Tyler and I release him. He falls backward, tears falling down his cheeks. Scarlett laces her hand with mine, and we leave him. I'll hand-deliver the phone to the police along with the code to get in.

Outside, Scar blows out a breath. "Thank you, Cross."

The smell of smoke tinges the air. There are sirens wailing in the distance, but they're not headed here.

I tug her to my side and kiss the top of her head. "Let's go home."

SCARLETT

ONE YEAR LATER

SAWYER and I get ready together at her place. Cross's and my place has been overtaken by his friends during senior week—our last hurrah as a class before we graduate —which means Sawyer has had to put up with me this week.

Not that I think she minds. Her cozy one-bedroom apartment is clean and very girly, kind of the opposite of my house.

Sawyer gives herself a once-over in the mirror. "What are the chances Cross is going to propose soon?"

I choke on my water. "He is *not* going to propose soon. I feel like we just got our parents to look us in the eye during our monthly dinners."

Sawyer grabs her keys as I toss my water in her pink— yes, pink—trash can. "And you think he cares about that?"

I think it over.

Of course he doesn't.

I mean, don't get me wrong. He is respectful when our parents are in proximity, but the dirty things we've done behind their backs, in their house, in public restrooms at restaurants…

A huff of air leaves me. "Probably not."

Sawyer laughs, and I join in.

The drive to graduation is less than a minute, and as soon as she parks the car, we both grab our caps to adjust them in the mirror. My blonde hair has grown in the last year, so long luscious waves flow over my shoulders to rest against my maroon gown. The diamond earrings my dad and Sofia gifted me with at dinner on Friday gleam through the strands, putting a smile on my face.

They gave Cross something less glamorous but surprisingly sentimental: a tactical knife.

I thought it was a joke, given that Cross had put me in danger—something my father likes to remind him of—but it was actually a job offer to work at the business with him.

The knife once belonged to my father when he was a field agent. He obviously retired it, and he now sits behind a big fancy desk to run the entire company, but he's kept it safe all these years. He and Sofia had it engraved with the words: *Earned, not given.*

Which was my dad's way of saying thank you, for saving his daughter's life.

However, Cross hasn't accepted the job offer yet.

"There are the guys." Sawyer nods to a large group of lacrosse players.

I spot Cross right away, his dark hair neatly styled underneath his cap with his eyes directly on me.

His lip lifts with a hot smirk, and I roll my eyes playfully.

Tyler catcalls Sawyer and me, and Cross elbows him in the stomach. A year older and they're still the same.

Cross's hands find their way to my waist, the silky

material of my gown snagging against his fingers. He pulls me in for a kiss, squeezing my sides gently.

He leans back and hovers his mouth over mine. "I've missed you."

"You saw me yesterday," I say.

A growl leaves him. "But I didn't sleep next to you. I don't like it."

I give him another quick kiss. "Me neither."

Tyler sighs. "You two make me sick."

Sawyer snorts. "You're just jealous."

"Fuck yeah, I am. Wanna be my girlfriend?"

We all do a double-take.

Sawyer pops her hip, curiously shifting her gaze around. "But you're gay."

Tyler shrugs. "I'd be straight for you."

Her lips flatten, and he starts to laugh.

"Come on." I place my hand in Cross's and lead us to our spots in line. "Let's go graduate so we can celebrate after."

"*Ohhhh.*" Tyler claps his hands eagerly. "And celebrate we will."

***

"Dad! Sofia!" I tug Cross by the hand toward our parents.

"Babe, wait." Cross tries to stop.

"Why?" I say, glancing backward at him. "You know they want the typical graduation day photo of us."

I laugh, and Cross shifts his gaze elsewhere.

My brows crease, and I spin toward him. "Is something wrong?" I drop my shoulders and lean in close. "You're not accepting the job, are you?"

Which is perfectly fine.

It's his decision—something my father and his mother reiterated several times.

Cross would be an amazing fit for the company, given his natural protective streak and honed ability to fight, but if that's not what he wants, then that's okay, too.

"This isn't about the job," he says.

"Then, what is it..." My words fade as I watch Cross dig into the pocket of his gown.

He isn't.

Is he?

I stand in shock, my eyelashes fluttering in disbelief, when he drops down to one knee, right there in the middle of graduation chaos.

"Scarlett Wallace..." He swallows, his throat bobbing up and down. "The first thing I thought when I laid eyes on you, standing next to your father on the altar, was that I'd be stuck with you forever."

Someone laughs from nearby, and I think it's Tyler.

"You were a part of my life whether I wanted you to be or not..." Cross opens the ring box and reveals a similar but larger diamond than the ones in my ears. "But *God,* am I glad you are."

I bite down on my bottom lip to keep it from wobbling.

"I couldn't imagine my life without you, and I never want to." He peers up at me. "Will you—"

"Yes." I nod quickly. "I'll marry you."

Cross lowers his voice. "Who's to say I'm asking you to marry me, Scar?"

I raise a brow, and he smirks.

"Will you marry me, Scarlett? Maybe change that last name so it isn't the same as my mother's?"

A laugh bursts out of me, and I nod again. Cross leaps

off his knee and wraps me up into his arms—my favorite place to be. With a shaky hand, he slips the ring onto my finger and kisses me so feverishly I forget that we're surrounded by our friends and family until my father clears his throat.

We break away just far enough for a tiny bit of air to slip between us.

"Congratulations, sweetheart," my father murmurs.

"Wait. I'm not done," Cross announces.

Everyone turns toward him, and he stands tall, seeming prouder than usual.

Sofia touches his arm. "What is it, honey?"

Cross looks directly at my father. "I want to accept your job offer but only under one condition."

I glance at my dad, his brow line heavy. "Go on."

"I want to pay you back for my junior year, when you stepped in and paid my tuition. You can take a percentage out of my pay."

My father is hesitant. He begins to shake his head, but Cross steps forward. "This is non-negotiable."

A few seconds of silence pass, all of us on pins and needles.

But eventually, my dad sticks his hand out. They shake on it, and Sofia and I smile at each other.

"Okay! Time to celebrate!" Tyler shouts. "Party at Cross's—" He eyes my dad. "I mean, Sawyer's!"

"Hey!" she interjects. "What?"

"Go." My dad flicks his chin toward our friends. "Have fun. *Celebrate*. Both graduation and engagement."

I squeeze Cross's hand, and he squeezes back.

"Thanks, Dad." I smile at him and Sofia. "I love you."

He grins. "I love you, too, kiddo."

And with that, Cross says goodbye to his mother, picks

me up into his arms, and we're rushing off to celebrate *our future.*

THE END

Thank you so much for joining us on our journey through Shadow Valley U! At this time, this series is now officially complete.

Catch S.J. Sylvis's upcoming release: https://a.co/d/gK7Lm0k

Join S. Massery's newsletter to keep up-to-date about her 2026 release(s)! https://smassery.myflodesk.com/newsletter

ABOUT THE AUTHORS

S. Massery is a dark romance author who loves injecting a good dose of suspense into her stories. She lives in Western Massachusetts with her dog, Alice.

Before adventuring into the world of writing, she went to college in Boston and held a wide variety of jobs—including working on a dude ranch in Wyoming (a personal highlight). She has a love affair with coffee and chocolate. When S. Massery isn't writing, she can be found devouring books, playing outside with her dog, or trying to make people smile.

Join her newsletter to stay up to date on new releases: http://smassery.com/newsletter

S.J. Sylvis is an Amazon top 50 and USA Today bestselling author who is best known for her angsty new adult romances. She currently resides in Arizona with her husband, two small kiddos, dog, and cat. She is obsessed with coffee, becomes easily attached to fictional characters, and spends most of her evenings buried in a book!

Join her newsletter to stay up to date on new releases: https://www.sjsylvis.com/newsletter-signup

ALSO BY S. MASSERY

Hockey Gods

Brutal Obsession

Devious Obsession

Secret Obsession

Twisted Obsession

Fierce Obsession

Hockey Titans

Into Ruin

Ruined God

Shadow Valley U

Sticks & Stones

Heart of Thorns

Cross the Line

The Christmas Playbook

Standalone Hockey

The Pucking Coach's Daughter

Fallen Royals

Wicked Dreams

Wicked Games

Wicked Promises

Sterling Falls

#0 Thrill

#1 Thief

#2 Fighter

#3 Rebel

#4 Queen

Sterling Falls Rogues

#0 Terror

#1 Nemesis

#2 Warrior

#3 Martyr

DeSantis Mafia

#1 Ruthless Saint

#2 Savage Prince

#3 Stolen Crown

Broken Mercenaries

#1 Blood Sky

#2 Angel of Death

#3 Morning Star

More at http://smassery.com

ALSO BY S.J. SYLVIS

Bexley U Series

Weak Side

Ice Bet

Puck Block

Chicago Blue Devils

Play the Game

Skate the Line

Rush the Edge

Test the Ice

Shadow Valley Series

Sticks and Stones

Heart of Thorns

Cross the Line

English Prep Series

All the Little Lies

All the Little Secrets

All the Little Truths

St. Mary's Series

Good Girls Never Rise

Bad Boys Never Fall

Dead Girls Never Talk

Heartless Boys Never Kiss

Pretty Girls Never Lie

Standalones

Three Summers

Yours Truly, Cammie

Chasing Ivy

Falling for Fallon

Truth